LIVE THE DREAM

LIVE THE DREAM

Claire Lorrimer

severn
House

This first world edition published 2016
in Great Britain and the USA by
SEVERN HOUSE PUBLISHERS LTD of
19 Cedar Road, Sutton, Surrey, England, SM2 5DA.
Trade paperback edition first published
in Great Britain and the USA 2016 by
SEVERN HOUSE PUBLISHERS LTD

British Library Cataloguing in Publication Data
A CIP catalogue record for this title is available from the British Library.

ISBN-13: 978-0-7278-8637-8 (cased)
ISBN-13: 978-1-84751-736-4 (trade paper)
ISBN-13: 978-1-78010-800-1 (e-book)

All Severn House titles are printed on acid-free paper.

Severn House Publishers support the Forest Stewardship Council™ [FSC™],
the leading international forest certification organisation.
All our titles that are printed on FSC certified paper carry the FSC logo.

MIX
Paper from
responsible sources
FSC® C013056

Typeset by Palimpsest Book Production Ltd.,
Falkirk, Stirlingshire, Scotland.
Printed and bound in Great Britain by
TJ International, Padstow, Cornwall.

For my darling sister, Anne,
with whom I have shared so many happy times, with love

ACKNOWLEDGEMENTS

I wish to thank Paul Ovstedal and his mother, the late author Rosalind Laker, for their assistance with information about World War II Norway. I would also like to thank Martin Johnsen for his advice and assistance and, not least, the team at Severn House, for their continuing interest in my wartime stories.

ONE

August, 1939

'War imminent stop You are to return home train leaving Munich 13.00 hours tomorrow stop Telegraph receipt of this instruction stop Father.'

The young Norwegian student, Kristoffer Holberg, handed the telegram back to the girl lying beside him in the long grass bordering the Lake Tegernsee where they had decided to picnic. The expression on his good-looking face was as downcast as hers.

'My sister says we'll just ignore it, the way we did last time when Father panicked, thinking there would be a war when Germany marched into Austria. We were going on one of our weekend skiing trips to Garmisch and we pretended we didn't get the telegram until we returned, by which time everyone knew the Austrians had welcomed them. Una says our Prime Minister is arranging a peace treaty with Herr Hitler right now.'

Kristoffer's face was momentarily distorted by a frown. 'I wasn't going to tell you but my father has written saying I should cut short my college course and return home.' He paused, his blue eyes thoughtful before adding: 'Being an MP, your father might have some inside knowledge about the political situation,' he said. 'Oh, Dil, darling Dil, I couldn't bear it if you had to go home.'

Tears filled Dilys' eyes as she contemplated the prospect of being parted from the young fellow student with whom she had fallen in love. Their developing relationship was not proving to be just a casual affair such as Dilys' twin, Una, was enjoying. Kristoffer, too, was serious: he talked of getting engaged when Dilys was old enough. At seventeen, she had not long ago left her girls' boarding school. She'd been allowed to further her education in Munich, where she and her twin boarded with a retired professor and his wife from whom they learned colloquial German and went to classes at college with all the young students from many other parts of the world. It was an idyllic, carefree life as groups of mixed nationalities went off together skiing in the winter months, bunking in mountain huts, having sing-songs to someone's mouth organ or accordion in the evenings. In summer they went on excursions, skated at night on the city ice rink, got cheap tickets for the events in the big *operahaus* and went to fancy dress and other parties.

The fact that there were such large numbers of uniformed men on the streets did not particularly concern them, for they were all polite and friendly to foreigners. They had heard stories of ill treatment, even of the deportation of Jewish people, but had not personally witnessed any atrocities. As far as they were concerned, the atmosphere in this beautiful city was entirely joyful, the students only interested in their personal pleasures.

As for Dilys and Kristoffer, from the day they had first met on the ski slopes when she had bumped into him and knocked him over, they had had no interest in anyone else. It was truly love at first sight, as she'd confessed to her twin.

There had been kisses and passionate embraces but they had never gone 'all the way' – a euphemism they employed at school for the kind of lovemaking that produced babies. Only those with brothers had even the vaguest idea of what this entailed. Such was their innocence that most were agreed babies went into and out of their mothers' stomachs via their belly buttons.

Kristoffer was aware of Dilys' innocence and had always controlled the passionate love he felt for her. Now, the prospect of their imminent parting became unbearable.

Alone in the field with the remains of their picnic lunch scattered around them, not only he but Dilys, too, was unable to think of anything but the agony of parting: of the prospect of not being able to see each other every day as happened now. Each morning when she ran downstairs to the hallway of the *pension*, she knew Kristoffer would be waiting for her outside the big house belonging to Professor Von Zwehl and his wife, who provided care, lodging and tutorials for them.

'I love you, Kris!' she now told him between his desperate kisses. His hands tightened round her and he pressed his body closer still to hers. There was no sign of any other people in the deserted spot Kristoffer had chosen for their picnic, and Dilys now made no objection when he lifted her blouse and, bending his head, kissed her breasts.

Unashamedly, she pressed herself even closer against him. 'Kristoffer, I want you to do it. I want you to make love to me. I want to belong to you in every possible way. Please, I know we shouldn't, but if I do have to go home at least I shall feel that we really do belong to each other . . .'

She broke off as she saw the hesitation in his eyes. He knew she was innocent and that there could be risks but he would be careful. He, too, wanted to cement their relationship, to make her his own.

He could feel her heart beating fiercely against his chest and, with all restraint gone, he quickly undressed her, his hands moving from her breasts down to her hips. It was Dilys who now struggled out of her skirt and helped him to remove her cotton knickers. Instinctively, her legs parted. Kristoffer had quickly pulled off his shorts and within seconds he was lying between her legs, his voice husky with desire as he kissed her gently and whispered: 'I shall try not to hurt you.'

Dilys was unsure what he meant, but whatever it was she didn't care. Uncertain though she was as to what would now happen, she never wavered in her decision to let him make love to her.

Kristoffer was as gentle as he could be, doing his utmost to curb the fierceness of his desire as he eased his way into her. She gave a small cry as he overcame her virginity and then, unable to control himself any longer, he allowed himself to move passionately inside her.

Despite the moment of pain and the strangeness of what had just happened, Dilys felt a great surge of joy at this astonishing but wonderful union of their bodies. And, reaching up, she pulled his head down to her and kissed him again, this time with a rush of tenderness.

Kristoffer's arm tightened around her. Very gently, he stroked the shining waves of hair he called the colour of burnished bronze from her forehead and said, 'You are so beautiful. I love you; I'll always love you.'

For several minutes they lay entwined and then Kristoffer slowly eased himself into a sitting position. The hot sun of the late afternoon was burning down upon them and both were damp with perspiration. A smile crossed his face as he shrugged off his shirt and said, 'I know, Dil, we'll cool off. Have a swim in the lake. There's no one around to see us.'

Returning his smile, Dilys stood up and shyly allowed him to take her hand. Together they ran down the glassy slope into the cold waters of the lake.

It was too cold to stay there for long but, refreshed, they ran hand in hand back to their picnic place, pulled on their clothes and sat with their arms around each other. There was a moment when Dilys knew that as yet in her life she had never felt happier than she did at this moment.

Almost reading her thoughts, Kristoffer said, 'I'll never forget this day. The day I made you mine.'

Momentarily the cloud crossed the sun and, as the shadow fell across them, Dilys was unhappily reminded of the time. 'It's nearly six o'clock, Kristoffer. We'll have to go back. I'll need to change for supper and one of the few times the professor is cross with us is if we are late for *abendessen*.'

Aware they would not be seeing each other again until the following afternoon, they were silent as, holding tightly on to each other, they walked back to the *pension*. Stealing one last long kiss, Dilys tore herself away from his embrace and hurried indoors.

Una was already upstairs getting changed when, her cheeks flushed, Dilys hurried into their bedroom. Knowing her twin almost as well as she knew herself, Una knew from one look at Dilys' face that something special had happened to her. There was a glow, a far-away expression in her eyes which made her ask impulsively, 'Dil, you and Kristoffer . . . you didn't go all the way, did you?'

For a moment, Dilys did not reply, and Una's thoughts turned to the two occasions when she herself had experienced this forbidden sexual activity, the first time being a hurried encounter with a French music student. He was almost as ignorant as she was and she had disliked the whole hurried procedure, which she had found both painful and embarrassing.

Nor had she enjoyed her second experience, this time with an extremely good looking, popular pianist who played the piano and sang romantically at the tea dances to which she was regularly invited. She had been thrilled when he'd asked her to meet him once the tea dance was over. He took her to a bar where he sat beside her in a quiet, secluded corner and filled her head with compliments, keeping his body excitingly close to hers and her glass of wine full.

Una had been kissed and fondled in the darkened room. It was a truly romantic evening, and when they left the bar in time for the professor's eleven-thirty curfew, he'd said he would drive her back in his car to the *pension* where she lived.

As Una's companion had promised he would have her back in time, she made no objection when, on the way, he parked in a deserted cul-de-sac and started to kiss her. At first, while she was responding to his kisses and caresses, he was gentle but, quite suddenly, he had exposed himself and made no attempt to conceal what he was doing as he hurriedly pulled on protection.

As embarrassed as she was shocked, Una had told him angrily that she wanted to go home immediately. At first he had laughed, telling her not to waste time teasing him; he'd had a long, tiring day and wanted to get home too. Una was now shocked as well as frightened, but her tears and protests had been ignored.

That experience was such that she had decided then and there to avoid sex in future. Guessing Dilys had experimented with her Norwegian boy, she could not understand how she could look so radiant, so happy.

Feeling that in some way, she herself was to blame for her unpleasant experiences, Una had decided not to confide in Dilys and to confine her light-hearted flirtations to the group of other young students she and Dilys mixed with during lectures.

For the first time in their lives, Dilys did not want to share her thoughts and feelings with her twin. What had happened between her and Kristoffer was too special, too private, too personal for anyone's knowledge than their own. Since their birth, she and Una had never been or wanted to be treated separately, or parted, even for an hour. As they had grown out of babyhood, Una had become the more dominant one, the leader, and Dilys her devoted shadow. It was only since they had come out to Germany to learn the language and Una had sometimes chosen to accept invitations from groups of young people that Dilys had preferred to go out alone with her good-looking Norwegian admirer.

'Dil, you did, didn't you?' she repeated.

'I don't want to talk about it, Una!' Dilys said. She added, with a note of defiance: 'Kristoffer and I are going to get married – when I'm old enough. We're sort of engaged and he gave me this ring and the chain so I can wear it round my neck. He guessed our parents would have a fit if they thought I'd agreed to marry him.'

Una sighed. 'We can but hope we'll get away with it again. After all, it all seems so stupid. Heinz, my Luftwaffe pilot, says of course Germany doesn't want to go to war with Britain, and if they do want to include Poland as part of the Reich there's no reason why Britain should get involved. It's really silly of Father to get such ideas! He should see how friendly everyone is. The German boys are just like us, even the ones in uniform. Last time we went home, Father was on about the black-shirted ones doing awful things to Jewish people but I told him this was nonsense because we've never seen anything like that here. I expect it's because he's a silly old MP!'

Dilys refastened one of her silk stockings to her suspender belt and straightened her skirt. Bending down to put on her court shoes, she said thoughtfully, 'Kristoffer said he thinks they do smash Jewish houses and steal from their shops but they make sure foreign students and foreigners don't see what they are doing. He says maybe it is true because he once saw a jeweller's shop with its windows smashed and the word Juden splashed across the door in white paint with a swastika in the middle.'

Una sighed as she sat down at the dressing table and brushed her hair. 'The trouble with our parents' generation,' she announced, 'is that they are still fixated on the last war. Father says "there is no such thing as a good German". I would just like him to meet Heinz, Wolfgang and Johann. I wonder that he ever let us come here! I suppose Mother persuaded him because she loved Dresden when she was there as a girl.'

Their conversation was interrupted by a knock on the door and Frau Von Zwehl came in with a telegram in her hand. 'Your father!' she announced, handing it to Una. 'He is arriving tomorrow morning and wishes you to be packed and ready to leave with him at midday.' Her voice broke and she wiped her eyes with a handkerchief. 'I am so sorry!' she added. 'You have been good guests.'

After she had left the room, Una shrugged her shoulders and said, 'That's it, Dil! Home we have to go. What a bore! I was going to a fancy dress party tonight with Johann – I suppose I can't go now.'

Dilys was beyond words as, trembling, she sank down on to the bed, her face ashen as she realized her separation from Kristoffer would be so very soon.

It was not until she was in bed later that night, listening to Una's soft breathing as she slept, that she allowed herself to remember what had happened that afternoon.

The next morning the twins took their usual places at the breakfast table and were enjoying the large cups of coffee brought in by the maid when they were aware of the front doorbell ringing. A moment later, there was the sound of the professor's voice welcoming a visitor.

'Dil, it's Father,' Una whispered. 'He . . .' She broke off as the portly figure of their father, preceded by the professor, came into the room.

He looked down from one of his daughters to the other, his expression stern as he said, 'When I received no reply to my telegram, and recalling last year when you chose to ignore my instructions, I have been obliged to cancel an important meeting and travel here in person to collect you. I trust you are both ready to leave?'

Una blushed as she pulled back her chair and stood up. Her heart beating fast, she said, 'Honestly, Father, Dil and I thought you were just in a flap like last year and you'd soon see there isn't the slightest chance of us English people getting involved. All the Germans are very friendly and Dil and I—'

Her father interrupted angrily, 'You don't know what you

are talking about! And I don't intend to take time now to begin enlightening you as to the current political situation. I have reserved seats for us on the one o'clock train. I shall settle up with the professor while you finish your packing. You will please both be ready to leave here with your luggage at midday.'

Neither girl spoke as they got up from the table and left the room. When the door of the breakfast room closed behind him, Una said crossly, 'He might have warned us . . . and he didn't even kiss us when he arrived. He's being absolutely horrid!' There were now angry tears in her eyes as she added, 'It's so jolly *boring* at home, and we'll miss the skiing at Christmas!'

Dilys' eyes were stinging with unshed tears of utter desolation. There was not even enough time left for her to say a last goodbye to Kristoffer. Nor did she have a telephone number by which she could tell him she was going home. When he called for her after lunch, she would not be there, and neither of them would know when they would meet again.

With a sigh of relief, Kristoffer left his uncle and aunt at their hotel after a long-drawn-out lunch. Quickly catching the next tram, he got off at the stop nearest to Professor Von Zwehl's *pension*. The maid opened the front door and regarded the good-looking young man who had called so frequently to see *fräulein* Dilys with concern.

'Very sorry, Herr Holberg,' she said. 'But the *fräuleins* is not here. They left this morning with a man, their father. *Fräulein* Dilys is crying!' she added.

Kristoffer's face was white with shock. 'You mean they've gone back to England?' he said, his voice choked with shock and dismay.

The maid nodded but, putting her hand in her apron pocket, pulled out a crumpled sheet of paper which looked as if it might have lined a dressing-table drawer. '*Fräulein* Dilys ask me to give you this,' she said.

Eagerly, Kristoffer took it from her. He did not unfold it then but thanked the maid and hurried back out on to the street. The pavement was dusty, warmed by the sun which glinted off the windows of the big houses lining the street. His heart beating hurriedly, Kristoffer made his way to the small square of grass and trees at the crossroad where the trams stopped and sat down on the bench. Only then did he unfold the ragged sheet of paper with hands that were trembling, and started to read in scribbled pencil:

Dearest, darling Kristoffer,
It is too dreadful . . . father has come to take us home . . . I asked him if we could go on a later train so I could say goodbye to you but he wouldn't even listen to me. I can't bear it. I love you. Please, dearest, darling Kristoffer, find a way to come to England as I know I won't be allowed to come and see you if you went back to Norway. Please write to me. It's so awful not even being able to kiss you goodbye and tell you I love you and always will. Please don't stop loving me. Don't forget me.
Your truly loving Dilys

The bottom of the paper was covered in crosses – childish kisses which brought a lump to Kristoffer's throat. He thought wildly that he would catch the next train to England. Then, as common sense returned, he decided that the best way he could deal with the situation was to return to Norway with his aunt and uncle when they left next day, explain to his parents his need to go to England, find Dilys and somehow persuade her parents to allow her to become engaged to him.

His thoughts went to the previous afternoon when they had taken that vital last step and he had made her his own. Last night he had lain awake thinking how wrong and irresponsible it had been of him to let it happen when he'd had no way of protecting her. He had consoled himself with the fact that it had only happened once and that he would not let it happen again, whatever the temptation. He loved her too much, too deeply, to put her at risk. Somehow he must persuade her parents to agree to an engagement and an early marriage, young though they both were.

At the age of twenty-three, there had been other girls in Kristoffer's life – casual flirtations and one ongoing relationship with Gerda, the daughter of his mother's best friend who lived on the same road as he did. They had played together as children and experimented with each other as teenagers with their first kisses and tentative embraces. Gerda was as tall as Kristoffer, with long, fair hair and eyes as blue as his. Physically a strong, healthy girl, she was every bit as good a skier as Kristoffer and, although quite heavily built, her features were pretty and her nature happy and outgoing. She was a good companion, easy-going and devoted to Kristoffer, her childhood friend. Their two families expected they would ultimately marry.

Kristoffer's father had determined that his only son would eventually take over the export side of his large timber company and, when his son left school, arranged for him to undertake a year's study, first in England, then France and then Germany in order to become fluent in each foreign language and familiar with their businesses and methods of management. Having also completed his year's compulsory army training, he was now in his third year of studies abroad before going home to start work in the family business.

Due to these years abroad, Kristoffer had only met up with Gerda on his occasional holidays at home. By then, he had enjoyed many flirtations with girls he'd met and had a brief, instructional, physical relationship with a Frenchwoman in her early thirties. Consequently he had matured in a way Gerda had not. Although still fond of her, he had not felt able to return the undisguised adoration she had for him. Using his long months abroad as a reason for not wishing their relationship to become serious, he'd been able to keep her at a metaphorical arm's length without hurting her feelings – something he'd hate to do.

Now, deeply and seriously in love with Dilys, he knew that when he went home he must make it clear to Gerda that there could never be anything more than a loving friendship between them. He had no doubt that she would soon find a husband among the other young unattached boys in Bergen.

At last, comforted by the thought that it might not be more than a few weeks before he held Dilys in his arms again, Kristoffer looked once more at her hastily written letter before folding it away. It was only then, with a horrible sinking feeling, that he realized that in her haste Dilys had forgotten to give him her home address and that he did not have the slightest idea where in England she and her sister lived.

TWO

Although England had been at war with Germany for the past four months, the customary Christmas routine remained unchanged at Hannington Hall and the twins woke to the familiar sight of stockings on the end of their white iron bedsteads. They sat up, smiling sleepily at one another.

'How much longer are our parents going to treat us like children?' Una exclaimed as she reached for her stocking.

'Well, I suppose technically we are still children seeing that we don't come of age for another three years!' Dilys replied. She pulled her pink dressing gown round her shoulders and handed the identical one to her sister. Sitting opposite one another on the side of their beds, they unwrapped their parcels: identical small ivory manicure sets, diaries for the coming year, a flannel wrapped around a bar of lavender soap and the traditional solitary tangerine, a walnut and a 'lucky' piece of coal.

Later in the morning, after returning from church, the family would gather in the drawing room close to the Christmas tree where they would exchange presents. There were also the customary ten shilling notes inside Christmas cards from their Uncle George, and the never varying small square box containing lace-edged hankies from their twin spinster aunts who arrived without fail in time for lunch in their chauffeur-driven Daimler from their house in the Dorset village of Compton Abbas.

Since Una and Dilys were first old enough to be allowed down from the nursery, where they'd usually had their meals, for Christmas lunch with the grown-ups, they could not recall a Christmas when their aunts had not been there, and the twins had always been a little frightened of them. Their aunts always wore sombre black high-necked dresses and resembled the widowed Queen Victoria. Somewhat inappropriately named Ivy and Rose, they monitored their nieces' behaviour with critical eyes and otherwise ignored them.

This cold Christmas morning, both Dilys and Una were shivering in their large unheated bedroom, such luxuries as a fire not deemed necessary for children. Una stood up and padded across the room to draw back the curtains. Sally, the maid, would be up presently with a jug of hot water for washing, as the only bathroom installed recently in Hannington Hall was being used almost exclusively by their parents, although twice a week the twins were allowed to have a bath – always provided the noisy, highly temperamental gas geezer had not decided to go on strike, when its supply of water was so tepid it was a matter of getting in and out of the bath as quickly as was humanly possible.

'Better hurry up, Dil,' she said as she removed her nightdress, fastened her brassiere and pulled on her Chilproof vest. 'You know what Father's like if we're late!'

Dilys did know. Both she and Una were still slightly in awe of Sir Godfrey Singleby, an upright, brusque Victorian man in his late fifties. He had married late in life and, as was customary for his generation, had rarely had any contact with his twin daughters when they were babies. He saw them only at mealtimes when they were old enough to be allowed to eat with their parents. Their upbringing was left entirely to their mother: to nannies or governesses, and only rarely was Sir Godfrey called upon when it had been necessary to tell them off for a serious lapse of discipline.

A self-important, proud man, he was the unchallenged Member of Parliament for his constituency and was frequently to be heard pontificating from the backbenches. He was the sole heir to Hannington Hall, the large family estate which was managed profitably by his steward. A dedicated Conservative, Sir Godfrey was an ambitious man who, having survived the last war, was hoping to be given a post in the Cabinet where he could play a more important role in running the country. Meanwhile, he attended Parliament whenever there was something of importance to be discussed, and in order to be able to do so, owned a service flat in Victoria.

His wife, Daphne, often as not accompanied him to London for lunch with friends or to go to her dressmaker or the theatre. She was quite content to leave the care of her daughters to a

nanny or governess until they were old enough to be despatched
to a private girls' boarding school on the Sussex coast. During
the holidays, if she was not in London, having discussed meals
with Cook and household affairs with the housekeeper after
breakfast, she would be content to work on the beautiful, intri-
cate tapestries she embroidered or to have tea with neighbouring
wives of a similar background to her own.

Now in her fifties, she had been over thirty and more or less
resigned to spinsterhood when Sir Godfrey had returned
unscathed from four years fighting in France and asked her to
marry him. Although he was far from being the handsome young
husband of her girlish dreams, she had almost given up hope
of marriage, so after a brief hesitation she had accepted his
proposal. On the whole, they saw very little of one another and
their marriage was very seldom intimate. Having produced two
daughters, there was an unspoken agreement that there was no
necessity to produce a son or further daughters. Absorbed in
his political ambitions, Sir Godfrey was as content as his wife
with their emotionless, distant but amicable status quo, and his
observance of his marital rights was now as rare as to be almost
non-existent.

Following their usual Christmas routine, the family always
attended the village church whatever the weather, together with
all the household staff, excluding Cook, who would be preparing
lunch. When the meal was over and cleared away, the servants
would be invited to assemble in the drawing room to receive
their presents, which had been bought and wrapped by Lady
Singleby. Following this small ceremony, the staff were then
required to lay a cold light evening meal under covers in
the dining room, after which they were given the rest of the
day off.

On this first Christmas of the new war when the British
Expeditionary Force was away fighting the invading German
armies in Europe, life at Hannington Hall remained unchanged.
Una's thoughts were concentrated on the New Year's Eve
dance their neighbours were giving as she finished dressing
for breakfast. She fastened her suspender belt round her waist
and pulled up her silk stockings. She and Dilys had purchased
these in Germany to replace the thick lisle stockings that had

been obligatory at school. Their school liberty bodices had also been discarded and they now wore the new Kestos brassieres. They had crisscross straps which went over their shoulders and supported their *brusts*, as their breasts were called in German.

Dilys also started to get dressed, her thoughts turning to the fact that it was nearly four months since her father had escorted her and Una home so peremptorily. There was still no reply from Kristoffer to the letter she had hurriedly written to him and left with Anna – the maid at the Von Zwehls' *pension*, to give to him when he called for her after lunch – before their unexpected, hurried departure. Although she had recalled with dismay that she had forgotten to give him her home address, she knew he could have asked the professor to give it to him.

Una had pointed out that with Britain declaring war with Germany only a week after they had come home, the postal services from Germany to England had almost certainly ceased to exist. She had suggested gently that perhaps Kristoffer had decided not to continue their relationship now they could no longer see each other every day and that it might be better for Dilys to forget him. She was, of course, unaware of how much further Dilys and Kristoffer had taken their relationship. She did, however, accept that it was still possible he would write when he returned home to Norway, where there would still be an active postal service.

Dilys fingered the precious ring round her neck and refused to give up hope. Twice a day without fail she hurried to stand at the window in her bedroom overlooking the drive, watching for the post boy to deliver the mail to Hannington Hall. There were nearly always letters for her father, a weekly letter for her mother from the aunts and once or twice a seasonal invitation to the twins to a party at one of the big houses in the neighbourhood. Since their return from Germany, Una insisted upon a reluctant Dilys attending such events in the hope that her twin would meet another young admirer and forget all about the Norwegian student she had been so keen on.

It was going to be difficult to celebrate Christmas in the usual way, Una thought. Their father would almost certainly be called back to London during the holiday, where contingency plans for the war were hastily being instigated. There were pictures in the newspapers of large numbers of London-based children with labels identifying them round their necks being sent on trains to unknown destinations in parts of the country away from the dangers of the bombing raids expected in the City. According to Sir Godfrey, the war was going badly at sea, the German submarines sinking so many Allied ships, resulting in a tragic loss of life and goods. Everyone now carried a gas mask and a buff-coloured identity card. Blackout curtains were obligatory at night, covering people's windows so no lights would show to help any German planes overhead.

'I can't believe this war is going to last for long whatever Father says,' Una remarked when they heard the gong summoning them down to breakfast – there was always a telling-off from their father if they were only a few minutes late. 'It all seems so silly! I'm absolutely sure Heinz and Wolfgang don't want to fight us.' She gave a mischievous giggle, adding: 'Johann wanted to make love to me! And Heinz was such fun. Wolfgang was a bit boring, talking all the time about the aeroplane he was going to fly round the world when he got his wings. I just can't believe all our German friends are now our enemies. It's all so silly!' she repeated.

As far as Dilys was concerned, the outbreak of war was not just silly, it was proving to be a personal disaster. She had no idea where Kristoffer lived in Norway, only that it was on the outskirts of a southern port called Bergen. Even if she did know, her father would never permit her to travel there to see him. She did not even know if he had returned home for Christmas.

Surely he had not, as Una had suggested, decided the distance between them was now too great to make their romance feasible? Or had he perhaps already found some other girl – prettier, more exciting, more grown-up than she was? Could he have forgotten that special last afternoon together when she had given herself to him believing they would love each other for ever?

As usual, their parents were already seated at the breakfast table when they went into the dining room. The sideboard was laden with dishes: porridge in a covered silver bowl; entrée dishes containing their father's favourite kedgeree; scrambled eggs, bacon and sausages. In silver pots were tea, coffee and milk which Sally, the maid, carried round the table, filling their breakfast cups. There were also bowls of stewed fruit grown in the garden, which the previous summer had been stored or bottled for the winter.

Ignoring the porridge, Una helped herself to scrambled eggs and sausages while Dilys stood staring white-faced at the dishes. She had come downstairs feeling extremely hungry and eager for her breakfast, but now, without warning, she knew she was going to be sick.

Hurriedly excusing herself, she ran out of the room and across the hall to the downstairs cloakroom. She arrived only just in time to retch into the toilet bowl. When the sickness passed, she stood up and wiped her mouth with her handkerchief, wondering as she did so what she could have eaten the night before to upset her. To her surprise, she was now feeling perfectly well again. When Una, who had been sent to see if she was all right, arrived at the cloakroom door, Dilys was able to smile at her reassuringly and shrug off the episode.

'Mother thought you might be sickening for influenza, there being so much about,' Una said. Linking her arm through Dilys' as they returned to the breakfast room, she added: 'Father said the Russians are fighting in Finland in blizzards and soldiers are dying of frostbite. Serves them right. He heard on the wireless this morning that the BBC forecast says England is to have the worst snowstorm for years. He said we must all listen to the king's message this afternoon after lunch. Father's going to return to the flat tomorrow in case we get snowed in here.'

The twins had on rare occasions gone up to London in the school holidays with their mother for a night or two – to buy school uniforms from Gorringes and shop for other clothes and shoes they needed from the Army & Navy Stores nearby or Harrods, and such outings always included a theatre, or cinema or even the ballet.

'Perhaps you should not go to church this morning, Dilys!' Lady Singleby said as her daughter sat down again at the table. 'If you have caught a chill, the cold in those draughty pews would just exacerbate it.'

'Really, I'm fine now, thank you, Mother!' Dilys said truth-fully. 'I assure you I'm really well enough to go.'

Sir Godfrey looked at his wife, frowning. 'Don't fuss, dear,' he said reprovingly. 'The girls aren't babies any more and it won't hurt them to toughen up a bit. There's a war on, you know, and we are none of us going to be able to mollycoddle ourselves. Una and Dilys may have to become VADs like you were in the last war.'

'You mean we may be conscripted?' Una asked, her eyes shining. Then she frowned. 'But I don't want to be a nurse. I want to do something more exciting – like driving an ambulance, maybe. Can we have driving lessons now we are home, Father? We are allowed to drive now we're seventeen.'

Sir Godfrey pushed back his chair and rose to his feet. 'I don't see why not!' he said indulgently. He was secretly quite proud of the way his two daughters had blossomed into attrac-tive young women. He had received many complimentary remarks from several of his fellow Members of Parliament when he'd taken them to lunch in the Members' dining room in the House of Commons. They were proving to be a talking point in his favour.

Una was in the best of spirits as an hour later she and Dilys walked behind their parents the short distance to Hannington village church. She whispered happily to her twin as they took their usual places in one of the front pews reserved for the family. 'Did you see James Sherwin, that vet from Fenbury?' she asked. 'He was staring at us as we passed him. He's really quite good looking with those big brown eyes and broad shoulders. Pity he's so old or I might have been keen on him.'

'He's not all that old!' Dilys whispered back. 'Sally's mother cooks for him so Sally knows all about him. She said although he is a widower he isn't yet forty. When his wife died Sally said he was heartbroken.' She broke off when a sudden wave of nausea engulfed her once more. Almost at the same moment, the service began.

Desperately trying to control the need to throw up, she whis-pered to Una that she was feeling ill and, pushing past her sister, hurried down the aisle as quickly as she could and only just managed to reach the deserted churchyard before she was throwing up the breakfast she had eaten after recovering from the last attack.

Una appeared by her side, saying anxiously, 'Mother sent me to see if you are all right. What's wrong, Dil? You must have eaten something I didn't have? You look ghastly.' She stopped as Dilys retched once again. Searching for a handkerchief in her overcoat pocket, at that moment a tall man appeared beside her.

'I saw your sister hurrying out of church looking quite ill,' he said. 'I wondered if I could be of any help?'

Una looked up at the would-be Samaritan. 'Oh, it's you!' she exclaimed as she recognized him and then quickly apologised. 'It's Mr Sherwin, isn't it?' She glanced quickly at Dilys and saw that she was about to be sick again. 'I think my sister is suffering from some sort of food poisoning. She wasn't well earlier this morning but she insisted on coming to church.'

'What bad luck on Christmas Day,' he said, his voice friendly as well as sympathetic. He smiled. 'I thought I recognized you both. The Singlebys' daughters, aren't you? You may not remember but we were introduced the summer before last at the village fête. May I ask which of the two I am speaking to?'

Una blushed. 'I'm Una,' she said, 'and my sister is Dilys. You're the vet, aren't you? Mr Sherwin? Dil and I recognized you in the church just now.'

He smiled once more, his thin, somewhat austere face lighting up, transforming his appearance to that of a much younger man. He drew a large white handkerchief from his coat pocket and, crossing the path to Dilys' side, handed it to her. She stared up at him, white-faced.

'If I may say so, young lady,' he said paternally, 'I don't think you should return to the church. If you don't have any transport perhaps I could run you home in my car?'

'Oh, we can walk home,' Una said, adding, 'but thanks all the same for the offer.'

He glanced once more at Dilys' white face, shook his head and said firmly, 'I'm sure you would prefer to be driven, would you not?'

For the first time since she had left the church, Dilys felt able to speak. She was no longer feeling sick but was shivering uncontrollably. Nodding her agreement, she turned to look at Una.

'Mother will be worrying by now. So if I go home with Mr Sherwin you can go back and tell her I am all right!' She turned back to her Samaritan. 'Father is reading the lesson and he wouldn't like it if Mother came out to see what was wrong and wasn't there to hear him.'

Ten minutes later, James Sherwin drove his elderly Morris estate car up to the front door of Hannington Hall and went round to open the door for Dilys.

The colour had returned to her cheeks and she looked up at him apologetically. 'I really feel like an awful fraud!' she said shyly. 'I'm perfectly all right now and I could have walked home. It was very kind of you to come to my rescue the way you did.'

Explaining that all the servants were in church so the front door would not be opened, Dilys took him round to the garden door which had been left unlocked. James smiled as he opened it for her but declined her offer to follow her indoors for a glass of sherry.

'Perhaps I can come another time,' he said. 'Please do remind your father that he and I are acquainted as he may be concerned at you driving off with a stranger! He brought one of his gun dogs to my surgery. Give him my regards and best wishes for the coming year!' he added with his charming smile.

When their parents returned from church Sir Godfrey recalled the vet when Una told him who had gone to Dilys' assistance. 'Nice chap! Decent fellow!' he commented. 'Good vet, too. Did wonders with poor old Jason's broken leg.' He turned to his wife. 'Maybe not quite one of us, but went to a good school, I seem to recall. We must invite him over for lunch next time I'm home for a few days. Quiet chap but I suppose that's to be expected, his losing his wife and child only a year or so after they were married. Didn't marry again, as far as I know. Now off you go, girls, and get tidied up before lunch. You are excused, Dilys, if you feel ill again. One o'clock sharp, and that doesn't mean five past.' He turned to his wife. 'Glass of sherry, my dear? I think there's just time.'

Una and Dilys disappeared upstairs. Una was agog with questions about James Sherwin and what he had talked about on the short drive home.

'Pity he isn't ten years younger!' she said as they brushed their hair. 'I bet he was really good looking before he got old.'

Dilys smiled. 'I'm sure Sally said he was only thirty-something. That's not really old.'

'Well, middle-aged then,' Una replied as, laughing, they went downstairs to greet the aunts who had just arrived.

Ten miles away, James Sherwin sat down in his empty dining room to eat the Christmas lunch his housekeeper, Sally's mother Mrs White had prepared the day before and left in the larder for him to heat up on Christmas Day. He, too, was considering his age and wishing he were young enough to be considered a suitable friend for the two pretty Singleby girls. It was now five years since he had been so prematurely widowed and he was indescribably lonely. It was not that he didn't see other people – his surgery was, if anything, too full of customers. It was the lack of someone, a person, to love and who loved him like the young wife he had so cruelly lost.

In the New Year, he now decided, he would start looking for an older vet to take on his practice, freeing him to volunteer for the army. Now the war seemed likely to continue, older, able-bodied men like himself would be needed, and it would be good for him to get away from so many sad memories.

His appetite had vanished, he realized and, pushing back his chair, he stood and picked up his half-eaten plate of food and carried it out to the kennel where he was boarding two Labradors recovering from distemper.

'Here you are, you two!' he said. 'It won't hurt you to have a bit of Christmas lunch for a change!'

Having watched them devouring his uneaten meal, he took them for a short walk before going to his armchair by the fire. Turning on the wireless set he had treated himself to last Christmas, he settled back to listen to the king's broadcast. His thoughts went back to 1936 to the king's brother, the uncrowned King Edward, who had landed his shy younger brother with the enormous responsibility of reigning over not just Great Britain but the vast British Empire as well. Edward had given up the crown, he'd said in his abdication speech, for the love of a woman, an American divorcee named Wallis Simpson who could not have been less suitable to be his wife and queen.

The fellow must love her very much indeed, James reflected, at the same time wondering whether he might, one day, find a woman he loved as much as the wife he'd so tragically lost.

THREE

K ristoffer walked to the end of the street and sat down
on the seat by the tram stop where he read Dilys' letter
a second time. As he reached the end, he realized how
stupid he had been not to ask the maid when the professor was
expected home. He, of course, would be able to give him Dilys'
home address. He hurried back to the *pension*.

That evening he was due to collect his aunt and uncle and
take them to the *Bahnhof* to see them on to the train home, but
if he missed his tutorial he would have time to call back and
obtain the precious information he wanted.

To his dismay the information was not forthcoming.
Unbeknown to Kristoffer, Sir Godfrey had questioned Herr Von
Zwehl about his daughters' progress and been informed that
Dilys had made less progress than Una in both her speech and
translation tutorials, due, he suspected, to her involvement with
the young Norwegian student. He and his wife had not thought
it necessary to inform her parents, as she was always obedient
where mealtimes or the nightly eleven-thirty curfew was
concerned. As a result of this information, Sir Godfrey concluded
it was just as well his daughter would no longer be able to
pursue the association which he deemed totally unsuitable for
a young girl of Dilys' age.

The professor, therefore, steeled himself not to feel sorry for
the anxious young man and, only weakening slightly, told
Kristoffer he could address his letter to Dilys care of her father
at the British House of Commons in London.

It was at least a lifeline, Kristoffer told himself as he hurried
to his uncle and aunt's hotel where he was to meet them.

'Are you not feeling well, Kristoffer?' his uncle asked two
hours later as he put down his empty coffee cup and stared
anxiously at his nephew's white face.

Kristoffer had been making an unsuccessful effort to pay
attention to what his uncle was saying about the possible threat

to Norway in the future if Germany invaded Poland as seemed likely. 'I apologise,' Kristoffer said. 'I'm afraid Dilys' sudden departure has been a bit of a shock. I do apologise,' he repeated.

His Aunt Ingeborg reached across the table in the hotel lounge where they were having a cup of coffee before leaving that evening to catch the train home, and patted his hand, exclaiming: 'What it is to be young and in love! You know, Kristoffer, your uncle and I always thought that you and your neighbours' child, Gerda, would marry eventually. Your English girl must be very special!'

Kristoffer smiled. 'She is, *Tante* Inge. We would have liked to become engaged but Dilys is still only seventeen and her parents would not permit it.'

His uncle raised his eyebrows and smiled at Kristoffer, saying, 'Never mind, m'boy. A good-looking youngster like you won't be without a girlfriend for long!' Unaware of Kristoffer's reaction, he added cheerfully: 'It is not as if your girlfriend has left you deliberately. In my opinion, her father is quite right to have made certain she and her sister go home. The situation is very serious, although granted the atmosphere here in Munich is undoubtedly a joyous one. At home we are genuinely worried. Not only did Herr Hitler take possession of Czechoslovakia, but he is now turning his attention to Poland. Next could be Holland who, incidentally, have mobilized their army. Some people are saying this is a madman whose ambition is to add all these countries to his growing empire. So ominous was the news when I spoke to my business partner on the telephone yesterday, he advised me not on any account to delay our return home, which your aunt and I had considered doing. I think you, too, should consider going home. You may be needed back in the army.'

For several minutes, Kristoffer was silent while he tried to estimate how soon he might expect a letter from Dilys once he'd written to her.

Having seen his uncle and aunt safely on to the train, and watching its lights chugging away into the darkening distance, Kristoffer stood silently, thinking with despair of the train that took Dilys and her father and sister at lunchtime from this same station. With an effort, he put his feelings of utter depression to one side as he consoled himself with the knowledge that he and Dilys could write to each other. He had her letter tucked safely in his breast pocket and he would go back to his *pension* now and write to her. Tomorrow morning, when the post office opened, he would buy suitable stamps for England.

Back in his room, he poured out his love and despair that they had not even had time to say goodbye. Somehow, he assured her, he would go to England to see her, and she must write back to him at once and give him her home address. After a tender reference to his treasured memory of their last afternoon together when they had sealed their relationship, he concluded with a vow to remain faithful to her for the rest of his life and had written his home address in Norway where she could write.

Sealing the envelope, he addressed it to her care of The Rt Hon. Sir Godfrey Singleby, House of Commons, Westminster, London, and put it on his bedside table ready to post first thing in the morning. With luck, he thought, Dilys would receive it within a week at the very most, provided, of course, that her father did not delay in giving or forwarding it to her at their home.

For the next few days Kristoffer managed to pass the time catching up on the German thesis he was supposed to be writing. In the evenings he met up with friends but without enjoyment. At night he found it difficult to sleep as he relived the times he had spent with Dilys. A week after her departure he stopped leaving his *pension* every morning and afternoon, waiting instead until the postman had delivered the mail, praying that there would be a reply to his letter to her.

On 3 September, Hitler's troops had marched into Poland. His landlady had tuned into the wireless and they heard the English Prime Minister Neville Chamberlain's broadcast announcing that Great Britain was at war with Germany. Kristoffer realized then that whether or not Dilys had written to him there would no longer be a postal service between the two countries and he was not going to get a letter from her. He packed up all his belongings, paid his *pension* bills, bought a railway ticket and by teatime was on his way home.

*　*　*

Back in England, Dilys, too, had watched for the postman's arrival as diligently as Kristoffer. She was blissfully unaware that his reply was now sitting in the in tray on the desk of her father's private secretary. Seeing the German stamp, she decided it should be seen first by Sir Godfrey before she forwarded it to his daughter.

Although it was addressed to his daughter, when he saw the German stamp Sir Godfrey, too, decided it was his duty to censor it. He had only to read the first adoring lines for him to shred it immediately, shocked as he was by the fellow's reference to their last day together when they had lain in each other's arms in the sun and declared their love for one another. That his young daughter could have allowed a man to lie with her in the open air where anyone could see them brought a rush of angry colour to his cheeks. Only one thing could be said to Dilys' credit: feeling guilty at her misbehaviour, she had had the good sense not to give the fellow her home address. Watching the shreds of paper falling into the waste-paper basket, he recovered his composure, knowing that he had put an end to the disgraceful relationship.

As he sat down once more at his desk, he pondered whether or not to reprove his daughter about her behaviour. Recoiling at the thought, he decided to leave it to his wife to do so but realized at once that doing so would be equally uncomfortable if he had to discuss sex with Daphne. By unspoken mutual consent, sex, passion and physical attraction were subjects they both avoided. Although they shared the same bedroom, he had his own adjoining dressing room so they were not obliged to appear naked in front of one another. Raised by strict Victorian parents, on the few occasions when he approached Daphne for his marital intimacies, as he called sex, it was carried out in the dark and not referred to the next day.

Down in the country at Hannington Hall with Una and her mother, Dilys' confidence slowly waned and she started to doubt that Kristoffer had ever truly fallen in love with her. He might already have relegated her to the past and found another girl to replace her after all.

Back home in Norway, Kristoffer had lost all hope of remaining in touch with Dilys. There were times when he began to doubt whether her loving declarations had been momentary: that, young and innocent as she was, she had mistaken her discovery of physical attraction for real love. He was forced to admit to himself that it was he, not Dilys, who had introduced the idea of a secret engagement and eventual marriage. She had been so sweet, so accepting of his passion, of his need to make love to her. Was she now regretting it? Was it possible, he asked himself, that she had just wanted to find out what lovemaking was all about? That now he was no longer with her she had decided to forget him? Or even worse, that she had already found someone else to love?

His thoughts tormented him as they vacillated between doubt and a deeper conviction that the vows they'd made to love one another for ever were valid still.

FOUR

On the first day of the New Year, the weather was so cold that permission had been given for a fire to be lit in the drawing room at Hannington Hall before lunch despite the shortage of coal. The twins were sitting close to it, Dilys' face pale and drawn while Una's was glowing with health. Her voice was full of concern as she leant over and grasped Dilys' hand. 'If you go on like this you're going to fade away!' she said anxiously. 'As Doctor Matthews thinks it's a grumbling appendix I don't see why he doesn't get on and remove it. I looked it up in that old medical directory of Father's and it said it is important to remove it before it bursts.'

Dilys attempted a smile. Her whole body ached with the constant vomiting every morning which sometimes now continued into the afternoon. She, too, wished their family doctor would be more positive. He seemed concerned that she had no pain, only the ache from retching.

Una's frown deepened. 'I heard Father say that Doctor Matthews was too old and Mother should take you up to London to see a specialist.'

Dilys shrugged indifferently. The fact was she felt too exhausted to care about anything other than the need to stop feeling so ill every morning . . . that and the continuing silence from Kristoffer. News on the wireless announced that the Russians were attacking Finland; and Germany, having invaded Poland, might well have Norway, Sweden and Denmark in its sights. Even if Kristoffer had not forgotten her by now, he must have many more urgent things to think about. As for the threatened appendix, she wished it could be removed and she could feel healthy and energetic again. It had even affected her once-regular monthly cycle, the absence of which she and Una attributed to the constant vomiting. They had not been able to account for the soreness of her breasts but Una thought that might be due to the fact that Dilys' new bust bodice was too tight.

Una suddenly scrambled to her feet, saying excitedly, 'Gosh, Dil! I never thought of it when I looked up "appendicitis" in Father's dictionary. I should have looked up "nausea". I'll go and get it!'

'Una, that old thing was published way back last century . . .' Dilys began when Una interrupted.

'So treatment might have changed now but the diagnoses won't have! Anyway, you can stay here if you want. I'm going to see what it says!'

It was nearly a quarter of an hour before she returned, a look of uncertainty on her face as she sat down once more by the fire. 'Took me ages because there were masses of causes listed . . .' Her voice suddenly deepened as she looked anxiously at her twin. 'Dil, there was a reference to "morning sickness" like you've been having but . . .' She broke off momentarily to lean over and grasp her sister's hands. 'Dil . . . Dil . . . you and Kristoffer . . . you didn't . . . you would have told me, wouldn't you, if . . .' She choked on the words, then, drawing a deep breath, concluded: 'You didn't let him *do it*, did you?'

The colour rushed into Dilys' white cheeks as she nodded. 'Once . . . only once! I know it was wrong but we love each other, Una. He does love me. I know he does! He gave me this ring, remember!' She reached beneath the collar of her blouse and held up the chain on which the ring was hanging for Una to see again. Then, as she grasped what Una's question implied, the colour rushed from her face and her voice dropped to a whisper as she said breathlessly: 'You don't think . . . I can't . . . *I can't* be going to have a baby!'

Seeing the look on her twin's face, which mirrored her own horrified feelings, Una said gently: 'It might not be that, Dil. It was just a thought . . . I could be wrong, but . . . oh, Dil, what are we going to do *if* I am right? We're going to have to tell Mother.'

Dilys' breath caught in her throat. She and Una gazed at one another in horror as they now pictured their mother's shocked face and their father's reaction. They recalled his long diatribes about the family having an exemplary reputation: flawless characters and the necessity to be known for their strict observance of the laws of good conduct. They had all been made aware of the seriousness of the responsibilities he had to his constituents and of his hopes for a seat in the Cabinet. White-faced, the two girls then thought of the utter impossibility of him having a daughter with an illegitimate baby.

'You're not to tell them, Una!' Dilys said violently. 'Not unless I'm sure. You might be wrong . . . it can't be true . . . we only did it once!' Then she burst into tears.

Una put her arms around her twin and hugged her. 'Don't cry, Dil, please!' she begged. 'I'm sure I was wrong, and if . . . if the worst came to the worst, we could find a way to tell Kristoffer and he could come to England and marry you. I know you are underage but Father would want you to get married.'

'Una, Kristoffer hasn't written to me,' Dilys said in a choked voice. 'I believed him when he said he loved me.' Her voice was almost inaudible as she added brokenly, 'He said so every time we were together. He wouldn't have given me this . . .' She fingered the ring on the chain round her neck once more. 'He said it was an engagement ring and when I was older we would be married. That's when we did it. But it was only once.'

Una remained silent as she listened as Dilys confided how wonderfully close she and Kristoffer had felt and how happy she was that her first experience had been with him. That although it had hurt at first he had been so gentle and caring.

'We truly loved each other, Una!' she wept now. 'We were going to spend the rest of our lives together. He loved me! I know he did!'

For a moment, neither spoke as Una considered the absence of a letter from Dilys' Norwegian boyfriend. If there really was a baby on the way, it was imperative he was told about it so he could marry her. It was now four months, she calculated, since Dilys could have conceived a child, and according to the medical directory a birth followed less than a year after.

If Dilys was having a baby, Kristoffer must be found soon but it was not going to be easy. Dilys could only tell her that he lived near a place called Bergen, that it overlooked a beautiful fjord and that his father owned a timber company. The only other fact she was certain about was that he had already done his compulsory military service.

'Kristoffer will come to England and we will be married!'
Dilys announced to Una. By then she would be eighteen and,
although not yet an adult, she had told Kristoffer she thought
her parents would agree to a wedding even if it meant her going
to live in Norway. 'Kristoffer had it all planned!' Dilys now
whispered. 'Oh, Una, what on earth am I going to do?'

Una drew a deep breath. 'You're going to stop panicking
and wait, Dil. Any day now you will have got the curse and
we'll be saying how silly we were to have got in such a
tizz about something which was never going to happen.
Meanwhile . . .' she smiled disarmingly at her twin, '. . . I'll
tell Mother I've now started being sick, too, and she'll think
you've passed on some sort of bug to me.'

Dilys hugged her. 'I suppose I was silly, Una!' she muttered.
'I mean, not to have told you about me and Kristoffer when it
happened. We always do tell each other everything and . . .'

'And I didn't tell you that I had done it, too!' Una admitted,
'but I was luckier than you because nothing has happened to
me since.'

For a moment, both girls were silent as simultaneously they
realized that Una's last words were all but an admission that
something *had* happened to Dilys, and that the 'something'
could only mean she was going to have a baby.

January and February 1940 gave way to March and there were
welcome signs of spring following a winter so cold that in
January even the River Thames had frozen for the first time
since the eighteenth century. Everyone now had ration books
and although meat was not yet rationed, other daily require-
ments were. The weekly ration of butter was four ounces, sugar
was twelve ounces and bacon or ham was three and a half
ounces. At sea, German U-boats were regularly sinking supply
ships and all the country's imports including war materials were
similarly at risk.

Albert, Sir Godfrey's chauffeur, had been called up, as all
men between the ages of eighteen and forty could now be
conscripted, so Henderson, a veteran of the last war who ran
the village garage, came up to Hannington Hall to give the
twins driving lessons in the family's Bentley. He also served

as the village taxi, and had been taking the twins to the secretarial school in Fenbury and bringing them back at lunchtime, but since petrol rationing had started the girls were going by train from Hannington Halt.

Neither of the girls were enjoying the course insisted upon by their father. Now eighteen years old, Una in particular missed the carefree, active life they had enjoyed in Germany, and she was still finding it hard to believe that their former German friends and companions with whom she had danced and skied and flirted were now her enemies. The war itself was going far from well and news of the terrible losses of shipping in the north Atlantic filled the newspapers. Sir Godfrey, now almost exclusively in London, forecast that the Germans would attack Scandinavia and the Low Countries before almost certainly turning their sights on Paris, attacking the French and British troops, and then invasion of Britain might follow. The situation was very grave.

Dilys was still without word from Kristoffer, and she had lost all but the very faintest hope that she would hear from him. Dire as the Allies' situation now was, her own frightening situation preoccupied her and, on her behalf, Una, too. She had even felt the baby move inside her.

Most of their friends in the neighbourhood had either joined up or were in jobs or on courses in London. James Sherwin was one of the very few people who called to see them at Hannington Hall. He had asked their mother's permission to take them out one evening to the cinema where the film *Wuthering Heights* was showing. Dilys had wept, her thoughts filled with her lost love, Kristoffer.

James drove them home afterwards and they had thanked him for inviting them. He had said that the pleasure was entirely his, and he hoped he might do so again.

'I think he's probably lonely living in that big Victorian house all on his own,' Una said. Their father approved of their friendship as James had treated his Labrador successfully when it had broken its leg and Sir Godfrey happily praised James' skills.

'It really is a pity he's so old! I might have fancied him,' Una had commented later with a grin. 'Not that I'd want to be the wife of a vet. I want to marry someone rich and important and travel round the world in my own huge yacht!'

Despite her dislike of the idea of marrying a vet, Una read in the local paper a few days later that James was looking for a replacement for his receptionist who had enlisted in the Land Army. Standing in the cold, unheated hallway outside the cloak-room where the telephone hung on the wall, she asked the operator to connect her to his surgery.

'James, it's me, Una Singleby!' she said when he answered. 'I've just seen your advertisement. Dilys and I have finished our secretarial course so we could start right away if you wanted. Would it be all right if we both shared the work? We'd only expect one of us to be paid.' Without giving James time to reply, she added: 'We're both bored stuck at home with nothing much to do. I'm sorry about the shorthand but we are both good typists. Dilys got ninety-five per cent for her exam mark and I got eighty-four.'

Una finally ran out of breath and, having got over his initial surprise, James was now smiling. He liked both of the twins and the shy, gentle Dilys slightly the better of the two. She only smiled rarely and more often than not left it to her twin to speak for them both. However, he had now been without assistance for two weeks and was becoming desperate. Two young girls were not the replacement receptionist he'd had in mind, but it was just possible that they could manage the work between them. They had pleasant, educated voices for telephone enquiries and appointments. He guessed that the dominant one, Una, might be good at dealing with impatient clients and the quiet one, Dilys, good with calming anxious ones and frightened pets.

'If it's all right with your parents, Una, I'm happy to give it a try,' he told her. 'The surgery is only a ten-minute walk from Fenbury Station, so it would be just a short walk here, and I could run you home in my car when I close the surgery at night. I should warn you that it could be quite late – six or even seven o'clock if there's an emergency.'

'We wouldn't mind that!' Una spoke for them both. 'As for the parents, they're mostly up in London now because of this silly old war. This horrible blackout everywhere is such a bore; surely a German bomber couldn't see the streetlights!' She gave

a quick snort as she added: 'We had the village ARP warden
come up to the house the other evening blowing a gasket because
there was a chink of light coming from our maid's bedroom at
the top of the house. He—'

She would have continued had James not been obliged to
interrupt her, explaining that he needed to get back to the surgery.
'Could you both come and see me in the surgery after lunch
on Saturday?' he asked. 'Then I can explain what you would
have to do. Meanwhile, it will give you time to discuss the idea
with your parents.'

Replacing the telephone receiver, Una turned to Dilys, her
expression now concerned. 'You do feel well enough to do the
job, don't you, Dil?'

She broke off as Dilys interrupted, saying: 'I really want this
job. Don't you see, if our parents won't let me keep the baby
I'll have saved some money and it will show them I can earn
my own living if they won't let me stay at home.'

With difficulty, Una hid her dismay. Stupid of her though it
was, she had been hoping that somehow the problem of Dilys'
baby would go away: there was no baby; the baby would die
at birth; Kristoffer would suddenly appear and marry her. That
her sister might actually have a baby was too frightening to
think about, still less their parents' reaction. Hastily putting
such thoughts aside, she decided to telephone her father about
James' job, praying that he would not disapprove.

They were over the moon when their father gave his approval.
'Do you girls good to find out what it's like earning your living.
Nice chap, Sherwin. Did a really good job on Bracken that time
he got run over.'

Sir Godfrey did not have time now to see a great deal of his
two Labradors. They were kennelled in the disused stable and
exercised by the gardener handyman, Norman, who had been
his batman in the last war. If either of the dogs was ill, James
was the vet called in to look after them. Since the outbreak of
war and the need for Sir Godfrey to spend so much more time
in London, Norman had been paid to take the dogs home with
him, which he was more than happy to do. He was also grateful
for any scraps from the kitchen which Cook gave him to supple-
ment their food.

The twins started work at the surgery the following week. James was surprised to discover how greatly they differed in character while resembling each other so closely in looks. Dilys, the quieter of the two, often had an expression which he could only describe as wistful. Una did all the talking and was surprisingly efficient. As he had anticipated, Dilys was gentle and capable with the sick and nervous animals and, indeed, their owners. Without understanding why he should do so, he began to feel concerned for her and in the brief moments when he had time to talk to the twins, he would feel quite pleased with himself if he succeeded in making her smile.

In point of fact, Dilys had absolutely nothing to smile about. She could no longer fasten the waistbands of her skirts and her breasts were fuller and tender. The movement of the baby inside her was more frequent and more pronounced. As Una kept saying, she could not put off telling their parents she was pregnant for much longer. By unspoken agreement, she and Una never discussed what might happen when they were told, although each had known that under no circumstances would their father allow Dilys to have the baby and keep it at home. Their job at the surgery was a very welcome diversion from their anxieties.

Dilys had finally given up hope of hearing from Kristoffer. She heard on the news that Norway was on the brink of being invaded by Germany. According to her father, British troops were being sent there to support their own army. She was now forced to accept Una's sympathetic but firm conviction that Kristoffer's feelings must have been a very great deal more transitory than her own.

'I expect he meant every word he said at the time,' Una had suggested gently, 'but . . . well, everything was different over there, wasn't it? It was all masses of students and young people like us having fun together. Just think about those Luftwaffe cadets,' she added, 'Heinz, Wilhelm and Konrad, who used to be such fun. Do you realize, Dil, that they are now almost certainly flying their beastly aeroplanes and trying to shoot down our boys? And your Kristoffer is probably trying to kill some of the other friends we made out there. I really do *hate* this war!'

At least while she was working at the vet's, Dilys thought, she was able to forget her condition for a little while. She enjoyed the variety of tasks she shared with her twin. Una had turned out to be efficient as a receptionist, and on two occasions James had called on her to act as his assistant.

'If either of you ever thought about a career with animals, I don't doubt you would both do very well,' he'd told them. It was something she would really like to continue doing, Dilys thought, before remembering with a sinking heart that she was soon going to be the mother of a baby and would not be having any kind of career at all.

FIVE

'For heaven's sake, Dilys, go and get out of that ridiculous smock!' Lady Singleby's voice was bordering on shock. 'You look like a dairy maid!'

The twins exchanged glances and Una reached hurriedly across the breakfast room table to grasp Dilys' trembling hand in hers.

'I'm afraid Dliys has some rather bad news to tell you, Mother. She is going to have a baby.'

For a moment, Lady Singleby was speechless. She pushed her plate of half-eaten toast and marmalade away, patted her neatly waved white hair absent-mindedly and stared at her twin daughters. Her pale blue eyes went from one to the other in disbelief.

She had arrived home late last night after a lengthy spell in London where she had been supervising help finding temporary homes for families whose houses and flats had been bombed, so consequently had not seen her daughters for three weeks.

The horrifying shock of Una's announcement filled her with dismay. She stared at Dilys' white face, her eyes travelling down to the recognizable bump beneath her daughter's ungainly smock. Appalled, she realized that not only was Dilys pregnant but that it was not going to be all that long before she gave birth. She was unmarried and only just eighteen. Her next, even more frightening thought was of her husband's reaction to the news. No one was more aware than she, his wife for over twenty years, of his lifelong, passionate desire to be promoted to the Cabinet, an ambition which she privately feared, replacing the far younger previous incumbent who had been called up and was now in the army. She knew only too well his almost paranoid insistence upon conformity, on the absolute necessity for his own and his family's impeccable reputation.

'You're telling me Dilys is . . . is pregnant?' she gasped.

Una nodded and Dilys burst into tears.

Her mind racing, it occurred to Lady Singleby that, ghastly though the news was, the present situation might yet be mitigated if Dilys could be married quietly before the baby was born . . . yes, married, but to whom?

'The father!' she exclaimed, staring at Dilys' white, tear-streaked face. 'You must be married at once. You can stay with your aunts. They can keep you hidden until the wedding. You can be married quietly down there and—' She broke off and grasped Dilys' arm. 'Who is he? The father? Answer me, child!'

As she waited for Dilys' reply, it crossed her mind that he must be one of the public school boys, the sons of their neighbours who the twins met at local dances and tennis club parties. Did the silly girl now think she was in love with this boy? No matter, he would have to marry her whatever his age. Sir Godfrey would see to that.

'Kristoffer Holberg. He's a boy I met in Germany!' Dilys whispered. 'He's Norwegian.' She broke off as tears engulfed her once more.

'Then your father must write to him at once . . .' Lady Singleby began, but Una broke in.

'Dil doesn't have his address, Mother, and he hasn't written to her since we left Munich. He doesn't know about the baby. With the war and everything, we don't think he wants to see Dil again.'

Lady Singleby's face turned pink. 'I don't imagine your father will care what the young man wants. He shall be made to do what is right, and you, Dilys, will do what your father tells you.' Her voice softened the merest trifle as she added: 'Why in heaven's name didn't you tell me this before? What on earth did you think you were going to do when that child is born? When is it due?' She turned to Una, saying, 'You have a more sensible head on your shoulders – why didn't you make your sister tell me about this months ago?'

'Partly because Dil didn't want me to say anything until she heard from Kristoffer, and also . . .' she added pointedly, '. . . you haven't been home often enough or long enough for there to have been a suitable moment. You're always in town now with Father or you're busy with that WVS thing you're doing. Besides, there didn't seem much point worrying you until Dil was certain about it. She didn't start getting big for ages!'

Dilys, now dry-eyed, said urgently, 'Must you tell Father? I mean, couldn't I go and live in a cottage somewhere where no one knows me . . . Scotland or Ireland or something? Una says she'd come with me.'

Lady Singleby drew an exasperated sigh. 'And just what did you think you were going to live on? Food costs money; houses, cottages cost money . . .' She paused before adding with difficulty: 'Babies cost money. And what chance do you think there would be of either of you ever finding suitable husbands in future?' She paused to draw a deep breath and then said forcibly: 'Of course your father must be told. However busy he is, he must come down this afternoon.'

She forced herself to look once more at her daughter's smocked figure. 'Heaven alone knows what that man you work for, Mr Sherwin, must be thinking! Being a vet, I imagine he has probably guessed you are pregnant, Dilys. I'm surprised he hasn't given you notice!'

James had in fact guessed Dilys might be pregnant. Not only had she started wearing the loose-fitting garments, but there was something about her which reminded him painfully of when his wife had been pregnant with their son – a sort of concentrated yet dreamy manner, in some ways as if in a private world. Her face had somehow changed, too, and recently she and her twin had become easily distinguishable.

Una was now considering enlightening her mother as to James' kind, friendly nature, but decided not to do so. Their mother was clearly deeply shocked and any further discussion about poor Dilys' future was better left for the moment.

Fighting the feeling of betrayal of her twin, Una was feeling an unexpected sense of relief that it was now her mother not herself who was responsible for Dil's' situation. The weeks since Christmas had flown by and sometimes it had seemed as if she, not Dilys, had been the one lying awake at night worrying how to solve her sister's problem, wondering what would happen when Dilys had the baby. Dilys had seemed astonishingly complacent and spoke frequently but irrationally about how she would love and care for this baby because it was Kristoffer's. No amount of cautioning from her, Una, as to the certainty that Kristoffer had long since forgotten his brief fling with Dilys had deterred her from the dream world in which she appeared now to be living. She even spoke of calling the baby Christopher if it was a boy or Christina if it was a girl.

Their mother's shocked reaction to learning the facts had not been quite as drastic as either had expected, but the thought of their father's was daunting.

'You will stay with me when Father gets home and calls me into the study, won't you, Una?' Dilys now pleaded as they went up to their bedrooms to get ready for the Sunday morning service at St Andrew's church. 'It's bad enough when he gets into one of his bates and he's bound to be terribly angry . . .' Her voice trailed away as she struggled into her coat.

Una understood exactly why her twin was so nervous. From time to time when they were growing up, although it had not happened very often, their father had lost his temper when they'd continued to commit the same offence after his first reprimand. The family cook at the time had been an ill-tempered woman called Mrs Kelley. She always complained to their mother if they left uneaten any of the starchy food sent up to the nursery for their meals. They had devised a nickname for her – 'Mrs Smelly-Belly' – which they'd thought so funny they had dissolved into the usual uncontrollable giggles when hearing their governess repeat it to their father. On the second occasion they were reported, Sir Godfrey had been angry enough to lose his temper. The two seven-year-old girls had been made to turn their palms up on his desk and been slapped hard enough with a ruler to set them howling. His furious purple face and angry voice had disturbed them as much if not more than their stinging palms. Small wonder now, Una told herself, that Dilys was afraid of his reaction when he arrived from London that after-noon and was told his eighteen-year-old unmarried daughter was going to have a baby.

The twins had every reason to be nervous. Sir Godfrey had been working overtime in London. After occupying Denmark and Norway, Germany was now invading Holland. In London the government was in conflict as to the planned strategy for the British Expeditionary Force. The probability that Hitler might next intend to include Belgium and even France in his list of conquests could no longer be ignored. Mining the beaches was mooted, as was the building of concrete gun emplacements on the south coast in addition to those defences already in place such as the issue of gas masks, the necessary blackout curtains in all the windows, the removal of signposts and construction of air-raid shelters.

When Sir Godrfey finally arrived home late that afternoon and his wife met him in the hall, he failed to give her the customary peck on the cheek.

'There had better be a good reason you have brought me back this afternoon, Daphne,' he said sharply. 'As I told you on the phone, I have important meetings tomorrow and I'll have to go back to town on the late train tonight.'

'Godfrey, I can assure you this disaster is not only important but extremely urgent,' Lady Singleby interrupted him as she followed her husband into the drawing room. She closed the door behind them and before either had sat down, she blurted out: 'One of your daughters is pregnant!'

Sir Godfrey's head turned sharply to look at this wife. 'What did you say?' he asked sharply. 'One of the girls is *pregnant*?'

Understanding his shocked disbelief, Lady Singleby remained silent as she urged him into one of the armchairs. She then crossed the room and poured him a glass of brandy before seating herself opposite him. Only then did she take her courage in both hands and, as unemotionally as she could, said, 'I'm afraid it's true, Godfrey. Dilys is going to have a baby. And if that isn't bad enough, the father is some unknown Norwegian boy she met in Munich and she doesn't even know where he lives, so we can't get in touch with him and insist he marries her.'

'Poppycock!' Sir Godfrey exploded, his face flushing a deep red and his pale blue eyes narrowing. 'There has to be a way to get in touch with the scoundrel. I'll get Smithers at the Foreign Office to locate him. He must be brought to England and marry Dilys as quickly as possible.'

Daphne clasped her hands together as if this would give her

the strength to force her husband to face the ugly truth. 'There's a war in Norway. Godfrey—' she began but he interrupted her.

'I am not without influence, Daphne: a fact you seem to have forgotten. My contact in the Foreign Office can trace this fellow's family and—'

Daphne interrupted him a second time. 'Godfrey!' she reminded him sharply. 'The silly girl does not know his address. Apart from the fact that their country is at war, there could be hundreds of Norwegians with the same surname and—'

It was Sir Godfrey's turn to interrupt. His mouth tightened as he said sharply, 'It not only "can be done" but "will be done". Meanwhile, Dilys is to be confined to the house. I will *not* have her going about the village where all my constituents can see her disgraceful condition. And she's to stop going to work at the vet's in Fenbury. Really, Daphne, it is beyond me why you have not supervised the girls' behaviour so this sort of disaster could not happen.'

Lady Singleby's face turned pink with indignation. With a huge effort, she bit back the reminder that it was her husband's idea they should go abroad to learn a language; that it was in Munich where Dilys had disgraced herself. Time had taught her to avoid Sir Godfrey's often irrelevant outbursts which could be quite violent, especially if he was tired and had had a few too many whiskies to revive him. She now forbore reminding him that her war job with the WVS would not allow her to remain at home to supervise all day. It would be far preferable for Dilys to continue her job at Fenbury and be away from the village. One thing was certain: the wretched girl could not go around in that awful smock. Hopefully none of the village women had seen her in it or they would already be gossiping when they met in the village hall for lessons in first aid on Wednesdays or to knit woollen squares to be made into blankets on Saturdays. In retrospect, she could recall now that the last time she had been home and had entered the hall, their chattering had ceased abruptly.

As she left the room to go and fetch Dilys and then get ready for supper, Lady Singleby faced the fact that on this occasion her husband was not going to be able to resolve the problems which lay ahead. This conviction that the baby's father could be traced was so unlikely in her opinion it could be discounted. Only the previous day on the six o'clock news, they'd been told Norway's army was incapable of repelling the might of the highly trained German forces. If the culprit was not found, what would happen to Dilys?

Lady Singleby had never been a doting mother, nor, indeed, in the least anxious to have any more children after the twins were born. Nanny had coped with them as babies and then a governess until they were old enough to go to boarding school. She had been rather flattered when her friends had commented on how alike they were and how pretty. Una tended to be slightly more forward and more adventurous than her twin, but Dilys was more advanced in aptitude. They were little trouble and she had been quite proud of them both on the rare occasions she, not Nanny or their governess, took them out with her. Now, suddenly, one of them was about to bring appalling disgrace on the family. The thought of her sisters, Ivy and Rose, learning the facts was almost as daunting as it had been telling her husband.

She hurried up the stairs on her way to the twins' bedroom where she must tell Dilys that her father was waiting in the drawing room to see her, and to be quick about it as he was catching the late train back to London. As she did so, it suddenly struck her that as there had not been any mention of Dilys being raped, she must have allowed the culprit to have sex with her despite the fact that she was an underage virgin. Recalling the unpleasant occasion when, on her wedding night, she had submitted to her husband's sexual demands, she failed to see why Dilys had submitted to the foreign student when he had no rights as a husband. In her experience it was certainly not an activity to be enjoyed.

Downstairs, Sir Godfrey was reluctantly shocked by the memory of the letter he had destroyed last September from the foreign student shortly after he had brought his daughters home. At the time he had considered Dilys much too young to be receiving that kind of sentimental rubbish, and especially from a foreigner. It occurred to him now that it had included an address to which Dilys was to have replied and was momentarily filled with regret that he had been so hasty in destroying it.

Not one to justify or dwell on his actions, he put the thoughts aside and awaited the arrival of his daughter. He would get on to his Foreign Office colleague tomorrow, who would undoubtedly be able to trace the whereabouts of the Norwegian. One thing was absolutely certain: he was not going to have his or his family's good name tarnished by the advent of an illegitimate child, of all things. War or no war, even if the culprit was a foreigner he must be found without delay and be made to marry his daughter.

Upstairs in their room, the twins had been sitting side by side on Una's bed, Una's arm protectively round Dilys' shoulders as they strained their ears to hear what was happening. The faint sound of their father's loud, angry voice had been just audible and then the banging of the drawing-room door. They were tense with anxiety when their mother came into the room to instruct Dilys to go down to the drawing room at once.

When Dilys returned to the bedroom ten minutes later, far from looking frightened or distraught, she was radiant. She flung herself down on the bed beside Una, saying, 'Father thinks he knows someone who can find Kristoffer. When he does, he is to tell him about the baby and make him come to England and marry me, and Una, I just *know* Kristoffer will want to come.' Yet again she fingered the ring hanging round her neck. 'I know you don't think so, Una, but I just know he does still love me no matter what anyone says.'

Una regarded her nervously. 'Wasn't Father terribly angry?' she asked. 'He sounded furious!'

'Yes, yes, I know!' Dilys replied, 'but when I told him I knew the name of Kristoffer's home town, Bergen, and that his father owned a large timber company somewhere there, he was certain he could be found.'

For the first time in the past eighteen years of their lives, Una did not share her twin's certainties – not regarding her beloved Kristoffer being found, but that when he was told he had fathered a baby and must come to England to marry Dilys, he would want to do so. Much as she wished, she could not believe that Dilys' faith in her beloved Kristoffer's undying love was justified.

SIX

It was with considerable difficulty that Kristoffer managed to hide his feelings of despair as his parents hosted a small party to celebrate their wedding anniversary. Gerda and her parents, Herr and Fru Magnusson were there, as were his aunt and uncle and two elderly friends of his parents. Pleading a need for some fresh air and exercise after the meal was over, he had managed to avoid Gerda's request to accompany him and gone out for a walk up into the woods behind the house.

It had been snowing in the night and the faint glimmer of sun did little to combat the cold to which Kristoffer was oblivious. His mind was filled with memories of Munich, that lovely city now embroiled in its country's war with the Allied countries, and the shock of losing contact with Dilys. For the umpteenth time he remembered that dreadful day when her father had spirited her away and his life had changed seemingly for ever.

Although he had returned to Bergen to work with his father at Holberg Tømmer AS, the family timber company, there were the evenings and nights to be endured with memories of what had been and fears that Dilys had not after all been in love with him and was deliberately not writing to him. Gerda was an almost daily visitor, suggesting they went to the cinema or a party, expecting their past affectionate familiarity to continue where it had left off when he met Dilys. He knew he should tell her he had fallen in love with someone else, but his feelings were too raw that even the mention of Dilys' name brought a painful stab to his heart.

With Great Britain at war with Germany, his plans to go to England to try to find Dilys were impossible, and so he had decided to join the army. He had been given three days' leave to go home for the family party and would be returning the following day to his unit. As he stood now beneath a fir

tree dripping snow on to his head and shoulders, he reflected
that he would not have gone home had he not hoped – irrationally
– that there might yet be a letter from Dilys.

Far from regretting his army life, not only did it distract him
from thoughts of Dilys but, like all his countrymen, he intended
to be active in defending his country against the threatening
German takeover of Bergen, among all the other Norwegian
ports. Presently, he told himself, he would have to return to the
house where his mother would give him those long, anxious
looks. He knew she had guessed that his relationship with the
English girl had been a lot more serious than he had told her,
but he had not been able to bring himself to confide in her,
knowing as he did that she, like her neighbouring best friend,
was hoping he would marry Gerda.

Gerda! He thought of her now. She was so affectionate, so
expectant of his response to her. Her smiles had faded momentarily when at the lunch party his aunt and uncle had referred
to 'the nice young English girl' he had introduced them to in
Munich. He'd replied in as casual a tone as he could manage:
'Oh, her father took her back to England the next day knowing
war with Germany was imminent,' and Dilys had not been
mentioned again.

Sighing, Kristoffer told himself once more that he was
fortunate to have been drafted into the army and could live
away from home and from Gerda's unspoken demands for
physical affection and his mother's anxious glances when any
reference was made to 'the English girl' he was friendly with
in Munich.

It was not the first time he had found himself in the difficult
position of having to parry a female's overt interest in him. At
the age of twenty-one when he had been studying in France,
his thirty-five-year-old female teacher, an attractive Parisienne,
had opted to teach him a lot more than the French language.
Unfortunately, her lessons, far from being academic, had come
to an abrupt end when, after an enlightening few months, she
confessed she had fallen in love with him. He had been both
flattered and embarrassed by her declaration. Subsequently he
came to realize that he was envied by his contemporaries because
he never lacked for female admirers.

Now, as Kristoffer looked back on those early years in his late teens and twenties, he recalled that there had been several times when he'd thought he was in love – a possibility he recognized was absurd once he met Dilys.

The pain of his loss returned yet again and he shivered, aware suddenly that he had grown cold. He tucked his gloved hands under his armpits for extra warmth. The sky had darkened and it looked as if it might soon start snowing. He must go back, he told himself. It was nearly four o'clock. Perhaps Gerda and her parents would have gone home and he would not have to face the inviting look in her eyes. In the old days before he had gone to Germany he would have walked her back to her house and stopped in her doorway for the customary kisses and intimate embraces.

Banging his gloved hands against his sides, he made his way back down the familiar path through the trees. The snow had stopped melting and there was now a light coating of frost on the branches. It reflected the cold emptiness in his heart, he told himself as he faced the unavoidable fact that the girl he'd wanted to marry may never have really loved him at all.

It had been a hectic day for Una at the surgery, having taken on Dilys' tasks as James' assistant as well as acting as his receptionist. When he finally closed the doors at half past six, she sat down on one of the now-empty benches and drew a sigh of relief.

James regarded her anxiously. 'Sure it has not been too much for you?' he asked. 'You look exhausted! That tiresome Mrs Campaign ought to be called Mrs Complain. I've told her a dozen times that there is nothing wrong with her Yorkie except that he's hopelessly overweight! Hopefully now with food rationing the unfortunate Twinkle will slim down despite his doting mistress's overindulgence.'

He smiled at Una, adding: 'How about coming next door and having a quick drink before I drive you home? I presume you are allowed to have alcohol? A sherry, perhaps?' His smile deepened. 'Medicinal, of course, as alcohol is taboo.'

He really was a very nice man, Una thought as she followed

him back across the hall to his drawing room. When she and
Dilys had first met him they'd thought he was a bit stuffy but
had since realized that beneath his confident, professional
approach to his clients he was quite shy. Since they had started
work at the surgery they had discovered both his delightful
sense of humour and exceptional depth of understanding of the
feelings of sick animals and their worried owners.

That innate compassion in his character was apparent now
when, having given Una a glass of sherry and poured himself
a whisky, he said gently, 'Forgive me for asking so personal a
question, Una, but I couldn't help noticing . . . your sister . . .
she's having a baby, isn't she?'

Una gasped. 'You know . . . I mean, you guessed?'

She broke off as James interrupted her. 'I guessed!' he said
quietly. Then added with the hint of a smile: 'Symptoms in
humans are very similar to those of animals! I guessed some
time ago.' He cleared his throat. 'Please forgive me for
concerning myself in something that is not my business, but
when you told me this morning that Dilys wouldn't be coming
to work again . . . well, I wondered—'

He broke off and Una felt a huge sense of relief that she
was not now going to be the one who had to enlighten him to
her sister's disgrace. She and Dilys discussed every morning
when they were getting dressed whether the clothes Dilys
was wearing were too revealing not just to their employer but
to the servants, the friends and neighbours who sometimes
came to see their mother on the rare occasions she was now
home. Lately, they had been forced to admit that none of Dilys'
clothes had waistbands large enough for fastening, and she
had been forced to add a strip of elastic and cover it with a
loose-fitting blouse and jersey. They had decided that as their
employer was a man he would not know how ridiculously
unfashionable her clothes were.

Impulsively, Una now decided to discuss Dilys' predicament
with James, who had sounded more sympathetic than critical.
Soon everyone was going to know if Dilys remained at home.
Even if Kristoffer was found by some miracle and was made
to come to England, he was an adult and could not be forced to
marry Dilys if he didn't want to. He might even be married

already for all they knew! And the baby was due to be born in little over eight weeks' time.

Her mind made up, Una gripped her sherry glass and, leaning forward, gave the man listening to her a brief summary of the events leading to her twin's present predicament.

Although not shocked by what he was hearing, James was surprised. Since their first encounter at Christmas and during the last few months they had been working for him, he had come to know the twins well enough to appreciate the innate differences in their characters. Therefore he would not now have been so surprised had it been Una, the more dominant one, who had got herself into trouble. It was far less easy to understand how the shy, gentle Dilys had, at the tender age of seventeen, willingly lost her virginity to a young man she had only known for a short while. Una had assured him that Dilys had not been raped or plied with too much alcohol; she had fallen in love with the young man and he with her.

James' thoughts winged back to the day when he was in his twenties, a student at veterinary college. He had fallen in love at first sight with one of the female students. They had been married six months later, and when a year later his young wife, Margaret, had produced their son, she had given up her plans for a career in medicine and stayed at home to care for him and their baby.

They had, James now realized, been no less precipitate than Dilys and her young lover: as certain as he and Margaret had been of their love for one another. In their case, tragedy had shattered his dreams when his wife and child had been killed in a car crash. Since then he had never remarried despite his intense loneliness. Was this young girl's love life to have a tragic ending, too? Would her loved one be found? And if so, would the Norwegian student really return her love and be eager to marry her, or had he forgotten her as Una feared might be the case?

James' face showed his concern as he looked at Una and said, 'You will tell me if there is any way at all that I can help? Please tell Dilys I am hoping that things will turn out all right for her.' He paused before adding: 'Meanwhile, Una, you will keep me informed, won't you? I've no need to tell you that anything you say will be treated as totally confidential.'

It was after seven o'clock and James insisted on driving Una home. Having thanked him for the lift and for the second time for his sympathetic understanding of Dilys' situation, she hurried upstairs to the privacy of their bedroom where she knew she would find her sister. As was now customary, her twin was sitting in a chair by the window reading a book. After removing her hat and coat, Una sat down on the bed and proceeded to tell Dilys of her conversation with James after he'd admitted he had guessed her condition. To Una's surprise, Dilys was not embarrassed as she had anticipated, but indifferent.

'What does it matter if James knows?' she declared. 'Soon everyone will know and be saying how awful it is me having an illegitimate baby, but I'm not sorry, Una. It's part of Kristoffer – the only part I have. I still love him . . .' And she burst into tears.

Una put a consoling arm round her shoulders but she could not think of anything to say to comfort her.

Lady Singleby returned home each of the following weekends and remained uncommunicative regarding Dilys' future. Sir Godfrey remained in London until 10 April when he arrived home in the evening. After spending half an hour alone with his wife in his study, he sent the maid to find Dilys.

When she came into the room he instructed her to sit down in the chair opposite him. He guessed by the eager, expectant expression on her pale face that she had been hoping he had located Kristoffer's whereabouts, which was not the case. He cleared his throat and a trifle less harshly than he had intended, stated, 'I'll get straight to the point, Dilys. My contact in the Foreign Office managed to find the timber company in Bergen but the owner told him his only son, who is in the Norwegian army, is expected to marry a childhood friend. So that's that, Dilys, and there is now no alternative but for you to go to the mother-and-baby home which your mother found for one of my constituents who was having an . . .' he hesitated for a fraction of a second before saying bluntly, '. . . an illegitimate baby. Arrangements have been made for you to go there next Wednesday.'

It was several minutes before Dilys could find her voice. The news that she was to be sent away to have her baby paled into total insignificance beside the news that Kristoffer was more or less engaged to be married to what sounded like his childhood sweetheart. Una had been right when she'd implied that her association in Munich with Kristoffer had not been a love affair on his part as it was on hers. Was it possible she had been so gullible, so stupid as to imagine that Kristoffer had only been pretending to love her?

'Dilys, did you hear what I said?'

Her father's angry voice brought back her attention as she assured him she was listening.

'Your mother will drive you to Chertsey after lunch on Wednesday. In the meantime, you will remain in your bedroom. The servants will be told that you are going into hospital for an overdue abdominal operation which, hopefully, will explain your present condition.'

Dilys caught her breath. 'But surely when they see me with the baby they—'

She got no further before Sir Godfrey, now purple-faced, broke in sharply: 'For heaven's sake, girl, there will be no baby! It will be adopted. That is the whole purpose of The Willows establishment. You will be taken care of until after the birth, when it will be handed over to its future parents. It is extremely discreet and—'

'No, Father, no!' Dilys shouted. 'I won't let them have my baby. It's mine . . . mine and Kristoffer's and I don't care what you say, he did love me and I loved him. I won't let—'

Sir Godfrey banged his fist down on the desktop and said furiously, 'Stop this nonsense immediately! Can you be so stupid as not to realize the harm you would be doing, not just to yourself but to your unfortunate twin, your mother and me if you came home with an illegitimate baby? The servants and our neighbours would be shocked beyond measure. As for my constituents, discovering that their chosen Member of Parliament who represented them was unable to control his own daughter's immoral behaviour—' He broke off momentarily, a look of horror on his face, then continued: 'I'd be made a laughing stock . . . probably lose my seat at the next election or be asked to resign. Moreover, Dilys, what decent young man would consider marrying you in the future, let alone your unfortunate twin. *Of course* you cannot keep the baby!' he shouted, his face now scarlet.

He was silent for a moment before finally he cleared his throat and, tightening his mouth, he ordered Dilys to go to her room and remain there.

Dilys was trembling but dry-eyed when Una came hurrying into their bedroom to find out what their father had had to say. Downstairs in the hall where she had been hiding behind the hatstand listening, she had heard his raised voice, his shouts and knew things had gone badly for her sister. Putting her arms round her twin, she hugged her, saying, 'No matter what, Dil, I'll be with you!'

Dilys returned the hug and, shaking her head, said sadly, 'I don't think you'd be allowed to come with me, Una. Not if they made me go to that place Father wants to send me – a place where they will take babies away after they're born.' She placed her hand on her stomach and added: 'I can feel it moving, my baby, and . . . and I love it. Even if Kristoffer is engaged to another girl, it doesn't stop me loving his baby. I won't let anyone take it away. I don't care what Father says! I'll run away somewhere and get a job and earn money and manage somehow . . . I won't let them take it!'

Una had been feeling anxious but now she was seriously concerned, realizing as she did that Dilys actually meant what she was saying. It was immediately clear to her that her twin meant what she had threatened to do and that there was no way she would be able to manage on her own if she left home.

'I'll help, of course, Dil,' she said. 'Maybe we could manage if I could get a job which pays a bit more than James does. But it wouldn't just be food we'd have to buy: we'd have to find somewhere to live and pay for that, and clothes and things . . .'

Her voice trailed away as she started to realize how hopelessly ignorant both she and her sister were about such domestic expenses or housekeeping. Neither had been to a domestic science college as had some of their school friends. There was also the insurmountable difficulty that they were both minors and if their father chose to have them followed then, however far they went, they would be forced to go home. If that happened, Dilys' baby would be taken away.

'We need to make a plan,' she said in as firm a voice as she could manage. 'Just give me a bit of time to think how we could manage on our own.' She put her arms around her twin's ungainly figure, hugging her reassuringly as she vowed: 'Somehow, Dil, I'll find a way to help you keep your baby!'

Twenty-four hours later, leaving Dilys locked in the bedroom by their mother, Una caught the small steam train at Hannington village halt and rode the short journey to Fenbury. As she walked to the surgery from the station, the early April sun was shining on the newly opened green leaves of the beech trees, she heard the chattering of birds looking for nesting sites, and she thought that had it not been for Dilys' dire predicament it would have been a day for rejoicing rather than anxiety.

Removing her warm overcoat, tam-o'shanter and gloves, she heard James call out to her from the small room where he performed operations. Although the surgery had only been open for half an hour, James was already operating on a dog with a broken leg and the reception room was already occupied by two women with their dogs. The one with the poodle was insisting that her dog was next to be seen and she was already late due to the emergency operation in progress; the other that her dachshund only needed the vet's attention for a few minutes so she should be first to see James.

Una was still calming the women when James came out of the operating room, his face beaming.

'The operation went really well despite me having no assistant.' His smile broadened as he looked at Una. 'Glad you're here on time, young lady. The patient is in the recovery hut if you'll go and take a quick look at—'

He got no further before both waiting customers were vying for his attention as they tried to push each other aside. In doing so, their two dogs became entangled by their leads. Una and James managed between them to separate the dogs and James was followed back into his surgery while Una was able to go and see James' patient. When she reappeared he was talking to the fat woman now holding her equally fat cairn terrier. With a wink at Una, he said, 'Be so kind as to give Mrs Forest our diet sheet for overweight dogs and a tin of that diet dog food, please, Miss Singleby.' Una stifled her desire to giggle as the thought struck her – almost as certainly as it must have struck James – that the diet sheet would be as useful to the dog's owner as it would be to her dog.

The second woman who had been obliged to wait her turn now followed James back into his treatment room. Within minutes she came out, her face rigid, and she stalked out of the door without speaking. James came back into the waiting room as Una returned and sat down at her desk. He was carrying her small black dachshund.

'I suppose you don't want to own a dog, Una, do you?' he asked. 'Do you know that wretched woman wanted me to euthanize this one. It's only three years old and as healthy as you or me.'

Before Una could reply, he added bitterly: 'The reason? Because it's a dachshund, a German breed! Her husband, a veteran of the last war, won't have it in the house now. It's his dog; she didn't want any dog in the first place!' Seeing Una's expression, he sighed. 'This sort of thing happened in the last war, you know. I have a book somewhere by a vet called Buster Lloyd-Jones who describes how he had been asked to put down dozens of German breeds – dachshunds, shepherds, schnauzers, you name it. Healthy pets who never had or would harm a soul.' He drew a deep sigh. 'I told her I wouldn't euthanize a healthy dog but I would try to find a home for him.'

Una's face brightened as she said, 'I'll ask my aunts. They take in stray cats so maybe they'd have him.'

The telephone started ringing and the day became very busy as it always was. By six o'clock, when the last person left, both Una and James were exhausted.

'Would you like to come next door for a reviver?' he asked her.

Reluctantly, Una shook her head. 'I'd love to but I must get back,' she said. 'Poor Dilys will have been alone all day and if I'm quick I might be able to catch the six-twenty train.'

'Nonsense! I'll run you back in the car!' James said, 'And don't argue,' he added with a smile. 'It's been a very busy day and you look shattered!'

As James' Morris estate car had room for animals to be safely transported in the back when necessary, he apologised for the doggy odour as he turned on to the main road leading to Hannington. He remained silent while, haltingly, Una confided in him about Dilys' predicament.

'I see why it isn't possible for Dilys to keep the baby,' she concluded, 'but she's absolutely determined to do so. Even if you increased my salary now I'm doing Dilys' work as well as my own, I don't think—'

She got no further before James interrupted: 'Una, the pair of you are still underage and you've never had to fend for yourselves,' he said. 'I've no doubt that your parents have always dealt with your expenses and neither of you have the slightest idea what living on your own would entail.' He glanced briefly at the young girl beside him. 'Una, I know you want to help your sister but unless your parents permitted her to remain at home I can see no way she can keep the baby.'

Seeing the expression on Una's face, he added: 'Is there no chance your parents might relent? Or a relative, perhaps, who might consider—'

'No, James!' Una broke in. 'There are only Mother's older sisters, the aunts,' Una interrupted. 'They never married and I dare say they'd love to have Dilys staying with them, but not – absolutely *not* – with an illegitimate baby. They are very Victorian, churchy, and . . . No, there's no one else. Father was an only child so we don't have relations on his side of the family.'

James turned the car into the gravel driveway leading up to the big Georgian manor house and tried not to let his voice sound too negative as he drew to a halt and said goodbye to Una.

'Try not to worry! Between us we might be able to think of something!' he said vaguely. 'Give Dilys my best wishes and tell her . . . tell her to read that poem called "Despair" written by that poet in the trenches in the last war. The last line says "Even the darkest night is followed by the light of next day's dawn".'

Una repeated it that evening when she and Dilys had gone to bed and were lying in the darkness.

Dilys was silent for a moment and then said, 'I suppose James must have found that comforting when his wife and child were killed.' Then she added sleepily: 'But no one is going to take my baby away . . . no one, ever.' And before Una could comment, she drifted into sleep.

SEVEN

D ilys awoke early the following Wednesday morning, the day her mother had resolved to take her to meet the matron of The Willows. Late last night, determined as ever that she would never allow her baby to be taken away from her, she had decided to lock herself in her bedroom and to remain there until her parents relented and agreed to some other solution.

Surely, she'd told herself, she could be hidden far away in a cottage and be given enough money to support herself and her child. She could live under another name so she would not bring any disgrace on them.

It was a wild idea, Una had told her. It was not beyond their father to have the bedroom door broken down, she had pointed out, and in any case Dilys would have to open it herself as she'd need help when the baby was born. Meanwhile, if she didn't go down for meals and food wasn't brought to her, she would starve as well as her unborn child.

When the alarm clock sounded at seven thirty to alert Una to wake up and prepare to go to work, she got out of bed and stood looking down at her twin. She was surprised to see Dilys too, was awake and seemingly perfectly calm.

'I've decided what I'm going to do,' Dilys said. 'I'll let Mother take me to that place and I'll stay there and have the baby, but as soon as it's born I'll go before they can take it away from me. You'll help me, won't you, Una? I've got it all planned. You can meet me in a taxi somewhere close by, drive me to the station and I'll catch a train to Cornwall and go to one of those little seaside guesthouses we saw that summer holiday in Newquay. I'll need money, but I have almost thirty pounds in my post-office savings account, and you'll lend me yours, won't you, Una? No one but you will know where I am, and if I can stay hidden until our twenty-first birthday, Father won't be able to make me give my baby away.'

When finally she stopped talking, Una's mind was working
furiously. It was a solution, but only a temporary one, she
thought as, shivering in the cold bedroom, she hurried into her
clothes. Of course she would give Dil her savings and, in due
course, she would send her the weekly salary James paid her,
but how long would that last? And how would Dil manage to
look after a newborn baby? Maybe there was a book with
instructions she could buy for her, but there would be no one
there to support her.

Una was close to tears as she kissed her twin goodbye
before going downstairs to breakfast. In all the eighteen years
of their lives, they had never spent a night apart. Now,
suddenly, in a few days' time they were to be separated: Dilys
would be at the mother-and-baby home until her baby was
born, and would then go to Cornwall, if she stuck to her plan.
For the first time in her life, Una's self-confidence vanished
and she felt very young and unsure of herself; unsure whether
she was about to assist her twin in heading for certain disaster.
She badly needed someone to give Dilys safe advice on how
to deal with her predicament. Suddenly, she knew exactly
who could do so – James. He was always calm, level-headed
and understanding of people's feelings. Her mind made up,
she could not wait to get to the veterinary surgery and confide
in him.

As Una reached the railway station, she heard the paperboy
shouting out the day's headline: 'British and French troops
land in Norway.' She just had time to buy a paper and read
that British troops had been sent to assist the brave Norwegians
who were desperately trying to resist the German occupation
of their country. Her thoughts went immediately to Dilys'
Norwegian boyfriend, the father of her baby. Almost certainly
he would be in the thick of the fighting, perhaps even dead.
When she had got to know him in Munich, he had seemed
such a likeable, genuine person that she had understood Dilys'
shock when their father had informed her that Kristoffer was
engaged to another girl.

As always at the surgery, they were extremely busy. James'
competence and affinity with the animals ensured he was never
short of clients. There was no opportunity, therefore, for Una

to have a private conversation with him until he had closed the surgery at the end of the day.

Una declined his offer of a restorative drink again but gratefully accepted his offer to drive her home. If Dilys had been taken to the mother-and-baby home Una was anxious to hear from her mother that her twin had not been too distraught.

In the course of her employment, Una had become perfectly at ease in James' company, and in the darkness of the interior of his car as he drove her home she told him of her sister's plan to escape to Cornwall with her baby when it was born. James heard her out without interrupting. When Una concluded by asking his opinion, he was silent for a few minutes while he tried to put himself into her parents' shoes. At the same time, he empathized with the young girl who wanted, bravely, to keep her baby.

Keeping his voice steady, he said to Una, 'I admire Dilys' courage, but I fear her solution would only be a temporary one. Your parents are not going to allow their young daughter to disappear into thin air. If your father did not wish the police to know about his private affairs, he would most probably have her found by a private detective. I'm afraid Dilys could not stop them removing the baby, which would be even more painful for her than if it was taken away at birth.'

Una listened to him in shocked silence before saying, 'So you think she will have to let it be adopted?'

It was a moment or two before James replied. Then he said quietly, 'I'm afraid so. Lawfully, she is still a minor.' He paused for a minute, and then suddenly his heart started racing. He cleared his throat and then heard himself saying quietly: 'Unless . . .' He then said hesitantly, 'Unless she was married.'

At first Una was too astonished to comment, and then, finding her voice, she said, 'But James, that's crazy! How could she be married? Who would marry a girl about to have another man's baby? I can't believe you said that. Were you joking?'

James drove on a short distance and then pulled up on the grass verge in front of a farm gate. Switching off the engine, he turned to look at the young girl by his side and said quietly, 'No. I wasn't joking. If Dilys was willing, I would marry her. If it was possible for us to be married quickly, her baby would not be illegitimate, and she and the child could be part of your family again.'

Una was effectively silenced by James' astonishing proposal. After a few minutes she said naively: 'But you don't love each other and . . . and you're miles older than Dil and . . . and I can see it would solve all Dil's problems, but why . . .'

'But why would I want to saddle myself with a wife and another man's child? Does sound crazy, doesn't it? But . . .' He paused, his eyes thoughtful and, after a moment, said quietly, 'The idea only just occurred to me, Una, but now . . . As you said, it would not be a love match but I would take care of Dilys and her baby. As for myself . . . well, there are several reasons which must have prompted my proposal. It's been pretty lonely living alone for the past six years. After my wife and boy died, I never wanted to marry again. I can't explain it but I felt if I did so I'd feel as if I was being unfaithful to Margaret's memory.' He paused again before saying, 'This . . . well, it would be different. I mean, we wouldn't live as man and wife. Dilys could have her own room and we . . . we would just be friends; keep each other company on those long, dark winter evenings.'

He turned suddenly and smiled at Una. 'Maybe Dilys would learn to keep house for me. As you know, my daily housekeeper, Mrs White, does the cleaning but she is also a good cook. She could teach Dilys; help her with the baby. The main thing is, Una, Dilys could keep the baby. I really loved doing things for my little boy. I love small children much the same way as I love all the animals who come to me for help. What do you think, Una? Would Dilys want to take this way out of her predicament? Do you think your parents would agree? I'd ask their permission first, of course.'

Yet again, Una was lost for words. The way James had put his spur-of-the-moment idea sounded plausible, but would it – *could* it – work? Was Dil so desperate to keep her baby that she would marry a man who was not that far short of being a stranger? A man so much older than herself? A man who was not her lost love, Kristoffer? A man she didn't love?

Much as Una liked James, and she really did, she herself wouldn't want to marry him, or any man, come to that. She wanted to have fun – the kind of fun she and Dil had enjoyed in Munich. Even though there was now a war on, people were still having fun. In London, tea dances and parties continued to take place as before. Theatres, concert halls and cinemas all remained open. According to their mother, London was full of servicemen and women in uniform. Had it not been for poor Dil's problems, she would have loved to accept an old school friend's recent invitation to stay with her and her family in Chelsea and go partying with her.

She badly wanted to see *Gone With the Wind*, the film everyone was talking about, and dance to Joe Loss at the Savoy. It seemed such a long time ago since they had danced in Munich last summer.

If Dil did decide to accept James' astonishing offer to marry her and legitimize her baby, she would be stuck in Fenbury, whereas if she had the baby adopted they could both go up to London, get jobs and join in the war effort. Dil would meet lots of new young men and forget all about her Kristoffer and the baby.

'It's enormously kind of you to suggest this James!' she said now to him, realizing as she did so that she sounded as if she were referring to a visit to a cinema or day at the races. 'Would you like me to ask her how she feels about it when I get home? Mother plans to take her to that Home to stay the day after tomorrow, although last night Dil said she was going to lock herself in her room and refuse to go.'

James cleared his throat. 'As you told me earlier that your father has gone back to London I will have to wait until he returns to ask his permission to marry Dilys, so perhaps it would be best for now if she goes to the Home. I will apply for a special licence so if the marriage can take place, it can do so before Dilys' baby is born. I'm not sure how long it takes to obtain a licence but I suspect it might be a week or so, after which it would be necessary to book a date at the town hall.' He broke off and after a moment's thought, added: 'Tomorrow, Una, if Dilys agrees to the marriage, can you make sure I am free of appointments so I have a time to make those enquiries?'

An hour later, having listened to her mother's furious account of Dilys' locked bedroom door, Una was permitted to go upstairs to 'knock some sense' into her sister and to warn her that if she did not open it the next day a locksmith would be called to do it. She found Dilys sitting by the window with a tray of half-eaten food which the maid had left outside the door on her lap. Una removed it, telling her sister that even if she wasn't hungry she ought to eat properly for the baby's sake. She then sat down beside Dilys and, putting a comforting arm round her shoulders, told her of James' astonishing offer.

Dilys' immediate comment was that she couldn't possibly marry James, kind as his suggestion was, because she still loved Kristoffer despite what her father had told her about the Norwegian girl he was engaged to. 'Even though he has stopped loving me,' she said in a shaky voice, 'I'm having his baby, Una. Of course I can't be anyone else's wife.'

'Dil, he isn't expecting you to be a real wife,' Una explained, and related the scenario that James had outlined. 'I mean, if you have your own bedroom, he can't be expecting to sleep with you, can he? I think he's just lonely and thinks it would be nice if you and the baby were there.' Seeing the doubtful look on her twin's face, she sighed. 'Maybe Father is right, Dil, and in the long run it would be best to let other parents have the baby, then you would be free to come up to London with me and we'd have loads of fun together. We could . . .'

She got no further before Dilys said in a harsh tone, 'No! I'll marry James if I have to but I'm going to keep my baby, Una. Just so long as he knows I can't be a proper wife to him then I'll do my very best to . . . to make it up to him for the help he's giving me.' She gave Una a quick hug. 'I'd miss you terribly if I went to live with him. I don't know what it would be like living without you. Oh, Una, how can I have got myself into this mess? Even if I do agree to marry James, suppose Father won't give his consent and . . .'

'He will!' Una interrupted her. 'You know what he's like, Dil! He's always on about his reputation, "the family good name" and all that. I sometimes think his wretched career and his constituents are more important to him than we are. He'll be only too pleased to have it all solved. That's why he arranged for you to go to that Home so you could get the baby adopted. Who knows, he might even end up liking having a grandchild if he can talk about his married daughter. As for Mother, she won't mind if Father has agreed to it.'

Two days later, Lady Singleby drove her silent, white-faced daughter to The Willows Home for Mothers and Babies owned and run by the matron, Mrs Marshall, an efficient, stern-looking woman in her fifties who was accustomed to dealing discreetly – and expensively – with girls from the upper classes. It was on her discovery that unwanted babies were very far from being the prerogative of the lower classes that she had purchased The Willows, furnished it expensively and quickly attracted the parents of daughters who had got into trouble.

Following the success of the Home, Mrs Marshall had added an annexe with a few private suites for the occasional society wife who did not want her husband to know the baby she was having was not his. Whatever the circumstances, she could be relied upon – and she charged – for her discretion.

Lady Singleby drew to a halt in the drive outside the front door of The Willows. Looking at Dilys' white, apprehensive face, she felt a rare maternal compassion for her delinquent daughter. She had left the problem of the girl's disgrace to her husband to deal with – in fact, she had had no chance to do otherwise – and had agreed that Dilys should be sent away to have her shameful baby discreetly delivered and adopted. Despite her concurrence, she had nevertheless been a little shocked by Dilys' adamant refusal to accept her father's solution and her determination to keep her illegitimate child and raise it herself . . . protestations she had not dared repeat to her husband.

Now, somewhat to her surprise, Dilys had suddenly stopped her hysterical responses and agreed to go quietly with her today to The Willows. Worried lest she should suddenly change her mind, Lady Singleby rang the doorbell and when the door was opened she hurriedly handed Dilys over to the matron's care. Having pecked her daughter on the cheek, she bade her goodbye and made her way back to her car.

Dilys allowed herself to be shown to a pleasant private bedroom where she was left to unpack and 'have a little rest' before going downstairs to tea where, Mrs Marshall told her, she would meet some other young 'patients', as she called the six other pregnant girls.

Dilys meekly followed the orders she was given obediently because of her near certainty that she would not be staying in the place for more than a week or two. Sitting down on the side of her bed, Dilys' hands went to the now sizeable bump. The taut expression on her face softened as she whispered: 'You're safe now! No one is going to take you away from me.' She paused for a moment, easing her back, which was aching quite often now with the weight of the baby, causing her to lean backwards. She wasn't sure when it was due to be born but she sensed it would not be long now. Would James be able to manage everything in time for them to be married before her baby was born? she asked herself anxiously.

Her thoughts returned to her last night at home. She and Una had stayed awake a long time talking . . . mostly about James and how much older he was than her. Would he order her around the way their father did when he was at home? Most often the topic was James' extraordinary offer to marry her, and was Una certain it was only because he disliked living on his own?

'I think it isn't just you he wants, Dil,' Una had said sleepily. 'I think he wants your baby! You know what he's like with puppies and kittens. Remember that orphaned baby goat? He looked after that himself when the farmer said he hadn't time and was going to get rid of it. James bottle-fed it just like a baby and I remember him saying how he had to get up in the night to feed it. It slept in the Keep Warm compartment in his Aga and he'd wake up to the sound of its little hooves tapping away on the kitchen floor while it bleated for him.'

Dilys had smiled as Una had said quietly, 'Bet he'll make a really good father for your baby, Dil.'

If Una was right about James being good to Kristoffer's baby, Dilys thought as she prepared to go downstairs for afternoon tea, she wouldn't mind living with a much older man. The thought calmed her and now she had more or less resigned herself to her future, she was able to accept that while she still loved Kristoffer, in spite of the fact that he was marrying another girl, she was going to be able to keep his baby thanks to the kind offer of marriage, albeit from another man.

EIGHT

Sir Godfrey remained in London for ten days, during which James waited impatiently to go to call on him at Hannington Hall to ask for his permission to marry Dilys. He was reasonably confident that her father would not refuse to give his consent. Although his veterinary practice was not one of the affluent upper-class professions, he was financially able to support a wife and child, and of an age to take on the responsibilities of marriage. He realized he would have to wait until the weekend to see Sir Godfrey but had used the afternoon Una had obediently left free of appointments to drive into Oxford to find out how quickly he could obtain a special licence. Although he discovered that he could get one within three weeks, he had been informed he would need to provide proof of Dilys' identity as well as her father's permission to marry him as she was still a minor.

Returning home later that afternoon, he told Una the marriage could take place provided he could produce Sir Godfrey's agreement to it and asked her if she would relay the information to her sister.

Undaunted, Una waited until her mother had gone up to London for the day and then caught the train to Fenbury and walked purposefully to James' house. She had taken a sheet of her father's headed writing paper from his study with her. Using James' typewriter, she typed out her father's permission for her to visit Dilys, her mother having told her that visitors were normally disallowed in order to ensure maximum discretion for all concerned.

The next day Dilys was overjoyed to see her. They sat side by side on the edge of Dilys' bed, their arms around each other.

'I'm so glad to see you!' Dilys said, her voice trembling. 'Una, I was made to see the doctor who looks after the patients here, and he says my baby is due very soon, maybe in ten days' time.' She burst into tears.

Una said quickly, 'It may still be all right, Dil! James has applied for the special licence. He still has to get Father's permission but I'm sure—'

She got no further before Dilys interrupted. 'Una, I can't . . . I can't marry James!' she said harshly. 'Mary warned me not to do it. She's one of the girls here like me, only she isn't a girl, she's married with three children. I sit next to her in the dining room which is where we all meet for meals. Mary's in a room with three other girls because her husband can't afford for her to have a private room and—'

It was now Una's turn to interrupt. 'Hold on a minute, Dil. You just said she was married, so why is she having her baby adopted?'

Dilys drew a deep breath and then said, 'Because it's not her husband's baby. She said she married her husband because he'd got her pregnant but she didn't love him, and then she met a man she did love and they did it – you know, they went all the way like Kristoffer and me – and when her husband found out he said she'd got to get rid of it or he'd divorce her and keep the children. So she had to agree to have the baby adopted. She said it was awful having to be a proper wife to a man you didn't love, and I'd be stupid to marry James because one day I might meet someone like Kristoffer I really did love and—'

Una's face was a mask of dismay as she broke in, saying doubtfully, 'Dil, you couldn't manage on your own, and besides, James would be terribly disappointed. He said he was having a spare bedroom redecorated so it would be all fresh and pretty for the baby, and last Sunday he went up to the loft and brought down the rocking horse which had belonged to his little boy. And . . . and anyway, you know Father won't change his mind and let you keep the baby.'

Dilys brushed the tears from her eyes and said tremulously, 'Yes, I know, but I've made up my mind. I'll have the baby here and then, immediately after it's born, I'll go away some-where where Father can't find me. Mary said I might be able to get a job as a maid in a hotel or as a waitress somewhere and find a poor woman to look after the baby when I was at work.'

For a moment, neither girl spoke, and then Una said forcefully, 'Dil, you'd absolutely hate being a maid or a waitress, and anyway, I don't think you could go anywhere where Father couldn't find you. He could get a detective to search for you. Don't you remember that story in the paper last year when detectives finally found that little boy who'd been missing for nearly a year? When you were found, Father would make you have the baby adopted and it would be even more awful because you would have got used to having it by then—' She broke off momentarily and then put her arms round her twin. 'Oh, Dil, darling, do you really hate the thought of marrying James? If you saw how excited he has been these past weeks, you'd realize how keen he is to marry you and not be on his own any more. I know he's rather old but he's one of the nicest people we've met. Everyone who comes to the surgery says what a kind, sympathetic person he is. I'm sure he'd make a wonderful father . . .'

She broke off as she saw Dilys draw a deep sigh before saying quietly, 'But don't you see, it wouldn't be fair, Una. I couldn't be a proper wife to him. I don't love him. I'll never love anyone but Kristoffer.' She reached up and fingered the ring on its chain round her neck. She sounded so despairing, tears filled Una's eyes.

'Maybe if it hadn't been for this wretched war, we could have gone back to Munich and found Kristoffer and told him about the baby. We have to face it, even if we did find him he might not want to marry you any more; not if he loves this other girl Father found out about.'

Dilys' expression hardened as she whispered, 'I've already thought about all that.' She paused and then added sadly: 'I truly believe Kristoffer did love me, Una, *really* loved me, but I suppose it just wasn't the lasting kind of love. Remember how we used to have "Best Friends For Life" at school and we'd cut our fingers and exchange drips of blood and promise to be true to each other for ever! Yet a year later we were best friends with different girls!'

They both smiled. Then Una said anxiously, 'What do you want me to tell James? Honestly, it seems to me you don't have much of an alternative as you are so certain you want to keep the baby. Whatever you decide you know I'll do whatever I can to help.'

Dilys put her arms round her twin and hugged her. Her tone of voice was wistful as she said, 'Mary made it sound possible for me to manage on my own, but of course she doesn't know Father the way we do. You are quite right. When he found where I was he wouldn't let me keep my baby.' She drew another deep sigh, adding: 'Oh, Una, if only I was twenty-one! If only there wasn't a war and I could have gone to find Kristoffer! Do you honestly think it would be fair of me to marry James not loving him?'

Momentarily she had a brief flash of memory, of lying by the lake in the sun in Kristoffer's arms, of feeling his lips on her breasts and the gentle way he eased himself into her and claimed her for his own.

The moment passed and even before Una spoke she knew what her twin would say – that she would be safe with James, her baby beyond her father's reach and, according to Una, much loved by the man she'd married. Una had told her that James was not expecting them to be anything more than friends: that maybe it was even possible that one day in the future she would learn to love him. Most important of all, she reminded herself, he would love her baby who would otherwise have no father to care for it. Was Mary wrong in suggesting she would hate being married to a man she didn't love? She had been perfectly happy without love before she'd known Kristoffer. She really didn't want that kind of love, that intimacy, if it wasn't with him. Maybe that was also the way James felt after his wife died. Maybe Una was right when she said he just needed someone to care for him and a child he could love as he had once loved his own little boy.

Quite suddenly, Dilys' mind was made up. 'All right, Una, I will marry James. I just hope the doctor was wrong when he said the baby would arrive in ten days' time!' She gave a sudden smile. 'Matron doesn't allow telephone calls except from husbands or parents, but maybe you could get a message to me as soon as you know if Father has agreed that James can marry me.'

Looking greatly relieved, Una nodded. 'Oh, Dil, darling, I

feel so much happier now I know that you are going to be safe. When you are living with James I'll be able to see you every day when I'm working at the surgery, and I'm sure James said I can stay sometimes for supper and perhaps spend an occasional weekend with you. He's such a kind person, I'm sure you will be happy living with him.'

Now that the decision was made, Dilys felt a swift sense of relief. All that really mattered, she told herself, was that as long as her father agreed to the marriage she would not be parted from her baby. For James' sake, she would do her very best to forget Kristoffer and be a good wife to him.

'It's going to be all right, Dil. I can't believe Father won't let you marry James. If he did refuse I'd tell him that you were going to run away, then I'd tell the newspaper reporters. Just think, suppose a newspaper printed the story, Father being an MP and everything! I'm sure he'll be only too glad to have it all settled quietly. Lots of people are getting married in a hurry now there's a war on in case their fiancés are called up and have to go abroad to fight. So it won't even look suspicious you being married so quickly. All we need is for Father to give his permission soon so you can be married before the baby is born.'

As it happened, James did get Sir Godfrey's permission to marry Dilys and he obtained a licence for the wedding to take place two weeks later. It was none too soon as Dilys' first labour pains began during the actual ceremony in the stark, business-like appearance of the town hall. Una was the only witness other than an attendant clerk, neither Sir Godfrey nor his wife being present. Fortuitously, James had allowed Una time off the week before to buy what would be needed for the baby. Una had used her own money to buy those necessities which had been outlined for her by the attendant in the chemist. James himself had ordered her a cot, pram and the furnishings which went with them on the same day as Sir Godfrey had agreed to the marriage. He had also, he told Una, made arrangements with his elderly housekeeper, Mrs White, to spend an extra hour every morning giving Dilys any advice and help she might need. The day before the wedding, he'd said with a smile to Una, 'Poor Mrs White nearly fell over when I told her I was getting married and that my future wife and I were expecting our first child at any minute! I'm afraid she was terribly shocked. Needless to say, I asked her if she would kindly keep the facts to herself. However, as she has been with me ever since I took over the practice when my wife died, I think she felt privileged that I had confided in her and trusted her not to gossip. She has seven children of her own so I'm sure she will be a fount of knowledge for Dilys.'

Una's liking for James had grown even greater at his thoughtfulness, and her belief that her dearly loved twin was doing the right thing by marrying him even though he was so much older was reinforced. In any case, all Dilys cared about was keeping Kristoffer's baby, so it really didn't matter that she wasn't in love with James, provided she liked him enough to live with him.

On her way back from the shopping expedition, it had suddenly struck her that before she and Dilys had gone to Munich they had always been united in everything they did, everything they experienced and felt. Now, quite suddenly, they had become two separate entities, Dilys having experienced real love and what it felt like to be having a baby. Was it 'real love', she asked herself, and if it was in Dilys' case, had it been in her beloved Kristoffer's case? Or had he gone back to Norway intending to marry his Norwegian childhood sweetheart? Maybe he had only imagined himself in love with Dilys. There was no other reason either she or Dilys could think of as to why he had not written to her. As Dilys had said, even if she had forgotten to put her address on the hurried note she'd left him, Herr Von Zwehl would have given their home address to him. It was of little help that although Dilys knew where Kristoffer's *pension* was – in which street and in which building – she did not know the name or house number, still less the name of the owner. 'I could take the right tram and walk there!' Dilys had said sadly, 'but I don't know where to write to him.'

Now, Una thought, Kristoffer would almost certainly have returned to Norway. The latest news was that British troops had landed in Norway and were helping their army to fight the invading Germans. In all probability, he, too, was defending his country and had forgotten all about poor Dilys.

Una had not been surprised by their father's consent to Dilys' marriage. James was not one of his constituents and Dilys wouldn't be living near enough for local people to gossip. Provided she kept away from Hannington Hall, Una had over-heard him saying to her mother, in a year's time no one would be suspicious about the age of Dilys' baby. Meanwhile, neither he nor Lady Singleby would attend the wedding but he would put one hundred pounds into Una's post office savings account on the understanding that she would be responsible for its sensible spending on her twin's needs.

As Una stood behind Dilys and James when they repeated their vows, she noticed that Dilys clutched James' arm from time to time as if she feared she was about to fall. When the moment came for the registrar to pronounce the couple man and wife, Una saw her clutch James' arm again and whisper something to him. He nodded, helped her to the table where they both signed the register and then turned to Una.

'Take Dilys out to the car,' he ordered. 'I'll join you in a few minutes.' He turned back to Dilys and in a low voice whispered, 'Don't be frightened! First babies very rarely arrive quickly. We'll get you back to The Willows in plenty of time.'

Dilys was frightened. She knew she was to have her baby in the Home like all the other women, but the contractions seemed to be coming at regular intervals now and were extremely painful, so much so that she gave no thought to the fact that she had just been married. She was sitting beside Una in the back of James' car and was clutching Una's hand, her other hand on her stomach in the hope of lessening the pains. James was reassuringly quiet as he drove fast but safely, over-taking the afternoon traffic wherever he could with a sharp warning blast of the horn.

When finally they arrived back at The Willows, Matron was also reassuring. They had a regular midwife on call, she told them, so Dilys would receive the best care. Her baby would be delivered in The Willows' special birthing room arranged for the purpose, so that expectant mothers need not go to the hospital. Maximum privacy could be ensured, Una had explained to James, adding that forty-eight hours after a baby's birth the new mother would return to her own room still with her baby for two days, after which it would be removed from its mother and given to its new parents.

'Dilys is very, very fortunate, James, that you're making it possible for her to keep her child, and I heard Father applauding the fact that you would be legitimizing it.'

Lady Singleby had introduced James to the matron when they had called to tell her that he and Dilys were getting married and that her daughter would be leaving with him after the baby's birth and taking the baby with them.

Despite Mrs Marshall's suspicions that James himself was responsible for getting the young girl pregnant, she did actually quite like him. Dilys, she reckoned, was a very, very lucky girl not to have been dumped, as so many of her patients were, by the men who had taken advantage of them.

Neither Dilys nor Una were aware that James had given the matron a handsome cheque 'for her charitable work' as he had termed it, while being somewhat cynically aware that it would probably line her personal pocket. All he had asked was that Dilys would have the very best care and comfort.

On midnight on her wedding day, after eleven hours of labour, Dilys gave birth to a baby, a girl with wisps of white-blonde hair and sky-blue eyes. When Una and James were allowed to visit her next morning, both leant over the crib to see the baby but only Una saw instantly why Dilys was looking so ecstatic. Despite the minor distortions of birth to her features, the baby was a living image of its father.

NINE

For the past five weeks since he had enrolled in the Norwegian army, Kristoffer had been with his unit, which was trying desperately to defend Trondheim against the invaders. Highly trained as the German troops were, they had already overrun Poland and Denmark. British and French troops had come to their assistance but the situation remained dire. During the course of the heavy fighting Kristoffer had suffered a minor wound to his arm and, with ten days' sick leave, had made his way back over the mountains to his home in Bergen.

After the noise and horror of the fighting, the quiet beauty of the mountains helped a little to combat the oppressive horrors of the war, not least the cries of the wounded and dying men around him. Without skis to assist him, it was heavy going through the winter snow which was still lying unmelted in the shade of the spruce trees.

As he neared the outskirts of Bergen, he met an elderly man travelling in the opposite direction who informed him that the Germans had landed in Oslo and now occupied the city.

It was inconceivable, Kristoffer thought, that his beloved country might have surrendered to the invaders.

When he finally arrived at his home on the Nordnes peninsular overlooking the harbour, it was to find the mellow timbered house unscathed by enemy shelling from the German boats surrounding the Norwegian coast. The town had surrendered to the Germans and already the occupying soldiers were busy taking over control of the population. The Nazi anti-Semitic dictates were already in force. So far, as far as Kristoffer could see, there had been no interference with the activities of Holberg Tømmer AS, the family timber company, but he assumed it was only a matter of time before that happened. Fortunately with the occupation of the city so recent, he was able to reach home without being stopped and asked for his identity papers.

He used the back door key he had kept in his pocket to let himself into the house, where he found his mother preparing the evening meal.

At that moment Kristoffer's father came into the kitchen. After he had joyously welcomed his son home, Herr Holberg related what was uppermost in his mind, namely that the Norwegian fascist, Vidkun Quisling, had been proclaimed by Hitler as the new Prime Minister and had asked King Haakon to confirm his position.

'Quisling is a traitor!' Herr Holberg said as he and Kristoffer sat drinking large glasses of beer in the warmth of the kitchen. 'He is known to be hand in glove with the Nazis and endorses their ideologies.' He sniffed dismissively and took another swallow of beer. 'Meanwhile, our government has evacuated to Hamar. But you may well know all this.'

Fru Holberg interrupted their conversation by suggesting that Kristoffer had a quick bath and changed out of his uniform into home clothes. When she called him to come and eat, sitting at the kitchen table listening to his father relating the local news, his euphoria at having reached home evaporated.

'It has to be faced,' his father was saying, 'that our country is no more able to stop the Germans than Poland, Denmark or Holland were. Nor, so I've heard, is there any good news of the Allied armies in Belgium. By the sound of it, they are in retreat and the Germans will soon be in France.'

Herr Holberg drew a deep sigh as he enquired if Kristoffer had heard about the battle going on further up the west coast at Aardanger. According to his neighbour, the occupants had been shooting at a German ship moored in the fjord. The Germans had promptly shelled the centre of the village and reduced it to rubble.

A smile crossed Herr Holberg's face momentarily as he added: 'The Aardangers promptly scuttled the German ship which they had captured and was moored in the harbour. There was a neutral Spanish merchant ship which had taken refuge there which they also scuttled.' His smile now gave way to a chuckle as he continued: 'Did you hear about it? Its cargo was a shipload of oranges which could be seen in their thousands bobbing about in the water all over the harbour!' His face regained a serious expression as he told Kristoffer, 'Apparently a number of men who had banded together to form a secret resistance force were responsible, their aim being to hamper the Germans in any way they could.'

Kristoffer regarded his father with eyes now alight with excitement. 'I know about these people,' he said, 'and if the Germans overrun our defences as now seems inevitable, I shall join them.'

Aware of the look of anxiety on his mother's face, he changed the topic of his conversation. 'What of Holberg Tømmer, Father?' he asked. 'I saw no sign of anyone in the forest, although I did hear the sound of chainsaws as I skirted the boundary.'

Herr Holberg gave a wry smile. 'Our German occupiers have commandeered our stocks and despite my telling them that spring is not the time to be cutting down trees, they are insisting we should continue to do so. The saw mills are still active but we have lookouts to advise when there are no Germans around. We conceal supplies of timber in the forest for our former customers and ourselves.'

'Isn't that a bit risky?' Kristoffer asked.

Herr Holberg shrugged his shoulders. 'So far we have not been detected, and I'm reasonably sure we don't have any "quislings" among our employees.' Seeing Kristoffer's expression, he grimaced, adding: 'That's what we all call those who collaborate with the Germans. All the employees of Holberg Tømmer are loyal compatriots, as you would expect.'

Herr Holberg told Kristoffer that Gustave, one of Kristoffer's old friends since schooldays, was already involved with a group of the Resistance. From the limited facts Herr Holberg knew Kristoffer gathered, there was an organization in London who were going to supply these groups with the necessary equipment, arms, ammunition and radios. These last were to enable the Norwegians to pass on any information about secret enemy emplacements or activity, to enable the British to take the necessary action to disrupt or destroy them.

Kristoffer did not need to hear more before deciding that he would try to find Gustave the next day. He would ask his friend the name of a contact for him to approach after he'd had a few days' rest and given the wound on his arm a chance to recover.

Sitting round the table eating the *lapskaus* his mother had cooked, Kristoffer tried not to assuage his hunger too quickly as he dipped his bread into the thick, tasty stew. As he ate, Fru Holberg told him about one of the Jewish families living further up the street. They had tried to escape to England in a fishing boat when the invasion seemed imminent, risking an attack by one the many German U-boats patrolling the North Sea. Close to tears, his mother expressed her fear that their friends might never have arrived in Scotland, as she had been unable to contact the fishermen who had transported them.

A brief moment of hope engulfed Kristoffer when it crossed his mind that perhaps he, too, might be able to get to Scotland and then to England and find Dilys, but his mother could give him no further details about the boat making such a dangerous journey. In any event, he told himself as he held out his plate for a second helping of *lapskaus*, it was his duty to remain in his own country and continue to resist the invaders as long as it was possible.

Replenishing Kristoffer's empty plate, Fru Holberg said, 'Whatever happens, *Far* and I will remain here in Bergen but we understand that you will wish to go on fighting the Germans in any way you can. But I do beg you to be careful, Kristoffer! Your father and I live all the time with concern about your safety.' She smiled suddenly as she added: 'So, too, does Gerda! She calls here every day to ask if there is news of you.'

As if Gerda knew Fru Holberg had just mentioned her, she walked into the kitchen using the key she'd had in her possession since childhood. Tall, fair hair plaited and coiled round her head, her face was wreathed in smiles as she hurriedly crossed the room and, bending over, threw her arms around Kristoffer and hugged him, taking care not to crush his injured arm, her eyes shining as she greeted him. Kristoffer stood up and, smiling, kissed her on both cheeks but drew back from any closer embrace.

'Your mother telephoned me to tell me you had just come home, Kris!' Gerda exclaimed, her eyes shining. 'It's wonderful to see you. We have been so worried about you haven't we, *Tante* Helena, when we heard Trondheim was now in enemy hands.' Frowning, she reached up and stroked his cheek. 'But how thin you have become! We must try to fatten you again while you are here on sick leave, should we not, *Tante*? It will not be easy now food is so scarce.' She smiled, adding: 'No matter. I have a little store set by and I will bake for you one of your favourite cakes!'

Without embarrassment, she leant forward and kissed Kristoffer's cheek again, unaware that he did not respond to her embrace. He stood silently, his eyes averted from her face as his mind filled with thoughts of Dilys. He knew he would have to tell Gerda that he had fallen in love with another girl and that the news would hurt her. Although nothing had ever been said about an engagement or his future marriage to Gerda, both families had assumed it would happen that way. However, now was not the moment to tell Gerda about Dilys – not while she was so happily rejoicing in his return home. He would be gone again very soon, and he would tell her before he left, he decided. Then she could turn her thoughts to someone else. Pretty as she undoubtedly was, she would not lack for attention from other young men once they knew he was out of the picture.

Only a year younger than Kristoffer, Gerda had completed her training as a teacher and now worked in Bergen in a junior school. There she was befriended by a cheerful English girl married to a Norwegian engineer. When Kristoffer enquired how she was enjoying the job, Gerda replied that since the arrival of the Germans Jewish people were being rounded up and that the fellow teacher was now hiding two children and their parents.

'*Mor* wanted to do the same but *Far* will not permit it.'

Their situation had become increasingly dangerous as the British were withdrawing all their troops, and news arrived that the Norwegian government had now been established in London. Both Herr Holberg and Gerda's father were now talking of an unstoppable defeat. No one mentioned the word surrender. Such a prospect was unthinkable, even if the worse happened and the entire country was overrun.

'It is no wonder,' Herr Holberg now said to Kristoffer, 'that people are talking of ways to harass the invader wherever and however they can.'

'*Far* says that the fascists under Vidkun Quisling are aiding the Germans,' Gerda declared, 'and they are to be despised by all of us who are true patriots! He has warned *Mamma* to be prepared for the inevitable occupation of Bergen, and has taught us both to fire a rifle so we can defend ourselves if it is necessary.' She sighed and then said regretfully that she must go home as she had promised her mother she would not be too long.

Kristoffer walked her across the road to her house as had always been his custom. As they approached the door Gerda asked anxiously, 'Is there really no hope we can get rid of the Germans?'

Kristoffer hesitated then shook his head. 'They have tanks and are skilled using aerial bombardments to decimate our troops. Unlike us they are highly trained and far better equipped than we are. It's carnage. They show no mercy and I've even seen them shoot the wounded. They don't care if their shells kill women and children, flatten schools, hospitals . . .' He shuddered at the memory. 'If . . . when . . . they reach the outskirts of the town, you and your mother and female friends must go and hide in the forests. Please, Gerda, promise me you won't risk your life trying to fight them. They are far too powerful to be resisted.'

For a moment, Gerda did not speak, and then she said softly, 'But you risk your life, Kris!' Seeing his expression, she added quickly: 'But I will be careful, I promise. And you must take care, too.'

They had reached the front door and, seeing Kristoffer hesitate, she said quickly, 'You are coming in, aren't you? My parents are longing to see you.'

'Yes, of course, if it isn't too late!' Kristoffer said, at the same time wondering how he could avoid time alone with Gerda when, as had always happened in the past, her parents made themselves scarce in order to leave 'the young couple alone'. He and Gerda had shared their first kisses and embraces when they were still in their teens. The embraces had, on occasion, become quite passionate, but after the evenings of such pleasurable but limited petting sessions, they were never referred to next day. Their school friends called them 'The Love Birds' and it was generally but unofficially assumed they would one day get engaged and marry. When there were parties or outings on steamers sailing up the beautiful fjord, or skiing in the winter in the mountains, they were always invited to join in as a couple.

It was now all too clear to Kristoffer that nothing had changed in Gerda's or her parents' lives while he had been away. They greeted him now much as his own parents had done, and despite his half-hearted protest they soon left him and Gerda alone in the living room.

As soon as the door closed, Gerda turned to Kristoffer, expecting him to put his arms round her and kiss her as he would have done in the past. Knowing him as well as she did, she realized at once that something was wrong. His hands were clasped tightly together and his face was turned away as if he was trying to find the courage to say the words he knew she would not wish to hear. With a sinking heart, she determined to find out why his manner towards her had changed.

Looking directly at him, she said, 'Kris, would I be wrong in thinking something has happened; something that has changed our relationship? Or perhaps something happened while you were fighting in Trondheim?'

Kristoffer bit his lip. He had anticipated that Gerda, who knew him so well, would realize very quickly that everything was different now: that for the first time in his life he had fallen in love. He'd known, too, as the months went by, that he would have to tell her that there would never be anyone to replace Dilys in his heart. Dreading the thought that Gerda would be distressed and hurt, he had put off writing to her. The brief moments when he had finally made love to Dilys flashed across his mind and, momentarily unaware of Gerda's presence, hot tears stung the backs of his eyes. Heartbreaking thoughts flashed yet again through his mind. Why had she not written to him? He'd never once doubted that she'd loved him as deeply as he loved her. How could she disappear back to her own country and just forget him? How could she have wiped him from her memory; treat their wonderful time together as no more than happy but unmemorable interludes? He had even questioned if it was possible that her father had withheld the letter he had written to her, that Sir Godfrey had opened it and seen his outpourings of love as inappropriate for his young, innocent daughter.

While Gerda stood silently beside him awaiting his reply, memories raced through his mind as he recalled the long, wakeful nights when he had realized that had it not been for the war raging in his country he would have found a way to go to England and discover where Dilys lived. It had even occurred to him that he could write another letter and, with luck, find a British soldier to take it with him when he returned to his own country.

Realizing suddenly that he could no longer delay replying to Gerda, he said awkwardly, 'It isn't just the war that has changed me, Gerda. Perhaps I should have told you months ago that I had met an English girl and . . . I fell in love with her. For a while I wasn't sure if she felt the same way as I did, but then we both realized that . . . well, that we wanted to be together for the rest of our lives.' Avoiding the look on Gerda's face, he steeled himself to continue. 'But Dilys was only seventeen and she knew her parents wouldn't consider her getting engaged to someone they had never met – a foreigner, too. So we kept our relationship a secret. I should have told you, Gerda, because . . . well, although we didn't have an actual understanding, I know our parents always assumed we'd get married one day. I . . . I suppose we did, too, although . . .'

'Although you never asked me to marry you, Kris,' Gerda interrupted, the tremor in her voice barely noticeable. 'I suppose I always assumed that one day—' She broke off and then forced herself to say in a level tone: 'But you never told me you loved me. I suppose I should have guessed that you'd fallen for someone else. I mean, it's not as if we were ever engaged.' She paused briefly, then added in a carefully controlled voice: 'I do hope, Kris, that this . . . this new love won't change our friendship. That really would make me very unhappy.'

Kristoffer felt a huge surge of relief as he deduced that from what Gerda had just said that she had not considered their relationship to be binding; to be loving, yes, but not the same kind of love he now knew could exist between a man and woman. As Gerda had just said, they were long-standing friends, loving ones. He turned, put his arms round her and hugged her.

'Dear Gerda, you will always be someone very, very special to me,' he said, meaning it sincerely.

It took her a moment to steady her voice before saying, 'Tell me about this English girl you love. She must be extremely special for you to feel so deeply about her.'

Kristoffer needed no second bidding to offload all his love and concern for Dilys. He listened happily to Gerda's reassurance that sooner or later Dilys would surely find a way to contact him: that even if she did not have his home address, the Holberg company was well known in Bergen and a letter from her would be bound to reach him as the postal service between the two countries must still exist, however unreliable.

Privately, Gerda was now hoping that Kristoffer might have read more into the young girl's responses than he had realized; that it had probably been the young girl's first experience of falling in love but, parted from him, she had quickly forgotten him when a new admirer appeared on the scene and lavished attention on her. Gerda's depression now vanished as she considered that she had only to wait and Kris would be hers again. Perhaps, at first, it might be for no more than consolation. Then, in time, he would realize that the two of them had always been destined to belong to each other.

'I will ask *Mamma* to invite you and your parents for supper tomorrow so that we can all celebrate your homecoming, Kris,' she said evenly. 'Last week a friend of *Pappa* brought him a haunch of venison from a deer he had managed to shoot in the forest and get it home without the Germans confiscating it. It will be a perfect time to enjoy it.'

She leant closer to Kristoffer and lightly kissed his cheek. The look on her face was now happily complacent as she realized that if she could maintain this casual approach to their relationship, all she needed to do was to sit back patiently and wait for Kristoffer to return his love to her.

TEN

I t was quite extraordinary, James thought as he looked at the pretty, flushed face of the young girl in the big iron bedstead, that he could be feeling such a rush of emotion. It wasn't love; he would never love anyone but the wife he had adored, but it was a fierce feeling of protectiveness, of tenderness which overcame him when he greeted Dilys in her room at The Willows.

Dilys was looking exhausted but deliriously happy as she gazed proudly at her newborn baby lying swaddled in the crib beside her bed. Above all, she looked so young and vulnerable that any lingering doubt that he might have done the wrong thing by marrying her now disappeared.

'The baby is very pretty although she doesn't seem to have your lovely red hair!' he said, smiling at Dilys as he bent over the crib. 'Have you thought of a name for her yet?'

Dilys returned James' smile, and then a shadow of doubt crossed her face. 'I had thought perhaps Christina?' she said hesitantly. 'It could be shortened to Tina!'

James nodded. 'Whatever you like!' he told her, at the same time recalling the name of the Norwegian boy who had got her pregnant.

Seeing his expression, Dilys said quickly, 'But if you don't—'

'No, no, Dilys, Christina is fine,' he interrupted. 'It's quite a long name for someone so tiny but Tina suits her very well.'

How much did James know about the past? Dilys wondered. She must ask Una what, if anything, James had wanted to know. It was ridiculous, she told herself, that they were now a married couple yet they knew so little about each other.

A wave of gratitude to him suddenly overwhelmed her. The baby daughter she had given birth to after many hours of almost unbearable pain was even more precious to her now than when she had been carrying her. But for James, she might now be awaiting an unbearable parting as Matron handed her baby to adopting parents.

Impulsively, she clutched James' hand. 'Thank you!' she whispered. 'I'll always be grateful, I promise. Always.'

Touched by her declaration, James cleared his throat and said, 'I am the one who should be grateful!' He smiled as he continued, 'You know how I feel about all newborns – puppies, kittens, etc. – tiny replicas of their parents, their helplessness, their vulnerability.'

It was this sensitivity which made him such a good and popular vet, and Dilys now understood why Una believed she could be happy married to this man. She was not only grateful to him but the better she knew him, the more she liked him. Shyly, she declared: 'I will try to be a good wife, James, I promise. I want you to tell me if I'm not doing things right. Una says you have been getting rooms ready for me and the baby, and . . . and I'm really looking forward to going back to Brook House with you next week. I hate it here. Sometimes at night I can hear one of the girls crying. She isn't going to be able to keep her baby. It's so awful, James, when people come to take one of the babies away.' She glanced briefly at her own baby daughter and said softly, 'Thank you! Thank you so very much for marrying me!'

Greatly moved, James cleared his throat and, rising to his feet from the chair by Dilys' bed, he said gruffly, 'I'll leave you to get some rest. Matron said you'd had a difficult time and were exhausted so I mustn't stay long. I told Una to cancel all today's appointments but to get a message to me here if there was an emergency which, thankfully, has not been the case. Nevertheless, as you know, clients don't come into or near the main part of the house so they won't see you and the baby and ask awkward questions. With the war, lots of chaps are getting married quickly before being sent abroad. I intend to put a notice on Una's desk announcing that my wife and I have had a baby girl, and if there are further questions she is to say, "Didn't you know, he and my sister were married some time ago".'

Yet again, Dilys' heart filled with gratitude. She had only thought vaguely of the difficulties there could be if she married James. It seemed now that he had sorted everything out.

'You aren't likely to be called up for active service, are you?' she asked anxiously.

'The news isn't good, I'm afraid!' James replied, his expression serious. 'The Germans are pushing us back towards the coast so it has to be faced – we are in retreat. If we can't stop the Germans it seems inevitable the troops will be the next target on Hitler's list. They have only to cross the Channel for it to mean every able-bodied man would be needed to defend ourselves. The Prime Minster, Mr Churchill, has already ordered the formation of a band of older men to be called the Home Guard to help our defence if there is an invasion.'

He broke off, realizing that he should not be relating this frightening news to the young girl lying exhausted after a difficult childbirth. In a lighter tone, he added: 'Don't worry, Dilys, I won't be called up in a hurry. I'd have to find another vet first to take over my clients.'

To distract her, he bent over the cot once more and stared at the baby who was sleeping peacefully. 'She really is very pretty, isn't she?' he repeated. 'Take care of yourself, my dear, and by the way, I forgot to tell you: Una will be in to see you this afternoon as soon as I get back to hold the fort.'

Exhausted yet strangely comforted by James' unexpected visit, Dilys lay back against her pillows and thought about the news he had given her. If England and France were losing the battle to halt the German's advance, what might already have happened to Norway? To Kristoffer? Was he still alive? Was he a prisoner of war? It was so dreadful not knowing even if he was alive. She would have given the world to be able to see him now, to show him his baby girl.

When Una arrived later that afternoon, they shared a tray of tea and cherry cake provided by Matron, who had been a great deal more accommodating since receiving the generous cheque from James when he had first visited The Willows. Sitting on the end of Dilys' bed, Una, for once, was being surprisingly unsympathetic as Dilys confided her fears for Kristoffer.

'Dil, you're married to James now and you've just got to stop thinking about the past.' Seeing Dilys' expression, she added quickly: 'I do understand how much Kristoffer meant to you, but you can never belong to him now – not even if he suddenly appeared. You've just *got* to forget him. I know it won't be easy . . .' Her glance went to the baby. The crumpled skin of the newborn had almost disappeared and the likeness of the infant to her father was unmistakable. 'But it isn't fair to James.' She leant forward and took one of Dilys' hands in hers. 'Dil, darling, he was so full of compliments about the baby when he got back to the surgery. He said I'd be sure to fall in love with her because she was such a sweet, pretty little thing and she hadn't cried once while he was here. He's going to love her, Dil and I know that's what you hoped for when you agreed to marry him.'

'Yes, you're right!' Dilys agreed. 'I will try harder to forget Kristoffer – I really will – but it isn't easy.' She paused momentarily and then said tentatively, 'Did anyone tell Mother and Father about the baby?'

Una nodded. 'I telephoned them in London but they knew anyway – Matron had already rung Mother. She said she and Father were "too busy" to visit you, but of course that was just an excuse.' She paused once more and then continued: 'I suppose you can't blame them.' A sudden smile lit up her face. 'Mother will have to tell the aunts, in due course. She'll probably say that you married James secretly and Tina is a honeymoon baby.'

Dilys was smiling now as they hugged one another.

'Was it ghastly giving birth?' Una asked as they drank their tea. 'Did it hurt terribly?'

Dilys nodded. 'I thought I was going to die but the midwife kept telling me everything was fine. She was really nice.' She put down her empty teacup and looked down at the baby beside her bed. 'But it was worth all the agony, Una. I love her so much! I never would have been able to let her be adopted the way Mother and Father wanted. I'll never stop being grateful to James for making it possible for me to keep her.'

There was a brief silence before Una said, 'Did James tell you that he thinks he will be called up? He has been in touch with the two other vets nearest to Fenbury to see if either of them would take on his regulars if he did have to go. He asked me, if that happened, whether I would like to move in and live with you and the baby. Of course I said yes, if Father would let me. At first Father said no, but he told me girls of eighteen were being called up for war service, not to fight but to work in factories and to help farmers and do nursing, as well as volunteering to join the army, navy or air force. So if I'm old enough to do all those things, I'm old enough to come and live with you if I want.'

Dilys looked at her twin's animated expression and smiled. 'It would be wonderful if you did come to live in Brook House, but . . . but wouldn't you rather do something more exciting? You could join one of the services – or maybe the new Air Transport Auxiliary and learn to fly an aeroplane like Amy Johnson.'

Una nodded. 'I saw the article about her too, in one of the magazines in the waiting room in the surgery. But I don't know if I'd be old enough to get chosen. Anyway, Dil, I wouldn't be able to live with you if I joined up. I hate it when we can't be together. Until you came here we were never apart, even for a single night – which reminds me, James says he will put two beds in the spare room so we can be together.'

Dilys returned her happy smile. 'You may not want to share,' she said. 'Not if Tina cries all night and keeps you awake.' Her smile faded as she added: 'Oh, Una, I'm so afraid I won't be able to look after Tina properly. I don't know anything about babies. James says his housekeeper, Mrs White, will advise me, and anyway, he says small babies are like newborn puppies: all they need is warmth, food and lots of sleep!'

They both smiled, and then Una said, 'Having raised his own baby, the poor little boy who died, he will know exactly what you need to do for little Tina.'

Dilys nodded, her eyes thoughtful. 'James has never talked about his wife or the child. It must have been so awful for him, losing them both so suddenly. Maybe Tina will sort of help to fill that gap.' She sighed. 'I really will try to be a good wife to him, Una. I mean, be a bit more affectionate than Mother and Father are. I don't think I've ever seen them kissing or even holding hands. I wouldn't mind holding James' hand or kissing him goodnight but . . . well, I couldn't be a real wife the way I was with Kristoffer.'

For a moment, neither of the twins spoke, then the maid came into the room to collect the tea things and reported that Matron had said she was to tell Una that visiting time was over.

Reluctantly, Una hugged Dilys and, after promising to come and see her again on Saturday afternoon when the surgery was closed, she kissed her once more, took a last look at the sleeping baby and left the room.

Tears, partly of weakness after the recent ordeal of the birth, trickled down Dilys' cheeks. Although Una's visit had cheered her in one way, there was still another whole week to go before she would be allowed to leave The Willows. The birth had not been an easy one, and she'd had several stitches which added to her physical discomfort. She tried hard not to let her thoughts return to Kristoffer and her desperate longing to see him – to show him the beautiful baby girl they had made together. The tiny child was so unmistakably his. She had his blue eyes and wisps of almost white-blonde hair. Even the shape of his mouth looked the same.

As if sensing her mother's need for comfort, the baby awoke and started to cry. Dilys leant over and lifted her warm little body into her arms. Almost at once, the baby stopped crying and nestled against her swollen breasts, seeking instinctively for a nipple. Dilys' tears dried instantly and she felt a swift surge of pleasure as her baby started to feed.

They were still lying in a gentle embrace, sleeping peacefully, when two hours later the maid returned with Dilys' supper. The middle-aged woman glanced at the young mother and baby as she placed the tray on the bedside table and was strangely moved by the peaceful look on both their faces. This was as it should be, she thought, aware that for once the mother would not have to give her baby away. She felt a moment of pleasure. The maid was more accustomed to seeing most of the girls and women here at The Willows crying their eyes out, their faces drawn, anguished by the knowledge of the coming parting with their babies. This young girl was lucky, very lucky, in that at the last minute the man she presumed to be the father had turned up to make an honest woman of the girl and to legitimize the child. The fact that the man looked almost old enough to be her father really didn't matter that much. At least this young girl did not have to give her newborn baby to strangers. Closing the bedroom door behind her, she reflected that The Willows, where she worked every day, was very far from being a happy establishment, but the pay was unusually good, and with six growing children and a husband who was away at war, she could not afford to be fussy, and happy days like this were a nice bonus. The picture of the young mother in the bed cuddling her baby was one she could, for once, happily take home when her long day's work ended.

ELEVEN

Christmas, the second of the war, was only two days away. James looked across the sitting room at Dilys, who was nursing her baby. Dilys' mouth, usually curved in a happy smile, was set in a stubborn line as she repeated: 'There is absolutely no way I'm going home for Christmas lunch if I can't take Tina. If my parents won't acknowledge my daughter, they can do without one of theirs!'

Una looked up from the rug by the fire where she was sitting wrapping a present. Turning to James, a worried frown on her face, she said, 'Dil won't listen to me, James. I've tried to explain that our parents aren't rejecting Tina, it's just that the aunts always come for Christmas lunch and if they saw Tina they would know immediately why Dil got married so quickly without them being told. They'd be fearfully shocked and disapproving.'

Dilys' head shot up and her cheeks flushed a deeper pink as she said, 'So their feelings are more important than mine! Well, I don't care and I'm not going!'

It was a moment or two before James spoke. Then he said quietly, 'I do understand how you feel, but you know, Dilys, they could have refused to see you again despite your marriage to me. Many turned their daughters out of their homes and banished them in similar circumstances. Others would have refused to allow Una to stay here with you whenever she wants. As far as Christmas is concerned, you yourself have told me that your aunts are very old fashioned and any suspicion as to Tina's illegitimacy they would see as scandalous?'

Dilys' expression softened slightly but her voice was still bitter when she declared, 'Maybe you are right about the aunts, but Mother hasn't once – not once – been to see Tina, not even when we had her christened.'

James exchanged glances with Una and then said gently, 'I do understand your feelings, my dear,' he repeated, 'but perhaps you should understand their concerns for the family's reputation. As Una says, you should try to see things from their point of view. It's important that the bridges should be maintained between you. You may require their support when Una leaves to join the Women's Auxiliary Air Force and becomes a WAAF, and I am likely to be called up soon, too.'

The thoughts of all three turned to the scenes on the recent cinema news of the thousands of soldiers from the defeated army trapped on the beaches of Dunkirk last June, waiting for rescue by the astonishing armada of little boats manned by their owners. The loss of life and the loss of huge numbers of men taken prisoner made it obvious that every able-bodied man was now needed to defend the country from the expected invasion. No one doubted that Britain was clearly Hitler's next objective. James had been lucky to find a much older vet in the adjoining village who was willing to incorporate his own veterinary practice with his.

James glanced quickly at Una, who nodded her agreement that this was a good moment to discuss the immediate future with Dilys. 'I had supposed Una would be here to keep you company when I was called up,' he said, 'but she will be leaving any day now. You will be on your own, and I'd be so much happier if I knew that you and your parents were properly reconciled; that you might even decide to return home.'

He paused to look tenderly at the now-sleeping infant in her mother's arms who he loved as much as if she had been his own. The seven-month-old baby was extremely pretty with her blue eyes and a surprisingly large amount of tight, white-blonde curls.

'As for this Christmas,' he continued, 'Tina is not going to know or care why she isn't coming to Hannington Hall with us. I guess she would far rather spend the afternoon here with Mrs White who, as you well know, will be only too happy to look after her on Christmas Day, give her her lunchtime bottle and tuck her up for her afternoon rest.'

That was unarguable, Dilys thought. James' housekeeper had been a tower of strength to her ever since she had arrived at Brook House with her newborn baby in her arms. Not only did Mrs White adore Tina but she had taken it upon herself to offer help and advice on all matters of baby care having reared six children of her own, all now healthy young adults. She was both capable and competent.

Reluctantly, Dilys finally accepted James and Una's advice that she should attend the Christmas lunch at Hannington Hall without her baby. Mrs White was almost as doting as she was, after all, and Tina would certainly not miss her.

She stood up and crossed the sitting room to take the sleeping baby upstairs for her afternoon rest, after which she would go to the kitchen and check on lunch for the three of them. James returned to his surgery pleased he and Una had managed to persuade Dilys to see the situation from her parents' point of view and leaving Una wrapping the last of the Christmas presents. He himself had no wish to quarrel with the twins' parents, who might well have chosen not to allow their daughter to marry a country vet, albeit it had been to legitimize the baby. Out in the kitchen it crossed Dilys' mind – as it had done so many times before – that her debt to James for marrying her and giving her and Tina a home was so vast that she feared there was no adequate way she could ever thank him. At least she had agreed to his wish for her to be present at the traditional family Christmas lunch, putting aside her resentment that her adored little girl was being ostracized.

Dilys' heart now swelled with love for her baby daughter, which she tried very hard never to think of as also being Kristoffer's child. Her marriage to James was working out far better than she had imagined. During the past seven months since she had moved in with him, he was always kind, caring, attentive and never intrusive. On occasions he had put his arm around her or kissed her cheek, but always as if she was his sister. His affection was comforting but what really made her happy was his obvious adoration of Tina. As the months had passed since her birth on 11 May, Tina had learned to sit unsupported and was even now trying to crawl and would soon be a toddler. She loved to be bounced by James on his knee and would cuddle up and hug him when he kissed her goodnight.

It was now almost the end of the year and she realized that, during the past months, her gratitude now included a very real affection. She found herself dreading the day when he would be going away to join the army; she hated the thought that he might be sent abroad where she might not see him for a long time.

So many dreadful things had happened these past months, she reflected. Although in September the success of the pilots in the aerial battles against the far more numerous German planes had halted the threat of invasion, thousands of German planes had started dropping bombs, including the horrific incendiaries, on London. Too many to be shot down by the depleted British squadrons, they were pulverizing London and other cities like Coventry and Bristol. German submarines were sinking the convoys bringing desperately needed supplies of food and materials for the factories which were working day and night to keep the forces supplied with wartime necessities. Women were now replacing the workforce in the factories in order to release the men to replace the huge loss of soldiers and sailors.

The whole of Europe was now in German hands and James had tuned in the wireless so she and Una could listen with him to Winston Churchill's broadcast. It was a stirring speech about the perilous state of Britain, which was now standing alone against the enemy. There was no doubt that Germany intended to include Great Britain in its list of occupied territories and he said that the nation would resist the invaders by whatever means.

It was after such a rallying broadcast that James had decided to join up as soon as he had transferred his practice to the neighbouring vet.

Meanwhile, Una had managed to find out from the father of one of her old school friends who worked in the Foreign Office what was happening in Norway. Vidkun Quisling was now working alongside the German Reichskommissar Josef Terboven, who Germany had put in charge of the country when it had finally surrendered last April. Her friend's father had also told her that most of the population were resisting the invaders in any way they could, and the resistant groups were continuing the fight and hiding in the forests.

Dilys had thought it highly likely that Kristoffer would have joined such a group, having so often spoken proudly of his devotion to his country. She tried not to think of the danger he might be in, although she had long ago accepted that even if he had never tried to find her, or had never loved her as she'd loved him, she still needed to know that he was alive.

Neither Dilys nor Una had ever shown the least interest in politics. The subject had not been on their school curriculum and they had always found their father's political diatribes exceedingly boring when he launched into current topical issues at mealtimes.

Their mother, like many other middle-aged women who did not need financially to work, chose to do something for the war effort and had become a member of the WVS, the Women's Voluntary Service. The women were on call to help in any emergency, manning canteens, arranging refuge, clothing and food for the survivors of the bombing raids whose homes had been destroyed. They had been responsible for the hurried evacuation to the country of children from London, and were available wherever voluntary help was needed. For the first time in her life, Lady Singleby felt she was of some real value to the country, and was surprisingly efficient at what she was required to organize or to do.

The dreadful bombing of the capital had not curtailed her social activities completely, and the theatres, opera, cinemas, tea dances and nightclubs still carried on despite the frightening air raids. These places of entertainment were filled by both civilians and uniformed men and women despite the frequent need to hurry down to the underground shelters when the air-raid warning sirens sounded.

The past year had changed Lady Singleby. Her frequent proximity to death and suffering, particularly of the poorer classes, had brought about a far less rigid attitude to the stringent class distinctions and moral ethics of her pre-war existence. Set against the magnitude of the suffering she saw on a daily basis, and not least the selfless devotion of mothers to their children, her feelings towards her wayward daughter had mollified.

On Christmas morning, when Dilys arrived with James and Una, she surprised her daughter by giving her not only her customary kiss on both cheeks but a hug, and exclaimed: 'Darlings, it's lovely to see you all. When I spoke to Una on the phone she said she wasn't sure whether you would be able to leave the baby. I do wish it had not been necessary but now I'm down here for the Christmas break I shall come and see her. The aunts aren't here yet so I can have you to myself for a little while.' She nodded at James and, wishing him a happy Christmas, she linked her arms through those of Dilys and Una and led them into the drawing room where a log fire was blazing.

Turning to Dilys, she said, 'How well you look, darling! With all this horrid food rationing I was afraid you might have lost weight. Perhaps your grateful customers bring you little thank-you presents, James – eggs and suchlike? Do you shoot? My husband manages to shoot a few pheasants or a partridge when he can take time from his work in London and get home. Our butcher is very good, letting us have the odd few sausages or a piece of liver, so we eat quite well here at Hannington Hall.'

She stopped talking momentarily to dispense glasses of sherry. James was amused to see how smart and fashionably she was dressed for a family lunch party. Lady Singleby was wearing one of her pre-war purchases, a maroon jersey silk dress with tiny jet buttons and a belt with a jet buckle fastened tight around her small waist. Her hair was immaculately waved and her face was lightly powdered and rouged.

Handing James a glass of sherry, she glanced briefly at his well-worn tweed suit and just managed to hide her disapproval. She forced a charming smile as she said, 'My husband is in the dining room carefully decanting the port which he insists is appropriate to complete Christmas lunch. Do say if you don't care for it, James. Una, dear, pop into the kitchen and see if Cook has everything under control. She gets in a bit of a flap these days but I suppose cooking a proper Christmas lunch for seven is a trifle difficult these days. She was complaining this morning that the fat and sugar ration is only a fraction of what she needs for what she called a "proper Christmas lunch".'

Dilys now handed her mother the box she was holding. 'One of James' grateful clients gave him these eggs, Mother,' she told her. 'We thought Cook might want to use that Isinglass stuff she puts in a bucket to preserve them if you don't need them immediately.'

Lady Singleby's carefully plucked eyebrows rose in surprise.

'I'd no idea you can preserve eggs. Cook spent the whole of last summer, when your Father and I were in London, bottling fruit and making jam and chutney, but she never mentioned eggs. Thank you, dear, and you, James. Thank goodness Cook is too old to be called up! Which reminds me, Una, have you heard yet when you will be joining the WAAF?'

She linked her arm through Una's again as she walked with her across the hall and down the passage towards the kitchen. 'I know you were disappointed to hear you couldn't be a pilot, but these "special duties" you said the officer had earmarked for you do sound quite exciting. Your father can't believe you have to sign the Official Secrets Act before you will be told what you will be doing! He says that, as you are still underage, he should be informed.'

Una smiled. 'I'm hoping I might be trained to be a spy!' she said. 'After all, Dil and I speak fluent French, and more importantly German, which could be jolly useful for spying!'

Lady Singleby looked shocked. 'I do hope you are not serious, Una. In fact, I'm sure your father wouldn't allow it. You are far too young for something dangerous like that. In the last war there was a Dutch woman dancer, Mata Hari, who was a spy. She was caught by the French and executed by firing squad just before the end of the war.'

'Well, she was silly to get caught, wasn't she!' Una replied. 'Anyway, I won't know what I'll be doing until they choose to tell me, and even then I can't tell you or Father.'

Seeing her mother's expression, Una quickly took the precious box of eggs from her and darted into the kitchen with it. When she rejoined her mother, she carefully changed the subject of her future war work. 'I'm so glad you are going to see Tina, Mother. She's such a beautiful, happy little thing, and she *is* you granddaughter!'

Lady Singleby paused, her expression embarrassed. 'Well, it's been a little difficult. Your father . . . Well, you know how concerned he always is about the family good name and that sort of thing, and if his constituents got to know Dilys and James had only been married a few days before—' She broke off, looking even more embarrassed. After a moment's silence, when neither spoke, she said, 'I think I can go over to Fenbury now your father is spending so much more time in London. He isn't using the car down here so I can use his petrol coupons. You and Dilys can expect me on Wednesday.' She took a deep breath, as if to be pleased to end the subject. 'This rationing is such a bore,' she announced more cheerfully. 'But I suppose it's necessary.'

Leaving her mother to speak with Cook, Una made her way back to the dining room to find her father. When Lady Singleby rejoined Dilys in the sitting room she sat down beside her on the sofa, patted her daughter's hand in an unfamiliar, intimate gesture and said, 'Any time you don't use your clothing coupons, my darling, I can always do with them! If the war and rationing go on like this I shall have to copy my friend's recommendation and buy my dresses from a titled woman she knows who sells her unwanted model gowns from her flat somewhere in Knightsbridge.'

Seeing the look of surprise on Dilys' face, no doubt at the mere thought of her mother buying second-hand clothes, she smiled. 'Nobody knows the woman's name but she has this big flat and I'm told one goes to it where her maid shows you all the dresses for sale laid out on the bed with their sale prices on them. One can try them on and pay the maid whatever amount is on the ticket. She then packs them up and off one goes with nobody the wiser. The clothes are quite gorgeous, I gather. Evelyn says they come from designers in Paris or New York, but Milady won't be seen in the same dress twice so selling them is the perfect solution for people like us now we have this horrid rationing. The woman is all right as she has a walk-in wardrobe with enough clothes to last a lifetime.'

She stopped talking as they were joined by Una and Sir Godfrey. He went over to the window where James was quietly watching a beautiful cock pheasant strutting boldly across the lawn, and somewhat to the twins' surprise he seemed almost at once to get along extremely well with James. After discovering that James' father had been one of his friends at prep school, he decided that perhaps Dilys' shocking behaviour had really not turned out to be the total disaster he'd feared and that James had proved to be a really decent chap, making an honest woman of his errant daughter.

To his further relief, when the aunts arrived and his wife introduced James as Dilys' husband, he saw they were quite excited by news of the whirlwind marriage and only critical of the fact that they had not been invited to, or advised of, the wedding.

'It was because of the war!' Daphne told her sisters smoothly. 'Godfrey and I hadn't agreed the couple should even get engaged, Dilys being so young, but when Dilys told us that James would soon be joining up and would almost certainly be posted off abroad somewhere, we decided to let them get married. It was just a quick registry office affair in case James had to leave at short notice. However, because he hadn't yet found anyone to take over his veterinary practice, the authorities agreed to delay his call up. You go in two weeks' time, don't you, James?'

Now mollified, Aunt Rose said, 'Well, congratulations to you both, but I do wish you had let us know, Daphne. At the very least, Ivy and I could have sent a telegram to wish them well.'

'And a wedding present,' Aunt Ivy added. 'Dear me, you must let us know what you would like, Dilys, dear child. What a surprise! Do you remember, Rose, in the last war how we stood at the drawing-room window and watched all those poor young boys marching down the street on the way to France and those dreadful trenches?'

Aunt Rose nodded. 'We had been presented just before the war started, and nearly all the eligible boys we'd met at our coming-out dance went off to France.' She sighed, adding sadly: 'And most of them were killed.' She turned to look at Dilys. 'Your Aunt Ivy and I had both met young men we had hoped to marry who, sadly, never came home. There were over two million casualties, you know. Looking back, I suppose that we, too, should have married before they went away.'

'Come now!' Sir Godfrey interrupted. 'We don't want this sort of talk today. Ah, there's the gong, so let's go in to lunch!'

Despite the absence of her baby girl, Dilys realized she was quite enjoying the family party. Somehow James was keeping them all laughing at his stories about some of his patients: the turkey who'd been brought to him in the summer with a broken leg and had become the farmer's family pet so he never got eaten at Christmas. Then there was the runt of a litter of piglets which an elderly lady had adopted when she heard the farmer was about to knock it on the head and eat it. She hadn't realized that a tiny, nine-inch-long piglet would grow into a huge sixteen-stone sow and had asked James to find it a good home.

'So what happened to it?' Aunt Rose asked anxiously.

James smiled. 'Well, by this time it had decimated their croquet lawn as well as the vegetable garden, so her husband said, not for the first time, 'We'll eat it!'

Sir Godfrey laughed but Aunt Rose looked horrified.

'Don't worry!' James reassured her. 'I told her I would find a good home for "Tinkerbell", so named after the fairy in that successful Peter Pan play because of the noise its tiny trotters had made on her flagstone floor. Well, you can imagine how inappropriate that name had become now it was a big fat sow.'

They all laughed, but Aunt Rose persisted. 'I do hope you did find a home for it, Mr Sherwin?'

'I gave it to a farmer I knew who said he could breed from it,' James told her, smiling. 'He was delighted to acquire a young healthy animal for free and he agreed never to send it to the market. So all ended happily.'

They were still smiling when the maid came in with the Christmas pudding, a sprig of holly on top and the brandy Cook had poured over it at the last minute flaming merrily.

'This is the last of the batch Cook made three years ago,' Lady Singleby said. 'Cook always keeps them to mature. Just as well now rationing prohibits the dried fruit and all those other ingredients. Goodness knows what we'll have next Christmas, so make the most of this one.'

In due course the crackers were pulled and the delicious box of crystallized fruits and the bowl of nuts were passed around. Both aunts were quite voluble after two glasses of Sir Godfrey's white wine and were even tempted to sip a glass of his excellent port.

At the far end of the table, Una was questioning her mother about the entertainments still being enjoyed in London despite the dreadful bombing raids, while Sir Godfrey was questioning James about the respective merits of Labradors or spaniels as shooting dogs. Sitting silently beside James, Dilys silently surveyed the now-untidy Christmas table, absorbing the relaxed, congenial atmosphere of this family gathering. It was surprisingly nice, she thought, to be here at home again. Not that she was unhappy with James at Brook House, but it was good to be reconciled with her parents; nice, too, that James was so at ease with them and so obviously approved of by the aunts. Most of all, she was happy that her parents were pleased with her marriage and that her mother had acknowledged Tina and promised that, when her actual age was less guessable, she could be introduced as a family member.

It was when Una came round the table to pull the last cracker with her and a child's bracelet fell out into her lap that Dilys' thoughts winged once more to Kristoffer. Automatically, she reached up to touch the ring she still wore round her neck and a wave of sadness and anxiety swept through her. Where was he this Christmas of 1940? What was he doing? Was he alive? And if so, was it possible he could at this very moment be thinking of her?

As Una looked at her twin's stricken face, she said anxiously in a whisper, 'Cheer up, Dil, darling! Everything has worked out really, really well.'

'I know! I know!' Dilys whispered back, reminding herself of the unfortunate girls at The Willows who would be childless this Christmas and the huge debt she owed James. She had no right to be thinking of Kristoffer and wishing he were there beside her. It was time she faced the fact that she would never see him again; and, more importantly, that she was deluded in imagining he had never loved her as she had loved him.

TWELVE

Kristoffer sat down at the table in the room above a jewellery shop in Bergen where he had just joined four other resistance workers in his cell. They were smiling as they congratulated themselves on the mission they had accomplished the previous day. Lorentz, their leader and radio operator, had informed the London headquarters about their successful destruction of a train carrying vital army equipment, and now London, where their Norwegian director was located, had decided to include them in a far more important mission.

'They want you to go over there, Kris, so they can spell out the details. Sounds more involved than usual.'

He and the other two men turned to look at Kristoffer, who said, 'I wonder why they specified me?'

'Because you're bilingual!' Lorentz replied. 'Your German is good enough for you to pass as one of them.' He was about the same age as Kristoffer and, like the other three men, his clothes and appearance were as unremarkable as possible. This enabled them to pass scrutiny without questioning when they attended their daily jobs in a factory now making ammunition boxes for the Germans. The owner was a fiercely patriotic family man. He had given them fictitious jobs which frequently took them away from the factory so they could be absent when their intermittent tasks as resistance workers needed them. He was as keen to hinder the German occupiers as they were and never hesitated to provide fictitious cover for them when they were absent.

'You're to go to London immediately,' Lorentz was saying. 'They are sending a plane to pick you up on Thursday night at the usual place, weather permitting. I have alerted Bertil to have his men ready to guide it in.' He smiled grimly as he added: 'Sounds a bigger job than we've done so far. I gathered that two other cells will be involved.'

Kristoffer knew that his four compatriots were anxious to be doing bigger and more dangerous jobs than those they had undertaken since last June when Norway had finally surrendered. By now a large number of men like themselves had formed groups all over the country who continued to hamper the invaders in any way possible. The population as a whole remained defiant, showing their feelings in simple, unpunishable ways such as refusing to sit down on a vacant bus or tram seat if it was next to a German. There were, however, a number of people now called Quislings after the German puppet, Vidkun Quisling, who fraternized with the enemy, but the population as a whole was intensely loyal and there were many like those in the Resistance who risked their lives harassing the invaders.

Kristoffer's heart was now beating fast with the news Lorentz had imparted. Not only was he to be involved in something of major importance but he was to fly to England – to the one place in the world where he could, hopefully, find Dilys. It was now nearly two years since she had been whisked away by her father and he'd never had a reply from her to the letter he'd addressed to Sir Godfrey. He clung to the hope that the memory of her commitment to him the day she had allowed him to make love to her had not been transitory. His spirits now soared as he realized that at long last he could search for her – that he could confront her father in person and ask him to reveal where he might find her.

Kristoffer's companions were now speculating as to what the important secret task might be. With Italy now allied to Germany, Britain being bombed night and day and the decimation of the shipping by Germany's U-boats, the Allies were looking perilously close to losing their lone battle against the enemy. Even in the Middle East the British army was being defeated by Field Marshal Rommel's forces.

Kristoffer bade his companions goodbye and made his way across the town to see Gerda. She was serving in a *kafeteria* near the harbour as one of the waitresses. It was also a 'safe house' – somewhere where active patriots could meet, pass messages to one another or simply disappear into a storeroom at the back if there was a sudden inspection. The ever-vigilant Germans made frequent visits to such places, demanding to see identity papers or looking for a Jew or a suspect resistant.

Gerda had changed her appearance as well as her name when she had joined one of the resistance cells. Her blonde hair was now cut short so that it could be covered by a dark brown wig. This double identity enabled her to move around freely as Ingrid without being recognized by relatives or friends when she was at work, something which would endanger their lives if she were caught when actively involved with the resistance cell who used the cafe for passing messages and making plans for sabotage.

Kristoffer was able to drop in for a drink or a meal as any casual customer might do, to pass on a message from his cell. They never discussed their clandestine activities when they were at home. Sometimes when he saw her in her brown wig he failed to recognize her for an instant when she came to his table to take his order.

On this occasion, the *kafeteria* was full, mostly of office workers who were snatching a quick lunch of whatever meagre unappetizing food was now available to the population. Kristoffer ordered only a cup of almost unrecognizable coffee and informed Gerda in an undertone not to expect to see him for several weeks.

After finishing his coffee he walked back to the drab single room he had leased in a dingy block of flats overlooking the harbour. On the opposite side of the town to his home, he used it whenever he was involved in resistance activities in order to safeguard his parents if the Germans were searching for him. In one corner of the single room was a wooden bunk, besides which was a shabby armchair. On a hook above the bed were the clothes he wore on occasions when he was working as a docker and needed a disguise. He now slumped down in the chair and allowed himself time to contemplate his trip to England.

The London headquarters had been set up by those in authority who had escaped to England before the final surrender. The premises were where cohesive decisions were now made for the increasingly large number of resistance cells dotted around the country. Coordinated in London, their isolated activities were now planned to cause more effective maximum disruption to German activities in Norway. Kristoffer's thoughts turned to the Norwegian in charge of these operations. According to a colleague who had already been to London to receive orders, the man was both charming and extremely knowledgeable about the whole of Norway, and highly efficient and sympathetic to the desperate needs of the resistance fighters for arms and equipment.

Kristoffer's excitement at the thought of his trip to England now gave way to a wave of anxiety. Would he be obliged to return to Norway immediately after his briefing in London and have no time in which to search for Dilys. To be in the same country as her but not able to find her would be unbearable. Even allowing for the fact that if he did so she might tell him she no longer loved him, he would rather know it than continue his life with such painful uncertainty.

Three days later, at two o'clock on a Tuesday morning as planned, an RAF Lysander made the hazardous landing in an isolated field in the safety of darkness. The men who had guided the plane in with torches hurried to unload the supplies requested by the Resistance. They then helped Kristoffer on board and the pilot turned the plane and taxied away, finally lifting off into the night sky. Kristoffer had been given a briefcase containing maps of strategic locations where considerable German activity was taking place, which would be of use to those in London planning future raids by the Resistants.

Undetected, the plane returned safely to its base in Scotland where Kristoffer was given a change of clothes, a meal and a warrant for his night train ticket to London. In the taxi the following morning taking him from Euston railway station to the address he had been given in Baker Street, he was shocked to see the devastation caused by the relentless air raids, rubble sometimes still being cleared from a bombed-out block of offices. The elderly taxi driver, a cheerful cockney, informed him that Hitler was wasting his time; England would never surrender. At the Norwegian offices, Kristoffer gave his name and was shown immediately into a small room where he was warmly greeted by a uniformed officer who shook his hand and introduced himself as *Kaptein* Martin Linge. Kristoffer handed over the package containing the maps and coded messages from Lorentz.

As time passed, Kristoffer became more and more impressed with the organization in London which had been set up to coordinate the various haphazard groups of men, and indeed women, who wished to continue the fight after the occupation. The maps he had delivered were apparently exactly what *Kaptein* Martin Linge wanted. He was now told about the fabrication of some parts for a new type of weapon which was being developed in a huge castle near Oslo. Along with the specialist German scientists employed there were several German foremen who supervised the work and a high-ranking German officer responsible for the overall smooth running of the factory, before the finished results were despatched to Germany.

Information had been sent to the London HQ to say that the parts made there, although sounding harmless, were actually intended for some revolutionary secret weapon cooked up by Hitler's scientists. It was now explained to Kristoffer that the Resistance were to blow up this place, eliminating its capacity to produce anything at all, ensuring that a considerable amount of time would be needed to rebuild the factory and replace the specific machinery they were using.

The job would have to be done at night, Kristoffer was told, when there was no danger of any Norwegian workers being on the premises. He was to be in charge of the actual operation on the site in conjunction with an explosive expert who would be co-opted from another cell. A sketch of the interior of the building and placement of the vital machinery was among the papers Kristoffer had brought with him. It had been produced by one of the Norwegians employed as an electrician, and a copy had been made and given to Kristoffer. He was to show it to the explosive expert as soon as possible on his return as it was known that a date had already been chosen for an inspection visit by a high-ranking German official to congratulate the staff on their satisfactory output. Security would be increased in preparation for his visit, Kristoffer was told, but despite this drawback it was hoped that the official and his entourage would be eliminated at the same time as the building.

It was an exciting project, Kristoffer thought as he left the building, and by the sound of it a very important one, although it was not yet known exactly what was the 'secret weapon' for which the parts were needed. Added to his excitement was the fact that he was told he could remain in England for the rest of the week as some of the false identity papers and equipment needed by the Resistance was not yet ready for Kristoffer to take back with him. Now, at long last, he was able to go and search for the girl he loved.

THIRTEEN

The first thing Kristoffer did when he left the building in Baker Street was to make his way to the Houses of Parliament where he attempted to see Sir Godfrey. After much scrutiny and questioning, he was finally taken to a small waiting room where, after a long wait, Sir Godfrey's secretary arrived to see him. A tall, thin, elderly woman, she regarded him suspiciously and appeared to disbelieve his insistence that he was a friend of Sir Godfrey's daughters. Were that so, she said coldly, she would already know of his name and address. It was some minutes before she relaxed when he explained his connection in Munich with Dilys and Una. She then recalled the shreds of the letter from Germany which she found Sir Godfrey had discarded, perhaps wrongly, in the upheaval following the news of the outbreak of the war. Feeling a trifle guilty, she now gave him the address of Sir Godfrey's London flat, instead of the family home in the country, leaving her boss to make the decision on whether to enlighten the young man any further.

Regardless of the cost, such was Kristoffer's impatience that he took a taxi directly to Greencoat Place rather than waste any time walking there. He had failed to consider the possibility that Sir Godfrey would not be at home when the porter informed him but, to his relief, he was then told that Lady Singleby was there. Without hesitation, Kristoffer insisted the porter telephone her to say he was on his way up to see her and, three minutes later, he stood outside the door of the flat.

His first impression of Dilys' mother when she let him in was that she bore no resemblance whatever to the girl he loved so dearly. She was a small, birdlike figure, her face thin, her chin pointed but, overall, she was not unattractive. She was fashionably dressed with a lot of jewellery and her hair was carefully waved.

Lady Singleby regarded the strange young foreigner calling

himself Kristoffer Holberg with a mixture of curiosity and approval of his exceptional good looks. He now explained to her that he had been a student in Munich at the same time as Una and Dilys and was anxious to look them up now he was in England. He did not say he was a Norwegian but she automatically assumed he was one of the very many foreigners who had escaped from their occupied countries to Britain, when they were miraculously rescued from the beaches of Dunkirk where they had been marooned by the unprecedented flotilla of small ships. These foreigners had joined the British fight against their common enemy, hoping for victory so they could return to their homelands.

When Lady Singleby realized exactly who Kristoffer was, and that he must be the father of Dilys' baby, her immediate instinct was to think of a way to stop him discovering her whereabouts. Mercifully, Dilys seemed happy in her marriage and she herself could see no good coming from a meeting with this young Norwegian boy. Hurriedly, she said the first thing that came to her mind, namely that both her girls had joined the air force and were now engaged in some kind of secret work which they were not allowed to tell her about, nor even where they were stationed.

Crushed with disappointment by the news, it was a minute or two before Kristoffer could find his voice. Then he said urgently, 'Please, Lady Singleby, if they should telephone you, would you be so good as to tell them that I am in London until the weekend, and if it is at all possible, to meet me.' Quickly he searched in his wallet for a scrap of paper on which he scribbled the name of his hotel and also his home address in Bergen and begged Dilys to try to get a message to him. He gave it to Lady Singleby, asking her to ensure Dilys knew of his visit and that he sent her his love.

Lady Singleby's immediate reaction was a feeling of anger as she recalled the disgrace this young man had so nearly inflicted on Dilys but, reading the note, her anger gave way to an unprecedented awareness of his good looks. Had she been Dilys' age, she thought, she might well have succumbed to the young man's attraction and charm. Her emotionless, almost sexless marriage had never awakened her to the kind of passion and pleasure hinted at by her woman friends. Now, however, she suddenly discovered herself understanding how her daughter could have been tempted to enjoy forbidden intimacies.

She shook Kristoffer's hand as he turned to go. 'If either does telephone me, I will pass on your message,' she said, at the same time knowing that it would not be in her daughter's interest for her to reveal the young Norwegian's presence in London. 'We must hope this dreadful war will be over in the not-too-distant future,' she added in an effort to uplift Kristoffer's spirits. 'Then we can all travel wherever we want and renew our fractured friendships again.'

Immeasurably depressed, Kristoffer left the building and walked dejectedly up Buckingham Gate, around the front of the Palace and on into Green Park. Coming out into Piccadilly, once more among the crowds of office workers out for their lunchtime break, he passed by the Royal Air Force Club without at first realizing its significance. He saw three uniformed officers approaching before stopping to chat to one another then disappear into the building. It struck him suddenly that it was just possible that Dilys and Una might belong to this club and someone there might know the whereabouts of two WAAF girls. It was a very long shot, he realized, but he had nothing better to do with his time.

He was about to go in when the doors opened and a young woman in WAAF uniform came out on to the steps, putting her uniform cap on her shining red hair as she walked down into the street. Kristoffer's shock was so intense that for a moment, he could not find his voice. Then he stepped forward and said huskily: 'Dil, it's me, Kris! Thank God I've found you!' He broke off as the slight frown of bewilderment left Una's face and was replaced by a wide smile.

'Goodness gracious me, it's Kristoffer! What on earth are you doing here?'

Finding his voice, he smiled happily, saying: 'Dil, I'd given up hope of finding you! I've just left your mother who told me you and your sister had joined the air force, but she didn't know where you were.' He paused, clearing his throat before saying huskily, 'Dil, why didn't you write back to me? Didn't your father give you my letter?' He broke off as Una put a hand on his arm.

'Kristoffer, I'm not Dilys, I'm Una!' she said awkwardly, her heart sinking. Kristoffer's words, the depth of longing in his voice, left her in no doubt that he was still in love with her twin. Dilys had been right in believing that the love they had shared was no transitory affair. How could she possibly tell him now that Dilys was married . . . married to a man who was not the real father of her baby . . . Kristoffer's baby.

His disappointment was palpable as he said, 'I'm sorry! I thought . . . Una, where can I find her? I must see her.'

When Una did not immediately reply, he added: 'She hasn't . . . she hasn't been hurt in one of these horrible air raids we heard about in my country? Una, please, tell me that she is unharmed. I have only two more days before I have to return to Norway. I'll go wherever she is. Please tell me where I can find her.'

Una tried frantically to think of some way to reply. One thing was uppermost in her mind, that it could only make Dilys desperately unhappy to know that Kristoffer was in England searching for her and that he had not stopped loving her. It would be kinder not to do so. As for Kristoffer himself, he'd said he would be returning to Norway in two days' time. Perhaps she should have told him Dil was married so he could forget all about her.

She had heard about the groups of men who had banded together to carry out dangerous acts of sabotage in France and Norway. A senior officer had told her about one such event which took place last April. A number of Norwegian secret resistance workers had blown up a train in the north of Norway carrying German troops and ammunition and almost completely destroyed it, but in doing so several Norwegians had also died. Awful though it was to contemplate such undertakings, it flashed across Una's mind that if Kristoffer were to be engaged in such dangerous activities he might not survive the war. It would be kinder to leave him in ignorance of Dil's marriage and to say nothing to her about his efforts to find her.

Una now told Kristoffer that her twin was engaged in the same secret work as herself: that she had not yet finished her training, after which she might be posted anywhere in the country where WAAFs were slowly but efficiently replacing their male counterparts for active service.

Kristoffer had one last hope. 'Your home in the country,' he said. 'If I write to her there—'

'I'm sorry but Hannington Hall has been requisitioned,' Una broke in. 'You could write to her here at the RAF Club. Address the envelope to me and I'll give it to her next time I see her. There's no other way I can put you in touch with her.'

Despite this grain of comfort, so great was Kristoffer's disappointment at the thought of not seeing Dilys that, for a moment, he could not find words to reply to Una. She was looking different from the girl he'd known in Germany but very smart in her blue WAAF uniform. Nevertheless, her facial resemblance to Dilys remained the same and it was a kind of torment for him to go on looking at her, knowing that she was not the girl he loved.

'I'll bring a letter for Dil back here later today,' he told her. 'I'm sure I don't have to tell you what a crushing blow it is for me not to see her. Do you realize, Una, that in three weeks' time it will have been two years since we last saw one another. I expect she told you I gave her a ring as we planned to get married as soon as she was old enough. I know it wasn't official but we were sort of engaged. Una, you must know . . . has she forgotten me? I know she meant all the things she said at the time, but perhaps at her age . . .' He paused to draw a long, painful sigh and then added: 'Perhaps she meant it at the time but then—' He broke off, his voice too choked with misery to continue.

Una's heart filled with pity. She said quickly, 'Of course she meant it at the time. She was for ever talking about the tremendous crush she had on you but . . . well, a lot has happened since then, what with the war and so many men dying on the beaches at Dunkirk, and the Blitz and everything. That wonderful year we had in Munich does seem to have faded into the past, doesn't it? I'm so sorry, Kristoffer.'

Reading between the lines, Kristoffer now realized that Una was trying to warn him that Dilys' love had not perhaps endured as had his own.

'I suppose it was silly of me to believe she felt as deeply as I did . . . do . . .' he muttered with difficulty. He was silent for a moment, not trusting his voice. Then he cleared his throat and said, 'I will put my home address in the letter I will leave here at the club for you to give to her. I realize she can't just post it to Norway, but she could address it to me at our government's headquarters in Prince's Gate, Knightsbridge, and I am sure they will forward it to me. I will write the address . . .'

Una held out her hand, saying, 'I'm afraid I'll have to rush off, Kristoffer. I'm meeting a friend for lunch so I'll have to dash or I'll be late. Otherwise you could come back inside and have a drink. I—'

'I quite understand!' Kristoffer interrupted. 'Can I try and get a taxi for you?'

Glad to be leaving the painful situation, Una said quickly, 'No, thanks! I'm only going to the Ritz so I'll walk.'

Guessing that Una wished to get away, Kristoffer announced that he was going in the opposite direction to buy a present for his parents at Harrods. He turned back down Piccadilly towards Knightsbridge, but at Hyde Park Corner he crossed into the park and walked aimlessly towards the Serpentine where he found a bench overlooking the lake and sat down, feeling more despondent than he had ever felt before. He was momentarily annoyed with himself for not having asked Una if she knew whether Dilys had received the letter he had written to her and addressed to Sir Godfrey, but on second reflection it no longer seemed relevant. Una would have told him if that had been the case.

It was now time, he told himself, to face the fact that those halcyon days in Munich he'd spent with Dilys were probably no more than a memory to her. It might even be as well if he, too, put them to the back of his mind in view of the life he now led in Norway. In a few days' time he would be back in his own country, ready to carry out what was clearly a very dangerous mission. It would be better both for him and the enterprise if he did not have anything else on his mind.

Angrily, he brushed away the threatening tears and, with his hands thrust deep into his trouser pockets, he stood up and strode dejectedly across the park back to his hotel.

FOURTEEN

James sat in his favourite armchair and looked across the room at Dilys. She had eighteen-month-old Tina on her lap and had been reading her a story, but the little girl was holding one hand in front of her face and playing peek-a-boo with him.

'I really don't know why I am wasting my time reading this,' Dilys said, laughing. 'Make up your mind, Tina: do you want a story or would you rather play games with Daddy?'

'Games!' the child said without hesitation, her large blue eyes sparkling.

'In that case,' Dilys said to James, 'she can sit on your lap while I go and get her bottle ready.'

Dilys stood up and, handing the child to James, she disappeared into the kitchen, a smile lingering on her lips. Watching her go, it struck James how greatly she had changed in the past eighteen months. The look of strain had disappeared, her movements were relaxed and she was perfectly at ease in his company. As for her child, little Tina had completely stolen his heart. It surprised him, each time she came running to him or held up her face to be kissed, that he realized he loved her as much as he had once loved the baby son who had been killed with his wife.

Now, as he settled Tina on his knees, it struck him that his feelings for Dilys, too, had changed. In those first difficult months following their hurried marriage, they had been of concern and understanding as to how sad she must be at the absence of the father of her child. From the start she had been completely honest with him about the fact that she still loved the young Norwegian student who had made her pregnant.

It had been largely pity for her predicament which had urged him on the spur of the moment to offer to marry her so she could keep her unborn baby. He knew most people would think he was out of his mind to have done so, but he had no doubt whatever that it had proved to be the right thing to do – not just for her and her child, but for himself, too.

Dilys was busy in the kitchen preparing Tina's bedtime bottle of milk which he loved to hold for the now-sleepy child. It had become a special time of day which he really looked forward to when he finished the day's work, closed the surgery and joined Dilys and Tina in the other part of the house. Dilys would have a drink ready for him, the child usually bathed and in her pyjamas, both greeting him with smiles of welcome and Tina eager for kisses and hugs. Dilys would be interested to hear about the day's activities, and to tell him what she and Tina had been up to. The look of strain and sadness had been replaced by a soft, maternal contentment.

Suddenly, as he sat there with Dilys' baby girl's arms round his neck, he was so intensely aware of his feeling of utter contentment that it surprised him. Catching his breath, he realized what had happened to him: he had fallen in love with the girl he had married. But almost at once, he remembered that in two days' time he would be leaving her – his call-up date had been confirmed.

James' thoughts turned uneasily to the desperate state the Allies were in. Apart from the huge numbers of men captured on land there had been a horrifying loss of men at sea: losses in the Middle East where the 8th Army was trying to keep the German army at bay, not to mention the loss of pilots and air crews. With the country in imminent danger of defeat, he'd felt he had no choice other than to volunteer his services. Not only men but women, too, were needed, replacing men whose jobs they were now doing, releasing them for more active duties. Una was already a member of the WAAF and was stationed near Bath, where she was engaged in secret work. Yet another new force had been created called the Women's Land Army, made up of girls and women who were replacing farmworkers. Other women had joined the Air Transport Auxiliary Service and were flying planes from the factories to the airfields where they were so desperately needed.

Knowing as he did that his neighbouring veterinary colleague was willing to take over his practice, James had been in no doubt he must offer his services. At the time he had done so, he'd been looking forward to it, but now . . . now suddenly he knew the very last thing he wanted to do was to leave his home, to leave the sleepy little girl on his lap and, not least, to leave Dilys.

That night, lying in bed in the darkness unable to sleep, James' thoughts went round and round in his head as he tried to fathom whether it was possible that a young girl not yet twenty might grow to love a man of thirty-six, sixteen years her senior. Not that he felt old. He felt like a young boy who had discovered love for the first time. It wasn't the first time, of course. He had loved his first wife, his childhood sweetheart. Their families and friends had all expected they would marry. It had been a quiet, gentle relationship, happy despite the years of arduous training. Their honeymoon had been postponed until after he had graduated but never took place because of the horrible car accident which had ended both his young wife's and baby son's lives.

He thought now of Dilys sleeping next door and felt a great surge of longing to hold her in his arms and make love to her. With a deep sigh of frustration, he knew his desire would not be reciprocated. If she was awake, her thoughts would be either with Tina, or Una, or with the three evacuees she had volunteered to take in under the scheme to protect London's children from the terrible bombing of the capital. Two boys and their sister would be arriving next week after he had left and would be company for her, Dilys had said, now he was leaving and Una had gone. She herself wanted to do war work of some kind but, after much deliberation, the plan to take in evacuees seemed the best way to help the war effort as Tina would not be affected.

When James awoke the following day, his last before his departure, Una arrived unexpectedly. She had a twenty-four-hour pass, she explained as she dumped her service cap and kit bag on a chair by the breakfast table. After kissing everyone, she sat down on one of the kitchen chairs.

'I was on night duty,' she said, her eyes twinkling, 'and as the weather had closed down and there was no flying, I wasn't a bit tired at the end of my shift, so I dashed back to my billet, grabbed my kit bag, thumbed a lift to the station and caught the milk train.'

She twisted round and lifted Tina out of her high chair on to her lap, hugged her, and over the top of the child's head, added: 'I've got a date with a Polish pilot in London this evening so I won't be able to stay the night, but I'll be here for lunch. I'm hoping the trains are still running. I heard on the wireless that last night's raid on London was pretty grim.'

Listening to her twin's bright, animated voice, Dilys realized suddenly how far apart they had grown since their lives had divided so precipitously. Whatever job Una was now doing, she was clearly finding it interesting and was enjoying her life in the air force. It seemed that when she and her fellow WAAFs were not on duty they were having plenty of fun. Most of the girls, like Una, were very young and, for the first time, were free of parental control. They now worked side by side with young men and girls from very different backgrounds, and were discovering how sheltered their own lives had been.

She stopped talking for a minute to play with the delighted child who thought she now had two mummies as Dilys and Una looked and sounded so alike. Una's gaze wandered to James, whose eyes were fastened on Dilys. His expression was so unmistakably one of love and longing that she turned quickly away.

Did Dilys know James had fallen in love with her? Una wondered. If so, how was her twin going to deal with it, insisting as she always had done that she would never love anyone but Kristoffer? One thing was absolutely certain: she must never tell Dilys that Kristoffer had been in England looking for her. She seemed perfectly happy married to James and with her adorable baby. It struck Una that her twin was in a kind of contented, middle-age, sexless partnership. If James had indeed fallen in love with her, was that cocoon now threatened?

It was not until James went off to the empty surgery to make sure all his equipment was safely stored, and the cat he was boarding had settled down quite happily, that Una had a chance for a quick chat with Dilys on her own. They took Tina up to her cot upstairs for a nap and, knowing they might not have much time alone together, Una went straight to the point. 'You do know James is in love with you, Dil?' she said.

Dilys frowned. 'I did know something had changed. I can't

explain what exactly – the tone of his voice, perhaps, or the
way he now wanders into the kitchen and sits in his chair chatting to me when before he'd sit in his armchair in the drawing
room and put the wireless on or read the paper.'

She looked anxious as she added: 'I kept telling myself I
was imagining that he was finding more ways to be with me.'

'Well, if I'm right, how will you cope?' Una asked.

Dilys followed Una back into the sitting room where they
seated themselves side by side on the sofa. After a moment's
silence, Dilys said, 'James leaves tomorrow. He seems to think
that after he has finished his training he will almost certainly
be sent overseas, but if that happened, he should get embarkation leave first.' She paused, and then said hesitantly, 'Do you
think I should let him make love to me before he goes, Una?
I mean . . . well, so far all the giving has been on his part. I
know he loves Tina and she certainly loves him, but I'm the
one who has had all the benefits from the marriage.'

Una shook her head. 'That isn't so, Dil. James led a pretty
lonely life before you came along. Remember how he used to
drive me home if I'd been working late or the weather was bad?
When I thanked him, he'd always tell me not to think about it
– that he had nothing needing his attention at home and running
me home was a useful way to occupy his time. He is very
lonely, and you and Tina have made his house a home.'

For a moment, Dilys did not speak, and then she said, 'I'm
really, really fond of James. He's a lovely person and I'd be
devastated if anything awful happened to him. I don't want
him to go away thinking I don't care, because I do!'

'Then sleep with him, Dil. After all, he is your husband and
what harm can it do? Unless you want another baby, then for
God's sake make sure he wears one of those thingummies! A
baby wouldn't be a good idea in the middle of a war and you
living here on your own. By the way, when do your refugees
arrive?'

For a short while before James returned, they spoke of the
recent terrible fires and bomb damage inflicted on London and
how these had persuaded those parents formerly reluctant to
take advantage of the government's evacuation scheme to part
from their children and ensure their safety in the country.

'I feel so sorry for them,' Dilys said. 'I don't think I could bear to let Tina go to strangers – people I'd never even met.'

Una's thoughts turned to the little girl who looked quite extraordinarily like her real father. It was fortunate that neither James nor anyone else in the family but herself had ever met Kristoffer and realized Tina was not James' child. For a fleeting moment, she wondered whether she had done the right thing by lying to the Norwegian so he could not find Dilys and upset the contented life she now had with her precious baby and the kind-hearted James. She could envisage a time when Dil learned to love him but she knew her heart was still with Kristoffer. For the time being, she knew Dilys still wore his ring on a chain round her neck and had not discarded it, even when James had put his wedding ring on her finger.

Una now found herself wishing that she could tell Dilys about her life and work in the WAAF. The radar system which allowed her and all the other girls on her shift to plot the movements of incoming enemy aircraft was so totally secret because the Germans did not have the same advantage and could not understand how the British fighters managed to be airborne and waiting for their bombers before they reached their targets.

The RAF area group where Una was based had not long had a Filter Room, and girls like herself were subject to RAF not WAAF discipline. The men were not as strict as the women admin officers. As long as they were on duty on time for their eight-hour shifts, remembered to salute officers when they saw them and obeyed the rules for keeping their kit and Nissan huts to the required standard ready for inspections they had few restrictions when off-duty. Their irregular shifts, which often meant they were sleeping after night duty, freed them from church parades, drills and other such activities. The male officers treated them as politely as they would civilian members of the female sex, although they were not, however, permitted to fraternize with non-commissioned WAAFs.

Una had found a way round this regulation when invited by an officer to go with him to the nearby city of Bath where there were regular dances at the Assembly Rooms. Unable to leave the camp in his car, she took a bus into the town wearing her uniform but taking with her a dress, shoes and handbag, and changed into these clothes in the ladies' room of one of the hotels where she had agreed to meet her escort. A young officer called Alistair McDonald was the kind of companion she loved. Light-hearted and determined to make the most of every moment, he was always laughing, joking and fun to be with.

His first attempt to join the RAF as a pilot had been turned down on a minor weakness in one eye, but after the dreadful loss of pilots in the aerial combats during the Battle of Britain, he had been told his renewed application had been approved. As a result, he was awaiting his call up and determined, meanwhile, to make the most of every moment to enjoy life.

Una understood why Alistair felt it necessary to make the most of life while he still could. All around her, news of boyfriends' sudden deaths was all too frequent an occurrence. Two of the girls on her shift had lost their fiancés; another slightly older girl had lost her husband. Others had lost civilian relatives in the bombing raids, although the war was only two years old. From the way the Prime Minister, Winston Churchill described the situation in his speeches on the wireless, the country was in for a very long, rough time with no prospect of an early end to the war.

Una liked Alistair very much, enjoyed his company and was only too happy to help him make the most of the time he had left to do so. Each evening she went out with him, and when the dancing ended he would drive her up to the surrounding hills where they would have prolonged necking sessions in his little car. Finally she had agreed to spend a forty-eight-hour pass with him at one of his friends' flat in London, and they had taken their affair a stage further. He proved to be an enthusiastic but considerate lover, and Una now told Dilys that she might even eventually have fallen in love, but neither chose to let the affair become more than a happy, pleasurable friendship, knowing that any kind of permanence was transitory.

It was strange how her relationship with Dilys had changed, she thought as James came into the sitting room having finished in his surgery for the last time. Their lives had taken completely different roads. Dilys denied that she wished she had been free to join the WAAF like Una. Even the suggestion that she might be having a more exciting life if she had not become pregnant elicited a violent protest from her that nothing, nothing at all, could ever make her wish to be without her child.

Her twin's vehemence worried Una and was on her mind as James drove her to the station to catch her train back to London. Was it, she asked herself, just Dilys' devotion to little Tina that made her so certain of her feelings? Or could it be that the little girl was a living link with Kristoffer, the man she still loved?

Una was sure, as James helped her on to the train and said goodbye, that she had done the right thing in keeping Dil and Kristoffer apart. Dil was happy now, and as for the man her sister had married, his love for her he'd been unable to hide.

FIFTEEN

Despite poor weather conditions, the Lysander managed, on the third attempt, to land safely. A strip of grass in an isolated field had been prepared by partisans who held torches to guide in the aeroplane, which was expected soon after midnight. Not unexpectedly, the landing had been precarious, not only because of the limited length of the runway but also because of a strong crosswind. Fortunately a German patrol had not been in the vicinity. Despite the rigid security practised by all those involved who assisted the partisans, there was always the risk of there being a Quisling among them ready to betray these nocturnal activities.

Kristoffer thanked all those who had brought him safely back to Norwegian territory and made his way on foot to one of the safe houses, a pig farm on the outskirts of Oslo. Reaching the farm shortly before dawn, he hid the bicycle he had been loaned in the hay barn. In the soles of his shoes were hidden precious diagrams of the interior of the *slott* thirty kilometres south-west of Oslo where their mission of destruction was to be accomplished. He grabbed a few hours' sleep in the loft.

The owner of the farm, a true patriot, was accustomed to finding strange men hiding in his outbuildings. Discovering Kristoffer asleep in the hayloft, he woke him up and went back indoors to tell his wife to prepare breakfast for him. Like all the other food producers, they were obliged by the Germans to hand over all but a tiny amount of their produce. Needless to say, they all managed to retain more than was permitted: eggs from their chickens, a piglet, and at this farm an old sow, which had been reported to have died of old age, had been turned into joints of pork and smoked up the chimney. Some of the meat was salted to make bacon, the offal was eaten at once and the head and trotters were made into brawn – all concealed in a pit below the floor of the dairy. Such concealments were very dangerous as the Germans made irregular inspections, and an erring farmer, and possibly his wife too, would either be shot or sent with other culprits back to labour camps in what they called 'the Fatherland'.

Kristoffer had encountered strict food rationing in England but the shortages here since the occupation were far more severe and, knowing the risks this patriotic couple took hiding produce to feed those like himself in the Resistance, he wished there was a way to thank them adequately for their courage.

Later that afternoon, he rode back to Oslo on his bicycle to meet Bjorn, the head of one of the resistance cells based in Oslo. He was then able to hand over the maps and information he had been given by *Kaptein* Martin Linge in London.

The Milorg resistance cell in Oslo, with which Kristoffer's cell was amalgamated, now learned of the plans that had been devised for them in London: they were to blow up specific rooms in Estridborgen, a huge twelfth-century castle thirty kilometres south-west of Oslo. Situated on the forested slopes overlooking Oslofjord, it was a grey stone edifice owned by an old Norwegian family who had moved out when it was requisitioned by the Germans. The village of Grulvik was two kilometres down the hill on the edge of the fjord. Its residents, without exception, were bitterly opposed to the presence of the German soldiers who were now occupying and guarding the castle while it was engaged in some highly secret activity. When they were off-duty they were permitted to go down to the village to requisition the best of the fishermen's previous day's catch. They also commandeered fruit and vegetables from the villagers' gardens and took the opportunity to ogle the women. In the evenings they would sometimes disobey the rigid rules of good behaviour with the residents and get drunk on the local beer and *akevitt*. A small number of the local women and girls had been employed by the Germans to clean and cook for the assortment of plain-clothed and uniformed men resident in the castle. The women were never allowed to go into the large reception rooms where the German specialists were carrying on their secret activities situated on the upper floor above the old dining room below. From time to time, German orderlies went as far as the closed doors of the rooms to deliver unidentified boxes and parcels, but even these uniformed men were not allowed inside.

Kristoffer was aware of all this, the details having been passed to Bjorn by partisans living in the forests surrounding the castle. What was not known was what went on in the rooms other than that both engineers and scientists were involved. In each case, they had total disregard to the former beauty and antiquity of the two adjoining rooms they were working in and damaged a number of the precious artefacts.

Word had filtered in that several extremely important government officials were due to arrive at the castle from Germany on 15 November to inspect 'a working model' of their secret apparatus.

This much information had been elicited from a German orderly by one of the patriotic local fishermen, who had made a point of befriending him. He had succeeded in getting the man drunk enough to reveal that the high-powered visitors would be staying the night there. He knew this, he'd boasted, as he'd heard his *gefreiter* instructing the cleaners to clean and prepare six more bedrooms. Fruit, soap, flowers and refreshments would be supplied the day of the visitors' arrival.

The German orderly, pleased with the interest the fisherman was showing, further related that the dining room on the ground floor of the castle was being prepared for meetings, with extra chairs and writing materials. What was not yet known, however, was the programme for the two-day visit, nor had any of the local women who worked as servants been able to provide comprehensive details regarding the interior of the building. It was these plans – architecturally accurate drawings of the ground and first floor and of the surrounding exterior – which Kristoffer had collected from London. They had been cleverly extracted from a large collection of guide books and photographs.

While Kristoffer had been away, Bjorn now told him, word had come in from another cell. A bilingual Norwegian Milorg resistance worker had found out from a boastful high-ranking German officer that the secret work being carried out inside the castle was the creation of a vitally important weapon which could speedily end the war in Germany's favour.

The news gleaned from one of the Norwegian gardeners, that the number of guards had recently been doubled, was now explained. News had also been received by the Oslo cell that the same German, General Haseneder, had been indiscreet enough to boast about his involvement at the castle to the patriotic Norwegian actress who had succeeded in charming him. Hoping to impress her sufficiently to agree to become his mistress, he had boasted about the importance of the proposed visit of the German VIPs who would be attending an extremely vital, high-powered meeting at Estridborgen together with one of the Führer's closest advisers. Further, to impress the beautiful woman he was escorting to dinner, he had added that he believed the work being carried out at the castle involved the plans for a new, highly secret weapon.

After reading all the information Kristoffer had been given by *Kaptein* Martin Linge in London, Bjorn admitted to Kristoffer that the proposed plan to blow up the dining room where the scientists, engineers and German VIPs would be gathered, and the rooms above where the secret work was being carried out, would inevitably mean that far more of the east wing of the beautiful, historic building would also be destroyed, whereupon they had agreed that if the proposed secret weapon was of such importance to Hitler it had to be destroyed, together with its inventors.

Now that they had all the details of the interior of Estridborgen, Bjorn arranged a meeting to discuss tactics for the forthcoming activities with the other members of Kristoffer's cell. Lorentz, his cell's radio operator, was to contact London to arrange for a Lysander to deliver the equipment they would need.

'It's going to be a very tricky and dangerous job,' Bjorn said to Kristoffer after the other men had left. 'As I see it, we are going to have to silence all those extra guards as well as the usual ones before we can get near the building itself.' He held up the letter included with the maps Kristoffer had given him. 'This tells us exactly where the dining room is – the one room where we can be certain they will all be together – and the passageway to it. Someone will have to find a place to put the explosives. Erik,' he named the head of the Grulvik area cell, 'wants someone reliable to be inside with the domestic staff

– someone who can alert us as to the plans for the VIPs' itinerary. Someone capable of giving us an indication of seating arrangements at the dining table, for example.'

He paused then turned to look directly at Kristoffer as he added: 'Erik has asked me to get hold of a suitable girl who could cope. I seem to remember you mentioning a girl called Gerda living in your street who wanted to join your cell. Did you not tell me that she wanted more dangerous work than she'd been doing for your lot?' He paused briefly to look once more at the papers he was holding, then said, 'We've got two weeks to go before the VIP gathering. Erik heard that extra staff would be needed, and his idea is to get the girl into the village in time to be recruited as one of the extra waitresses they will require. Time's short, Kris, so you need to see if your girl is willing as quickly as you can. She'll be a pretty important part of Erik's plan. Ideally he hopes to get her on the domestic staff employment rota at the castle as well. I have an identity card ready; it only needs a photograph. She'd be Katja, the daughter of a local fisherman.'

His face broke into a smile. 'Fifteen days doesn't leave us a lot of time but we will succeed. I'll get a message to Erik to let him know you are here. We'll meet up with him in two days' time after dark. Meanwhile, Kristofffer, do your best to contact the girl before then; hopefully she can come along with you to the meeting.'

'I'll do my best,' Kristoffer replied. 'I haven't seen her in ages but I'm pretty sure I can find her. One thing I can tell you is that she's a very determined character, and if she says she will do something you can be sure she will do it properly. I'll get word to you if I can't find her.'

Bjorn nodded, his expression thoughtful as he said, 'She's a pretty integral part of our plan so don't hide the fact that it will be extremely dangerous from her. She'll need to get out of the building within a couple of minutes of giving us the signal to blow it up, and that won't be easy. Erik has already got the wiring in place.' He smiled again as he told Kristoffer that one of the local cleaners had deliberately stained a large patch on the dining-room wooden floor. The housekeeper, part of Erik's cell, had then reported it as damp so that the village carpenter could go and replace the floorboards, making it perfect for the visitors.

This job had enabled him to lay a long length of cable beneath the floor of the dining room, ready to be connected to a plunger hidden outside the castle walls. It led to the huge window, where he'd bored a pencil-thick hole in the left-hand side of the window frame which he concealed behind the beautiful, heavy brocade curtain. In due course, on the night before the planned explosion, a cleaner would pull out a length of cable and feed it through the hole where it would drop to the ground, hidden among the leaves of the thick creeper covering the wall.

Bjorn smiled as he added: 'It seems Erik has planned it pretty well. He has even got one of the gardeners standing by to spend a day "pruning" the creeper on the appropriate day, to guide the cable over the stone archway leading to the kitchen garden. In his wheelbarrow, together with his hedgecutters, a second long length of cable will be hidden to run among the creeper along the wall, over the top of the arch and down to the hedge bordering the fruit bushes. There it will lie hidden beneath the hedge, waiting for the plunger to be attached to it. As if tailor-made for the purpose, the ground falls away behind the hedge down through the forest to the fjord far below, affording excellent cover for the proposed VIPs' visit.'

'If we can pull this off,' Bjorn said, 'apart from destroying their new invention, we will be getting rid of the Germans' top brains, which will be a huge contribution to the war effort. It's tricky, of course. So many things could go wrong. The wires could be discovered, for instance, or perhaps your Gerda cannot for some reason give the signal saying when everyone is seated at the table and the waitresses are out of the room.' He broke off, sighing. 'Ah, well! There's little we do which isn't risky! Let's hope this girl is right for the job as you say, Kris. It certainly sounds as if she's up to it if she's keen to "Kill the *tyskersvin*" – pigs is an apt description!' he said derisively. 'Meanwhile, how was London? By all accounts taking an awful pounding.'

For a moment, Kristoffer could not speak, his meeting with Una and failure to see Dilys uppermost in his mind each time he thought of his brief trip to England. Then, pulling himself together, he replied, 'As you can imagine, the bomb damage everywhere is pretty grim – gaps where houses used to be, streets with big bomb craters, pedestrians picking their way through rubble from the previous night's raid on their way to work, men and women, some in foreign uniforms, hurrying about their business despite the devastation. Everyone was friendly, strangers ready to talk to and help one another. The most depressing sound,' Kristoffer related, 'was the wail of the air-raid sirens! Their rationing regulations are similar to ours but food, although severely limited, is still available in the hotels and restaurants. As for the people, in spite of all the horror and danger their spirit is as defiant as ours.'

He drew a deep sigh before adding: 'Brave as they are, I couldn't help wondering how long it will be before they are forced to give in. A shocking number of supply ships and their escorts are being sunk by the wretched German U-boats. With food so scarce, every bit of land capable of growing vegetables, even people's gardens, is now being used for that purpose. There's a black market of course, but then we have one, too, don't we? I came away praying that they can hold out and not be forced to surrender as we Norwegians had to do.'

Bjorn nodded, his expression thoughtful. Then he patted Kristoffer on the shoulder, saying, 'At least we in the Milorg are doing what we can to make things difficult for the enemy. Glad you are safely back. See you here the day after tomorrow, after you've had a chance to see your parents and speak to your friend Gerda. There is one of our fishing boats leaving tonight for Bergen and they have been warned to expect you. You will be safe with them.'

When Kristoffer walked through the door of his home early the next morning he was welcomed by his father and mother who, as always, had been concerned for his safety. They told him that Gerda, too, had come back home and had not been very well.

Having changed into his ordinary clothes and eaten the meal his delighted mother had hurriedly prepared for him, he went across the road to Gerda's house. He found her sitting in an armchair by the window, an unopened book on her lap. Her face was very pale and her fair hair hung limply round her cheeks.

'Gerda, it's me, Kris!' he announced, as she had not turned her head when he'd opened the door. Hearing his voice, she swung round and, recognizing him, burst into tears.

He hurried to her side and put his arm round her shoulders, holding her until her tears stopped. Then he said gently, 'What on earth has happened to you? I've never in my life seen you like this. Tell me what is upsetting you.'

For a moment she remained silent, then, brushing away her tears with the back of her hand, she whispered, 'He . . . they . . . they raped me . . . they . . .' She broke off, starting to cry again.

It was several minutes before Kristoffer was able to calm her. Then he learned the facts. Gerda had been returning late one night to the room she rented near the *kafeteria*. It was three minutes after curfew. Two German soldiers who happened to be passing had seen her reaching in her bag for her door key, and with several shots of *akevitt* inside them and nothing better to do, they had apprehended her for her tardiness. Hoping to escape retribution, Gerda had smiled at them as she apologised. It had been a mistake as immediately the more dominant of the two had told her that they would not report her for breaking the curfew if she agreed to go down a nearby alleyway with them for a 'goodnight kiss'. Guessing what they intended to do to her, she had refused to go with them, at which point their jocularity became nasty. Each taking an arm, the two soldiers had dragged her to the alleyway and taken it in turns to rape her. After they had done so, they had dragged her back to her doorway, joking with one another in their guttural German voices.

Gerda's voice suddenly hardened as she continued, 'When I managed to unlock my door, they followed me inside and raped me again. Finally they let me go and threatened that if I told anyone what they had done they would say I was lying in order to get back at them for not letting me break the curfew.' After a slight pause, she continued in a more level tone of voice: 'The next day, I went to see Lorentz and asked him if he had a job which involved killing Germans. It was all I wanted to do; felt I must do. He wouldn't promise anything but said he had something in mind and would let me know, but it might be dangerous. When I came home, I couldn't tell *Mor* or *Far* what had happened to me. They would have been so angry, so distressed and anyway, there was nothing they could do.' Her voice trembled slightly as she added in a whisper: 'I have such horrible nightmares, Kris!' She started crying again but then stopped abruptly and announced in a firm voice: 'I shall never get married now. Never! I always thought that one day you and I . . . well, no matter. I'll never let a man touch me . . . not even you, Kris!' She managed a weak smile. 'I was terribly jealous when you told me about the English girl you met in Germany. Did you manage to see her when you were in England last week?'

Kristoffer pulled up a chair and sat down beside her, still holding her hand. 'No, no, I didn't see her, but I gathered from her twin that both she and Dilys had joined the English Air Force. Una said her sister never spoke about me, that it was over two years since we were all in Munich together and she thought I'd virtually been more or less forgotten – not that she put it quite like that.' His voice broke and he concluded sadly, 'Oh, Gerda, it hasn't been a good year for either of us, has it? I'm so sorry about your horrible ordeal. I wish there was something I could do to help you forget it!'

Gerda suddenly sat up straight, the colour returning to her cheeks. 'There's nothing you can do, Kris! I won't feel better until I've killed some of those German pigs . . . preferably long, slow, hideous deaths where I can hear them beg for mercy . . .'

She broke off, her cheeks now flushed an angry red, her fists clenched. Although Kristoffer fully understood why she needed revenge, he was shaken by the ruthless depths of her emotions.

'Maybe I can give you a little comfort after all,' he said quietly. 'I've been asked to vet you, Gerda, for a very dangerous job: one where you will need to be very calm and your timing exactly right for the plan to succeed. You would have to be working in an old castle full of German soldiers as a waitress, catering to their needs. You would have to smile in a friendly fashion and be deferential. I realize it won't be easy for you knowing how you feel now about the brutes who attacked you.'

There was a strange smile on Gerda's face, almost, Kristoffer thought, like that of an animal stalking a prey. A phrase shot into his mind – 'the smile on the face of the tiger'. Then she stood up and turned to him, her voice now calm and controlled, and said, 'When can we leave? Tonight . . . tomorrow? I don't mind how dangerous the job is, and I won't care if I even have to clean their filthy boots! I'll do anything, anything at all so long as I can wipe some of them off the face of the earth.'

Two days later, their orders all finalized, she and Kristoffer left Oslo together to take the train to Grulvik and Estridborgen, where the destruction of the German secret ammunition development and the scientists involved was to take place.

SIXTEEN

1941 had been a momentous year, Dilys thought as she sat by the wireless listening to the shocking news of the Japanese attack on Pearl Harbour, killing 2,403 Americans and destroying a large part of their fleet. For a moment she paused in her task of wrapping Christmas presents. With another three weeks to go before Christmas day, she had decided to start her preparations early while she had a few moments to spare.

Time was passing surprisingly quickly, she realized, looking across the room to where her daughter was playing happily with the old doll's house brought over from Hannington Hall. Each day she was busy looking after little Tina who was getting into whatever mischief she could find and caring for Betty, Archie and Joe, her three evacuees from London's East End. Most people in the village had only been able to accommodate one or two children, but James' large house had room enough for the two boys and their sister, so they had been able to stay together.

Although Mrs White still did all the cooking, washing and ironing – her contribution to the war effort, she said proudly – it fell to Dilys to stand in the long queues outside any of the shops open in Fenbury village which had an unexpected supply of offal or fish or other supplements to the meagre ration allowance. The children were always hungry and thanks to Mrs White and Dilys' efforts, the evacuees had added weight to the skinny frames they'd had when they'd arrived from the heavily bombed East End of the City.

It hadn't been easy when the three children had first arrived. Bewildered and homesick, they found themselves suddenly in the totally unfamiliar surroundings of the countryside. They were unaccustomed to so many things, from running hot water to nightly baths, to milk from the cows at the nearby farm instead of bottles from the dairy. The little girl, Betty, aged five, was desperately homesick at first, her only comfort her rather grubby ragdoll from which she refused to be parted when Mrs White suggested washing its dress. The boys, aged seven and eight, were all but unmanageable at first, having been allowed to run wild in the bombed-out ruins of their streets, their schools closed. Their father had been called up and was abroad somewhere in the army, and their mother was working long hours at one of the factories now hurriedly making uniforms, parachutes or parts for munitions. Gradually, Dilys and Mrs White between them had calmed them down, Dilys earning their total devotion by allowing the boys to have one of the farm puppies and Betty a kitten.

Dilys smiled to herself as she recalled how the little girl had changed almost unrecognizably from a shy, weeping, scrawny waif to a smiling, happy, plump child who considered herself Tina's guardian, mothering her as she had once fussed over her now-discarded ragdoll. Tina adored her, seeming sometimes to prefer Betty's company to her own. Not that she minded, as it was lovely to see them running round the garden hand in hand, or to watch Betty with a book she could not in fact read, pointing out the pictures, frequently identifying an animal wrongly and making up names when necessary. Dilys realized that one day, when Tina started school, she would have to unlearn these fictitious identities, but for now nothing mattered except the children's happiness. She was not even concerned by Tina's imitation of Betty's cockney accent.

Busy as she was, Dilys had very little time to consider whether she, herself, was happy. James had now been a lieutenant in the Royal Army Veterinary Corps for the past two months and was somewhere overseas. She received infrequent airgraphs from him thanking her for her letters and Tina's scribbles and telling her the little that the censor allowed about his activities, but not that he was in North Africa facing the German General Rommel's far better-equipped army. She guessed he played down the danger he was in and was touched by his unfailing expressions of how much he missed her company and how often he thought of her and Tina.

Despite the fullness of her days, she, too, thought frequently of James and of that last night before his call-up departure date the next day. He had been unusually silent throughout supper;

such comments that he'd made nearly all concerned his satisfaction with the way his busy practice was now being handled by the elderly vet in Oxford. The man had managed to obtain an extra petrol allowance to enable a van, equipped with James' accoutrements, to travel once a week to the outlying villages. Every letter from James ended unfailingly with the simple phrase: 'With all my love.'

Invariably, reading those words left Dilys feeling uncomfortable, forcing her to face the fact that she was not in love with James although she had possibly let him think so. She remembered how Una had suggested that as James had so obviously fallen in love with her, Dilys might consider allowing him to sleep with her before he went off to war and was maybe killed. It would be a way to repay him, Una had said, for being her saviour, for marrying her so she could keep Tina and subsequently doing everything he could to keep her happy.

There had been many times when Dilys had considered doing what Una had proposed, but she had kept putting off the decision to do so. Always at the back of her mind, stupidly, was the feeling that she would be being unfaithful to Kristoffer. She knew such thoughts were ridiculous but until that evening she had not needed to reject them. Suddenly, time to think about the past had run out and she'd realized that it was James', not Kristoffer's happiness she must consider.

After Una had returned to London, Dilys had taken her courage in both hands, and when it came to her usual bedtime, she had crossed the room and held out her hand to James, saying, 'I'd like it if you came up and said goodnight to me later, if you aren't too tired.'

James had looked up sharply, his eyes searching her face with a questioning look. She'd known she was blushing as she added quickly: 'Only if you want to, James!'

A smile now lit up Dilys' face as she recalled how awkward that next hour had been, but how pleased she was afterwards that she had taken Una's suggestion to heart. James had been so gentle, so thoughtful, so controlled that she had no memory of Kristoffer's passionate lovemaking. James had demanded nothing from her, making love to her in silence. It was afterwards he'd told her he had fallen in love with her.

It was something he had never expected to do, he confessed, and he had not intended to tell her. Now he would be able to take with him the memory of his last night at home, and it would ensure that he came back to her when the war was over.

Three weeks later, James had been given forty-eight-hours' embarkation leave, during which he had made love to her again in his quiet, gentle way, requiring Dilys' acceptance but no passionate response. This obvious happiness and satisfaction left Dilys feeling she was at last repaying James for the huge debt she owed him for safeguarding her and her child.

Now, reading his latest airgraph, her memories of him were both caring and tender and intensified by her gratitude for his marrying her so she could keep the beloved little daughter who brought her such joy every day. Telling herself that in many ways she had grown to love James, at the same time she knew that it was not the deep fundamental love she'd felt – and still felt – for Kristoffer.

On the evenings alone by the fire, Una far away on some distant posting and the children safely tucked up in their beds upstairs, her mind would wander back, uncontrolled, to the days in Germany she'd shared with him: so many long, happy days, dancing, skiing, skating, singing in the trains returning to Munich after weekends in the mountains and picnics by the lakes. Colouring every moment were the wonderful hours in his arms, his kisses, his caresses and the exciting plans they had made for the future once they were married.

Such memories would bring stinging tears to her eyes which she brushed aside, forcing herself to think how much she had to be happy about. Not only did she have James' faithful, obliging Mrs White to help her cope with the house and the children, but now the three young evacuees had settled happily in her care. Exhausting though they were, and constantly up to mischief, they were no longer homesick, making friends at the village school and enjoying country life. Dilys had become genuinely fond of them and tried not to worry that her small daughter copied both their London accents and their not always desirable manners.

Once the war was over, Dilys often thought, and the evacuees had returned to London and James was safely home, she might have another baby – James' child. He would be pleased, as would Tina, who would miss the children even more than she would. After the war! When would it be over? she asked herself as she sat darning holes in the children's socks. The war in the Far East was escalating, more and more shipping was being lost at sea and the 8th Army were suffering terrible losses in their fighting in North Africa where the German Field Marshal Rommel had the advantage of far better-equipped troops. Although James' letters were censored and he never referred to the danger he must be in, it was always a relief when one of them arrived saying he was well.

Dilys' thoughts returned to the Christmas present for her father she was wrapping – a precious package of cigarettes, which were in desperately short supply, that she had managed to hoard over the past six months. For her mother, Dilys had wrapped two large Kilner jars of fruit from the garden, picked from the plum tree the past summer. She had found some lavender talcum powder in the village shop for the aunts, and at the village jumble sale she had acquired some second-hand games and toys for the children, and had saved her sweet ration so they would all have extra sweets in their stockings.

With nearly everything now either rationed or unobtainable, it had become a world of make-do-and-mend or go without. Nevertheless, few people complained as everyone was aware that a shocking number of sailors were dying as their supply ships were routinely sunk by the U-boats as they struggled to bring vital supplies back from countries like the United States.

It was quite remarkable, Dilys thought as she put away her sewing basket and prepared to go to bed, how their cigar-smoking Prime Minister, Sir Winston Churchill was managing to keep everyone's spirits up with his moving tirades against Hitler. There could not be a person in the British Isles who owned a wireless set who did not listen to his rallying speeches and, without fail, to the Home Service six o'clock news. Dilys' father had told her that, whenever possible, the broadcasts were listened to by the people in occupied countries despite the dreadful penalties they would incur if they were caught doing so.

Was Kristoffer listening to the news? she always asked herself. Did he ever wonder what was happening to her in what was known as this last bastion of freedom from the Nazi yoke? She always put such thoughts quickly from her mind but, with little Tina growing more and more like him every day, it was not easy for her to forget him. Una, too, had not failed to notice the resemblance and said it was fortunate that neither James nor anyone else in the family had ever met Kristoffer.

This Christmas was to be the last family gathering at Hannington Hall. The house was to be finally occupied by the Guards, after several months of bureaucratic delay, at the beginning of the new year – something her parents had agreed to as they came down to the country less and less often. Not only was her father so busy in London but the train services were all too frequently disrupted by the bombing raids and were completely unreliable. Her mother was equally prepared to brave the bombs in London, absorbed as she was in her duties in the WVS. Never a day passed when she was not required to cope with a newly bombed-out family needing clothes and accommodation. She was frequently exhausted and was glad to have their spacious flat in Victoria, where she could snatch a few hours' rest before a further call for help.

The life Lady Singleby now led was the very reverse of the pre-war days when she'd occupied her time meeting with other friends for luncheons or going shopping or to a beauty parlour, frittering time away at theatres and at seasonal events. Unlike so many others who rushed to take cover in underground shelters or cellars, she continued with whatever she was doing when the air-raid sirens wailed their eerie warnings, maintaining she would rather die above ground than be buried alive. Although bombs had fallen further up the road from the town flat she and Sir Godfrey occupied, his office had so far escaped the relentless nightly attacks. Curiously, her former fear of death was eliminated by the horrors she so often encountered following a raid. Resolute as she was, people, including her fellow workers, turned to her for guidance and were reassured by her calm, self-confident manner.

Although Lady Singleby saw Una occasionally when her daughter was in London on one of her short leaves, she seldom had time to go down to the country to see Dilys. Una's breaks were usually taken up with dates, invitations from army, navy or air-force officers on leave and wanting to forget the war and enjoy the entertainment London bravely continued to provide in the blackout. Not even the horrific bombing of the Café de Paris, which killed every one of its staff and customers, deterred others from braving the possible air raids in order to make the most of their too-short leaves in the few restaurants and cinemas which remained open.

Dilys had neither the time nor the desire to take Tina to London, so all Lady Singleby knew of her little granddaughter was Tina's piping treble on the telephone. With calls rationed to three minutes, they remained strangers to one another. Quite often bomb damage to the communication system made even phone calls impossible, and such lines as remained undamaged after a raid were kept for emergency use only.

Despite these limitations, Lady Singleby had now come to acknowledge the hitherto 'shameful' existence of the child's birth and, busy though she was, frequently sent an expensive present, usually from Hamleys or Harrods' toy department.

Una managed to spend most of her leaves with Dilys and Tina and was able to coincide a visit with Tina's birthday in May. The little girl was old enough to recognize Una, who she adored, partly because Una always had time to play with her and partly because she found it funny that Una looked so like her mummy that she would often mistake one for the other. On this birthday visit, not only did Una bring with her her grandmother's present, a doll complete with an entire wardrobe of clothes, but accompanying her aunt was a laughing, handsome, funny man in smart tartan trousers and a jaunty beret, the uniform of a Scottish airman.

Lieutenant 'Scotty' Hamilton was based twelve miles away from Fenbury. The tiny airstrip that had existed in peacetime was being hurriedly enlarged to accommodate the air force with their Spitfires and Hurricanes, their crews and administrators.

Una had recently been promoted from the ranks and had met Scotty Hamilton in the RAF Club in Piccadilly where she was on leave, enjoying a drink with a colleague at the bar. Tall and good looking, with laughing brown eyes, Scotty lost no

time in asking her if he could buy her a drink. On finding that
Una's twin sister was actually living not far from his base near
Fenbury, he had insisted that they further their new friendship
whenever she visited Dilys. Furthermore, he extracted a promise
from her that she would advise him whenever she was next on
leave in London.

Now, two months since their first meeting, they had been
in regular contact and Una had finally been persuaded to spend
one of her forty-eight-hour leave passes with him in a hotel
in Hertfordshire where they were unlikely to be seen by anyone
Una knew. Like so many of the young servicemen Una met,
Scotty risked his life almost daily on bombing raids across
the Channel, always in danger from anti-aircraft fire and the
skilled German fighters sent up to intercept them. In her job
in the Filter Room, all too often a badly damaged plane was
plotted making desperate attempts to limp home, praying to
reach land before they came down in the 'drink', as they called
the sea.

Scotty, like nearly all pilots, never used the likelihood of his
death to persuade a girl to have sex with him. However, the
huge loss of life of the air crews had gradually corroded
the strict morals appertaining to unmarried girls, namely that
they remained virgins until they were married. Now, when
loved ones were about to go overseas perhaps never to return,
or for pilots like Scotty, it seemed cruel to deny them what
might be their last – and in some cases their first – opportunity
for sexual comfort.

For the first time in her life, Una was enjoying a regular
relationship. Scotty was immense fun, always laughing and
joking and ready for any suggestion Una might make. Tina
positively adored him, and not, Dilys said, laughing, just because
he always managed to bring chocolate bars with him when he
visited. This he did quite often, riding over in a Jeep from his
base when he had time on his hands but no chance of seeing
Una, who was not due any leave.

'Just looking at you makes me feel I'm closer to my girl!'
he told Dilys as they settled down to eat the delicious cold ham
he had brought with him, together with half-a-dozen eggs. 'I'm
just crazy about your sister. You know, honey, when this hateful

war is over I want her to marry me. I've never felt this way about a girl before.' His expression became anxious. 'Do you think I'm in with a chance? Una has never actually said she loves me but she swears there's no one else. As that old song says, she's driving me crazy!'

He was smiling again and Dilys found herself torn between two opposing wishes: one that Una was in love with this charming Scot, the other that she hoped not if it meant she would end up going to live in Scotland after the war. Then she thrust such thoughts aside, telling herself that the war was very far from over and, knowing her sister, it was highly unlikely she would still be attached to the same person when it did end. Scotty, too, might have found someone else to love by then.

Love, she told herself, was not always the euphoric blessing it was supposed to be. Many of the renowned poets wrote of torment when they had been rejected by the objects of their adoration. Now, in wartime, lovers were parted, sometimes for ever. Who could be happy when no one could be certain they would live to see the following day? Perhaps she was fortunate that, great though her affection was for James, she would not feel suicidal if he were reported killed in action. Every night she prayed for his safety but never with quite the same fervour as she prayed that Kristoffer was not in danger. The last good-night kiss she gave their little daughter was always a deep reminder of the love they had shared that unforgettable summer before the hateful war had started.

She would touch his ring on the chain round her neck involuntarily, wondering what had happened to him since the German occupation of Norway, praying that he was still alive and that one day she might see him again.

Dilys knew that such a meeting, if ever it were to happen, could not be happy, much as she longed for it. She was James' wife and, even if Kristoffer still loved her, she could never belong to him. The memory of their cruel, abrupt parting brought tears to her eyes, but despite the pain a second parting would bring, she was never able to stop herself longing to see him, even if it was only once more.

SEVENTEEN

Surprisingly, the train compartment in which Kristoffer and Gerda were travelling to Grulvik contained no German soldiers, only an old woman with a basket on her lap containing a live goose which, they presumed, she had purchased at an Oslo market. She got out at the next station and they were then able to converse without fear of being overheard.

'We will take the opportunity to rehearse once more,' Kristoffer said. 'We are brother and sister and our names are Katja and Gunnar. We are visiting our aunt who has been ill. Our aunt has told you there might be a chance of employment for you as Estridborgen has been occupied these past six months and the occupiers, Germans, will be needing extra staff shortly when they expect a number of important visitors who will be staying there for several days.'

He paused briefly, aware that Gerda was stifling a laugh. Before he could reprimand her for not taking his words seriously, she said, 'I'm sorry, Kris, but I cannot look at your moustache and those big round spectacles without laughing. You look so much like . . .' She fought for a suitable personage but failed to find a name. He was quite unrecognizable as Gunnar Jensson, which was, of course, his intention. Gerda, too, was disguised, her blonde hair dyed a light brown. It had grown long and was coiled in two plaits round her ears. She might well pass as a country girl, there being no make-up on her pretty face. Her expression had lost its haunted look, which had been replaced by one of excitement. On several occasions, Kristoffer had had to remind her that their aunt was supposedly very ill and Gerda was not supposed to be happily anticipating this timely opportunity to contribute to the death of a number of individuals of the same race as those who had defiled her.

'Pay attention, Gerda!' Kristoffer said sharply. He fingered the identity papers and travel passes in his breast pocket, adding in the voice of a German interrogator: 'Your name? My name?'

Unsmiling now, Gerda replied, 'My name is Katja Jensson and this is my brother, Gunnar.'

Kristoffer's voice was surprisingly Germanic as he proceeded to question her, and for a moment or two, fear replaced Gerda's former enthusiasm for what lay ahead.

Satisfied that she had all the right answers instantly ready, Kristoffer continued to brief her as to the part she must play. Hurriedly produced by a talented resistance worker, Gerda had in her possession a very complimentary reference from the fictitious owner of a restaurant in Sweden, recommending her for her capabilities not only as a waitress but as a hostess welcoming guests and ensuring that the dining room ran smoothly.

This would ensure her temporary employment at the castle, Gerda having been advised by her aunt that several local women and girls had been offered jobs there as extra help would be needed for the VIP visit. Despite being as deeply antagonistic towards their German invaders as were most Norwegians, they had willingly applied for jobs as domestics.

As expected, two Germans boarded the train at the next station, and then a third who checked travel permits and identity papers. Despite scrutinizing their papers for an unnervingly long time he eventually went away satisfied and Kristoffer and Gerda were able to continue their journey without further incident.

Safely installed in the typical wooden house of a patriotic farmer and his wife, Gerda in the only spare bedroom and Kristoffer with a makeshift bed in one of the outside barns, Kristoffer took her to meet Erik and several other men in his cell in a house in Grulvik. After the introductions, the planning was further defined. One of the group had managed to form a slight friendship with the chief mess orderly and would now mention Katja's arrival. Katja had a German boyfriend in Oslo, he would report, and he was sure she would be willing to offer her services as she could still stay here with her aunt if she was needed. Katja was to go up to the castle the following morning and ask for him. The man had let slip that the visitors were in close personal contact with Herr Hitler and the meeting at the castle had been instigated by the Führer himself.

'You will have a huge responsibility on your shoulders, Gerda. We know four of the local females employed there and it is imperative, therefore, that they are well clear of the dining room when we blow it up. You will have to devise a way to ensure this in such a manner as not to cast the slightest suspicion that something is about to happen. There will, of course, be a very large number of extra guards but we have found there is a cellar door on the north side facing the forest. It is at that side of the castle where there is no view and only the vegetable garden to see that the staff rooms are situated. It is unlikely this will be heavily guarded and our men will see they are silenced if any guards are there.'

He paused briefly to offer Kristoffer and Gerda glasses of *Brennevin* and poured a glass of the strong spirit for himself before continuing: 'You will both have to make your way up to the *hytte* where you can lie low for a few days after the explosion. It will be far too dangerous for you to get away by train as all escape routes will be scrutinized. When the dust settles and we think it's safe, we will send a man up to the *hytte* to tell you and you can go home. I hope all this is clear to you both as you, Gerda, will not only have to find a way to safeguard the other waitresses, but you will have to find out exactly where the cellar is and if a key is needed for the outside door.'

Kristofffer met Erik's anxious gaze. 'I've known Gerda all her life,' he said quietly, 'and if anyone can carry this off, I assure you she can. She has more reason than most to hate the Germans. If we have anything to fear as far as her capability is concerned, it is that she might want to hang around and stick a knife into any survivors! Isn't that so, Gerda? Not surprisingly, you are without fear for your own survival, aren't you?'

Gerda nodded. As they made their way back to the farm, Kristoffer reflected on the remarkable change these last few days had wrought on Gerda. The white-faced, tearful, almost hysterical girl he had found at her home had been transformed into a bright, upright, eager and determined female who made him think of some of the figureheads on the old Viking ships as they braved the stormy seas. She laughed when he told her so and said she hoped he would have cause now to be proud of her.

'You told me of the bravery of the British women who you saw going to work every day, leaving their precarious bomb shelters to struggle over the debris of the previous night's air raids, not knowing which of their colleagues might not have survived or even if their factory was still standing. Well, I, too, have courage as you will see – as much as the British women you admire!'

Kristoffer wondered if perhaps Gerda was a little jealous, thinking that his praise of British women included Una and Dilys, who he had told her were doing secret work in the Royal Air Force. He resolved not to mention Dilys' name again, although he had already made up his mind to return to England as soon as possible. Many young Norwegian men were slipping out of the country and making hazardous journeys in small fishing boats to cross the Channel to the Shetland Islands and then to Scotland. Once safely on the mainland, they went to Brahan Castle, north of Inverness, where the Norwegian Brigade Command was stationed, and there they joined the Norwegian army regiment or enrolled to train to be pilots.

Since the occupation the twelfth-century castle Estridborgen had been requisitioned by the Germans. All that was known about the present occupants was that, surprisingly, most were not uniformed Germans but civilians reputedly engaged upon some highly important secret activity. Adding to this mystery was the fact that the castle was always heavily guarded by soldiers. The four women from the village, who were employed to clean the bedrooms and collect, wash and return the laundry, were the only local inhabitants allowed on the pathway which led up the forested slopes of the mountain.

As Kristoffer had expected, Erik was impressed with Gerda's obvious intelligence and enthusiasm. Within twenty-four hours of their arrival at Grulvik, Gerda managed to get up to the castle, where she was taken by the mess orderly to be interviewed by *Hauptmann* Weiss, the German officer responsible at Estridborgen for the security and smooth running of the VIPs' visit.

Erik had provided her with a faultless background of local family history, which *Hauptmann* Weiss had accepted with surprising ease, being impressed by her Nordic prettiness and charming accent when she spoke his language. He agreed at once that, with her flirtatious smile and charming manner, she would be an ideal waitress in the dining room. He had then introduced her to the four female domestic staff already recruited from the village in time to prepare for the arrival of the important visitors, all of whom would be staying for the night. Without exception, the women were all violently resistant to their German occupiers, and had readily agreed to work as domestics for the Germans up at the castle if it assisted Erik's plans. They were delighted to meet Gerda, under whose authority they would be when the VIPs arrived and the secret plans were executed.

For the next few days Gerda devoted herself to memorizing every aspect of the building, so that when Kristoffer and Erik interrogated her she could prove that she knew all of the interior. She could find her way blindfolded from room to room and, more importantly, to the cellar by which exit she and her fellow domestic staff would escape when the planned destruction of the east wing of the castle took place. How this was to be done they had not yet told her.

For the most part, Gerda was finding these preparations both exciting and diverting. She was not, however, too happy when an order arrived from *Hauptmann* Weiss for her to attend him in his office. She and Kristoffer had seen him one evening when they had gone to the neighbouring village for a drink. The man was on his own and, ignoring Kristoffer, he had tried to engage Gerda in conversation. He had clearly had too much to drink and his red, sweaty, lascivious expression clearly indicated his attraction to her. Fortunately, being only too aware of Gerda's recent ordeal, Kristoffer feigned the onset of violent stomach cramps, quickly paid for their drinks and hurried her away.

As a rule, the German occupation officers, although autocratic and dominating, behaved reasonably well towards women in public. But isolated as they were in foreign countries for months on end, they would take advantage of any available female company willing to be friendly with them.

When summoned to one of the offices, Gerda feared she was being called for a private interview with *Hauptmann* Weiss, and it was a great relief when she was confronted by another of the officers, a charming, elderly, grey-haired man with a military moustache. He could not have been more courteous, despite his greeting her with the customary Nazi salute. All he wanted was for her to remove the blue anemones and yellow aconites from all the vases as he had an antipathy to them. Gerda supposed that he was one of those few who disapproved of the ruthless Nazi regime but as a regular soldier must obey orders. She found herself almost wishing that he would not be blown to bits when Erik's men blew the east wing of the house to smithereens.

The part she was to play was simple, comprising no more than drawing back one of the heavy curtains as a signal to the men concealed outside. This was to enlighten them that the German hosts and their guests were all seated at the table and no Norwegian other than herself was in the room. She would then be given exactly sixty seconds to leave the room carrying a heavy silver platter from the sideboard. This was to be dropped in the passage immediately outside the dining room as a signal to any Norwegian servant in the kitchen to stop whatever they were doing and hurry out of the room, ostensibly to help clear up whatever had fallen. So precise was the timing that they then had only half a minute to race along the passage and down the flagstone steps to the cellar where Kristoffer would have opened the heavy oak door into the vegetable garden at the back of the castle.

It was assumed by Erik that at the sound of the explosion and debris flying from the east wing, all the guards and security personnel would rush to that area of the castle. He had estimated that the female staff from the village could quite reasonably be able to hurry back to their homes as fast as they could get away from the building. Hopefully, Gerda's and Kristoffer's escape would not be noticed as they made their way up through the forest to the *hytte*, one of the many cabins built high up in the snowy mountain peaks offering refuge in winter for climbers or skiers lost or marooned by bad weather. Bjorn seemed satisfied that Gerda and Kristoffer would be safely hidden up the mountain until the search for suspects had died down and they could make their way back to the safe house in Oslo.

Down in the village, Fru Nielsen, Gerda's fictitious aunt, had been coached by Erik to account for Gerda's sudden absence by saying that she had been wounded in the explosion and her brother, Kristoffer, had taken her to a hospital for treatment. Fru Nielsen would not know which one, but think it was across the fjord near where the pair lived. If she were subsequently questioned further as to their address, she was to say that they had recently moved; that her nephew had promised to write it down for her but in his hurry to catch the ferry across the fjord with his wounded sister, he had forgotten to do so.

The photographs for their identity cards had been taken of them in their disguises, which they would discard when they left the mountain *hytte*, thus making it far less likely that they would be apprehended on their eventual return to Oslo. Erik, who had lived in Grulvik all his life, was confident that every one of the occupants of the small fishing villages was prepared to swear that they had known Fru Nielsen's nephew and niece since they were young children and it was their habit to visit her three times a year, so they could not possibly be imposters.

Kristoffer was far more nervous than Gerda when Erik announced that the detonation should take place the following lunchtime. Erik told the group gathered around him that God was definitely on the side of the Norwegians: that a German *gefreiter* had been sent to the village that morning to collect freshly harvested salmon as there were to be three extra guests from Berlin arriving for the weekend and the fish were required for the luncheon party the next day. This information enabled his men to get everything in place that night for the detonation the following day.

Gerda returned from the castle that evening announcing that she had been instructed to see that six extra bedrooms were prepared and that the cleaners were to pay special attention to all the reception rooms. Erik had already been informed that the eighteen-foot-long pine refectory table in the dining room had been polished until it shone and the visitors' rooms had been readied for the occasion which, he had gathered, was by way of a celebration of the success of whatever enterprise the present occupants had all been working to achieve. They were not military personnel but men in civilian suits, with conventional collars and ties, and they were now gathered in the drawing room, smiling as they congratulated themselves on the successful outcome of their work.

Although most Norwegians had been taught German in school, it was wrongly considered by the boffins that the women from the small fishing village who worked at Estridborgen were uneducated and therefore unaware of the meaning of anything they overheard. The need for one hundred per cent secrecy had been impressed on the boffins but they were finding it difficult not to exult at the successful outcome of their hard work. Along with the promises of great honours from Herr Hitler if they were successful in their achievements, they were too exalted by the expected arrival of the Führer's representatives the next day to concern themselves with caution.

As Erik now said, it was already obvious that something special was happening as the guard surrounding the castle had been doubled. The children in Grulvik had been given the day off school and flags with swastikas on them to wave as two big Mercedes cars arriving from Oslo military headquarters drove through the village and up the two-kilometre rough road to the castle.

However, at eleven o'clock next morning, there was not a single child to be seen. Their parents had by mutual agreement sent them all off for the day by ferry to Borre, where they could see the old Viking burial mounds and picnic in the woods. The German *Oberstleutnant* who was supposed to be overseeing the safe arrival of the visitors was incandescent with anger at the obvious insult but there was no way he could get the children back. He decided to order the villagers themselves to line up where the children should have been in order to wave the flags but, faced with smiling apologies, he was informed the children had insisted upon taking their flags with them so they could wave them on the ferry. Needless to say, the flags would either end up in the sea or be left behind on the Viking graves. It was typical of the way all Norwegians other than the Quislings managed to defy their German masters.

Up at Estridborgen, Gerda had been detailed to stand by the front door and receive the visitors' coats and hats. It was an honour for her, *Hauptmann* Weiss had said with a leer, because all men appreciated a pretty face and a curvaceous figure. Somehow she had managed to smile back at him, content with the knowledge that in a few hours' time hopefully he, too, would be dead.

When the hour came and luncheon was served, Gerda realized that the task was not going to be as easy to carry out as Erik had supposed. The German mess orderlies were acting as waiters and the women were carrying the trays of food from the kitchen along the passage to the dining room and taking empty ones back, the reverse of what had been expected. Thus the Norwegians who were to be alerted by Gerda to remain out of the room when she gave the signal were not in the same place at the same time. She, herself, was responsible for refilling any empty wine glasses, smiling prettily at the men as she leant over them to reach the table. This instruction had been demonstrated to her by *Hauptmann* Weiss, and she had been hard put not to hit him when he had deliberately brushed against her breasts.

It was nearly twenty minutes after the meal had begun before a moment came when she could hurry over to the window to straighten the curtain and give the signal to the waiting men. As she did so, she could imagine how tense and agitated they must be, wondering what was going wrong. Now, knowing how little time she had before the east wing would explode, she hurried out of the room, dropped the tray and, together with the waiting women, raced down the passageway towards the flagstone steps leading to the cellar.

They had barely started their descent when one of the women tripped and fell headlong down the stairs. Gerda jumped down to where she lay by the cellar door. There was a deafening explosion followed by the sound of falling masonry and timbers, and a cloud of dust rolled down the staircase, covering them. It was several minutes before human sounds could be heard, men's voices shouting and someone screaming, then the noise of heavy boots racing along the passage above their heads.

Gathering her wits, Gerda tried to lift the fallen woman to her feet but she cried out, saying her leg was broken. It was twisted beneath her and Gerda realized she had two options: to leave the woman where she was to be found by the surviving Germans or for the four of them to carry her outside where hopefully Kristoffer would be waiting. Knowing she could not leave the woman, not from compassion but because she could reveal the plot to the Germans who found and questioned her, Gerda opened the door into the cellar and instructed the two women to help her lift the casualty across the cellar floor and out through the heavy wooden door into the open.

To her immense relief, Kristoffer was waiting; the body of the German sentry he had killed lying not far from him. From the front of the house there came sounds of furious activity, men shouting as those who had survived the explosion began trying to douse the flames which were now emerging through the roof. The slight wind was blowing the smoke up over the roof towards them, where it disappeared among the tips of the pine trees on the mountainside.

As soon as he realized what had happened to the woman, Kristoffer signalled to one of Erik's men who had been detailed to remain hidden in order to provide cover for him and Gerda as they escaped up into the forest. Fortunately he was a strong farm labourer and able to carry the injured woman on his back. Kristoffer ordered him to take one of the little-known paths back down the hill to the village, making as little noise as possible while the uninjured women screaming and crying were to run down the road ahead as any terrified female would normally have done.

It was a tense four minutes, each of them aware that at any minute guards might decide to come round to the back of the castle. Fortunately, as Erik had gauged, all rescue work was being concentrated outside the shattered remains of the east wing. There was no telephone connection to the castle and communications had been by field telephone and relayed to the Oslo headquarters. Erik knew that it would be quite some time before help could be sent to Estridborgen. It was a very old, beautiful building and it was feared by all who were aware of its proposed part demolition that any subsequent fire could destroy it completely. To this end, Erik had arranged that any able-bodied person in the village would go up to the house to help fight a fire if there was one. Their willingness to help would also serve to support their supposed ignorance of a plan to blow up the place. His objective would have been achieved – namely to kill the scientists, engineers and planners who were using their vast brainpower to produce a weapon deadly enough to wipe out any enemy.

Gerda had not been up into the forest but Kristoffer had used his free time to explore and had found the tiny wooden cabin several hundred metres high up where snow had already fallen and where he and Gerda were to hide until the hiatus following the explosion had died down. It had taken him half a day to get there and he knew that he and Gerda must now make haste if they were to get there before dark.

They had been climbing for little more than half an hour before Gerda stopped, saying she could not go on any longer. The aftermath of tension had set in and she was trembling. Kristoffer sat down beside her, produced a small flask of *akevitt* and held it to her lips.

'It will give you strength!' he said gently. 'We can't afford to stop here as I know I could never find the *hytte* in the dark. We must have shelter as it gets extremely cold up high after nightfall.' He waited for her to drink and then helped her to her feet. 'We'll pretend we are just going off for a picnic!' he said, smiling as he tucked her arm in his, and he started to hum a Norwegian folk song they had both learned at school. It was a long walk, mostly through densely packed pine trees but higher up, on rocky grassland, a chill wind was blowing. They were both silent now and Kristoffer was trying hard not to worry that if he lost the way they could end up without shelter of any kind.

Dusk had crept over the mountainside when the simple wooden cabin loomed up ahead of them. There was a light scattering of snow on the roof and frost had made the locked door hard to open once Kristoffer had found the key hooked under an overhanging wooden tile. Both he and Gerda were familiar with these cabins which could be found at high altitude on any mountainside if climbers or skiers needed shelter. Inside, the bare necessities for survival were always available: wood bark for lighting the stove and logs for heating; eating and drinking utensils; coffee, tinned biscuits or dried food of some kind; matches, candles, cloths. In the bedroom adjoining the main room were a couple of wooden bunks with sleeping bags for the occupants.

Kristoffer hurriedly lit the stove and carried in a supply of logs for the night. Gerda, now shivering uncontrollably in her light wool skirt and pretty blouse worn for the lunch party, crouched in front of it, trying to restore her circulation. He then found for her a thick wool jersey and a pair of knee-length red ski socks in a cupboard, after which he went outside and filled a saucepan with snow and, bringing it quickly to the boil on top of the stove, he made a jug of coffee for them.

Gradually Gerda stopped shivering and smiled weakly at Kristoffer, who was now trying to boil some *spekemat* which he had found in the cupboard, a kind of dried salted meat, to make a hot soup. She watched him coping so capably with a surge of admiration. He, too, must be as cold and exhausted as she was, but he was humming cheerfully and turned every now and again to smile at her. Her heart began to beat more swiftly as she realized that for at least the next few days she would be alone here with Kristoffer, and that if he was ever going to respond to her love for him, this must be the opportunity; he would see now that she wanted more than affection. She knew from him that when he went to England he had not been reunited with the English girl he had adored and that it was now nearly three years since their brief affair in Munich. She was certain that by now he had ceased thinking about Dilys and was ready to turn to her, Gerda, his childhood sweetheart, for the love she longed to give him.

They were both exhausted after the long, hard climb up the mountain which had followed the tense, exacting moments of the destruction of the east wing. It would be a long wait before they were back among other people who could tell them if the German's invention had indeed been destroyed, along with its inventors. They decided to have an early night. By the time they had both been out of doors and washed their faces and hands beneath a sky now studded with stars and taken their turn in the tiny outside shed that served as a toilet, they were both shivering. The warmth from the stove had not yet permeated the bedroom next door and Kristoffer suggested

they carry the sleeping bags from the bunks and lay them
on the floor in front of the glowing logs, a suggestion instantly
agreed by Gerda.

Having leant across to give Gerda a gentle goodnight kiss
on her forehead, Kristoffer curled up in his sleeping bag and
was asleep within minutes, unlike Gerda, who was tense with
frustration. When Kristoffer had suggested they sleep side by
side, her hopes had soared that this might lead to hugs, kisses
and then the sexual intimacy she craved. She was now twenty-
five years old and the only sex she had known was the brutal
raping of her virginity by the drunk Germans. She now wanted
desperately to put the dreadful memory from her mind and
replace it with the sweet, thoughtful loving Kristoffer could
give her. In their teens, they had explored each other's bodies
and kissed and caressed one another hungrily without overstep-
ping the rules for unmarried couples. Kristoffer may have
forgotten those evenings of exciting exploration but she had
never done so, and that childhood adoration had turned all too
easily to love. She'd thought her heart was broken when he'd
told her how madly in love with the English girl he was, and
of his intention to get to England as soon as he could and marry
her. Her heartbeat quickened as, lying so close to his sleeping
body, she heard him murmur Dilys' name.

Kristoffer was indeed dreaming of Dilys. They were hand
in hand walking up the mountain fields where he and Gerda
had been that day. They were searching for a secluded spot
where they could stop and make love. He could smell the scent
of the wild flowers around them and feel the warmth of the
summer sun on his face. Suddenly, Dilys reached out her hand
and found a way to cover his fiercely beating heart. He was
filled with longing for her, and she moved her hands and his
to her bare breasts. Her nipples were hard and he caressed and
kissed them. As he did so, he felt her hand move down beneath
the open waist of his trousers to caress him tantalisingly
between his legs.

He had not made love to a woman since he had gone back
to the flat of a girl he met at a Christmas party who was obviously well accustomed to enjoying casual sexual relationships.
That girl had found him attractive for that night but had had

no wish to make their association permanent. Kristoffer had been perfectly happy when she declined to see him again. He was a young, healthy male and his body now responded instantly to the feel of soft fingers encircling and stroking him. He was about to press his mouth hungrily to what he believed in his dream were Dilys' lips when he heard Gerda's voice, deep and husky, begging him to invade her willing body.

It was only then he realized he had been dreaming and that it was Gerda whose half-naked body was lying beside him and her hand which was between his legs, stroking him. With a deep, aching feeling of disappointment, he began to draw away from her, murmuring pointless apologies.

Her cheeks flaming, Gerda cried out: 'No, please, Kris, I want you to make love to me. I know you don't love me but I still want you—' She broke off for the briefest of pauses, and then said, 'Don't you see, I need you to dispel those awful memories of what the men did to me. Please, Kris, help me to forget.'

For days afterwards, Kristoffer tried to convince himself that he had only had sex that night with Gerda for her sake, but he knew in his heart that this wasn't altogether true. He had been aroused by her before he had woken from the dream of Dilys and had not been able to subdue that need for release when Gerda had continued to press her body against him, her tongue in his mouth, her hands teasing every sensitive part that increased his need for release.

After it was over and he had apologised and she had wept, he feared that his guilt at having betrayed both her and Dilys would prohibit any return to his normal friendly relationship with Gerda. To his relief, however, the following day, although pale and a little red around her eyes, she had behaved as if nothing had happened, and gradually he had been able to relax. The following ten days passed without further incident, the only reminder being that at night-time they each, by unspoken agreement, retired to their separate bunks in the bedroom.

EIGHTEEN

Dilys was sitting in the hot August sunshine watching the land girls loading the stooks of corn on to the conveyor belt carrying them into the threshing machine. She knew most of the girls who occasionally dropped in for a glass of homemade lemonade and a chat in the summer evenings when they had finished the day's tasks. Dilys was pleased to see them, the house seeming relatively deserted after her evacuees had returned to London at the start of the New Year. The first half of 1943 had been a mixture of good and bad events. At the end of January the Russians had defeated the German army at Stalingrad and the Germans were finally driven out of North Africa. As a consequence the dreadful German 'wolfpacks', as they were known, were having less success as the Allied ships and aircraft carriers were released from duty off the coast of North Africa and were now escorting the allied Atlantic shipping, their planes able to hunt and destroy the U-boats. But there had also been a dreadful civilian tragedy in April when hundreds of people were crushed in Bethnal Green underground station shelter after a daytime air raid warning caused panicking Londoners to rush down the stairs, smothering those ahead. Sadly, Una's delightful boyfriend, Scotty, had been shot down in a raid over Germany, and the wonderful actor Leslie Howard had presumably drowned when his plane was lost somewhere over the Bay of Biscay.

At home, shortages of nearly everything had made daily life more difficult, although mercifully the better summer weather had lessened the misery of the everlasting cold resulting from the shortage of fuel and rationing of electricity. However, all these discomforts and concerns paled into insignificance when she was notified by James' colonel that he had been wounded and taken prisoner during the July landings in Sicily.

It had been a long and anxious time before she'd had further news a few days ago, this time from the Red Cross, saying he was in a German field hospital north of Pisa but was not well enough yet to write to her. Dilys worried about his recovery and whether, once he was stronger, he might be repatriated. A few days ago she had received an airgraph from a fellow officer who had been a patient in the same hospital as James but had managed to escape back to his regiment. He was keeping his promise, he'd written, to let her know that James never stopped talking about her and their little girl, but his head injuries made it impossible for him to write. The standard of medical care was not good and he hoped for James' sake that the British would soon reach the north and James would receive the treatment he needed.

Dilys worried constantly. There was no one she could telephone to enquire about James' progress, and sometimes, when she was feeling depressed, it crossed her mind that he might even have died and she would not know it. Sometimes, she found herself thinking of Kristoffer, most particularly at this time of year when the fields were full of buttercups and poppies and the woods were carpeted with celandine. Their bright colours reminded her all too vividly of the mountain and the lakeside where she had lain so wonderfully happily in Kristoffer's arms and he had told her about his native country and how they would live there once they were married.

There was, too, the daily reminder of him whenever Tina lifted her sweet little face for a kiss or came towards her smiling to show her some treasure she had found and wished to share with her mother. With the three evacuees no longer there to be cared for, no Scotty to drop in for a relaxing hour or two of home life and only a few short visits from Una, who had been posted to 12 Group to work in the Filter Room there, Dilys was often lonely. There were constant invitations to dances and parties at Scotty's airbase but she had no wish to become friendly with other aircrew only for them to get shot down and killed like Scotty. Una had been devastated when she'd heard the news but now, six months later, she was dating again.

War was so cruel, Dilys thought as she helped Tina fold some wheat stalks into the shape of a doll. All around her the countryside was so beautiful and calm, so peaceful in the drowsy summer heat of the afternoon. How could evil monsters like Hitler manage to achieve such power over everyone's lives? News had filtered back from Germany that Jews imprisoned in a Warsaw ghetto had been systematically massacred and recently there were pictures of children Tina's age standing bewildered, clutching their parents' hands, watched over by beligerent-looking German soldiers brandishing rifles.

She thought sometimes of the charming German boys she and Una had met in Munich, the friendly, happy days dancing, skiing and singing. Were they, too, doing these dreadful things to people? Killing other young men like Kristoffer? Was he still alive? One of the land girls had met a Polish soldier who had escaped from his country and was in England fighting with the British. Was Kristoffer here among the many Norwegians who had managed to get away to continue the fight against their invaders?

When such thoughts came to her mind she tried quickly to dispel them, telling herself that it was utterly ridiculous to dwell on the memory of a few isolated months when she was still a young girl in her teens. Reminding herself she was now twenty-one, mother of a three-and-a-half-year-old child and a married woman, she would turn her thoughts to James and the brief life they had shared when he was still a practising vet and she and Una worked for him as his assistants. Even then, she was obliged to recall that she was pregnant and desperately afraid she might not be able to keep her baby. Her debt to James was too big ever to be repaid, but if he came home an invalid, she would spend the rest of her life taking care of him.

It was now nearing six o'clock and Dilys could see that Tina's energy was finally flagging.

'Come on, darling. Time to go home!' she said, struggling to her feet and reaching for the picnic basket she had brought with her. As the child's mouth drooped, she added quickly: 'And it's high time you shut those chickens in for the night. Maybe there will even be a nice fresh egg for your tea.'

Tina loved all the animals and felt delightfully grown up

when her mother put her in charge of the rabbits as well as the new clutch of ducklings. Fortunately she was unaware that from time to time, usually following a visit from a land girl, one of her charges would go missing; nor did she make the association when there was a particularly nice lunch the next day. Chicken and duck were known on the table as 'fowl'; rabbits and lamb as 'meat'. She was very tender-hearted, very caring towards the dog and the cat which the evacuees had had to leave behind them.

Dilys had received somewhat grubby but painstakingly written letters from the children saying how much they missed their conker gathering beneath the chestnut trees. When they had first arrived they had not only missed their parents but the hustle and bustle of the busy streets, and the friends who lived in the same road where they all played when the bombs weren't falling. The big open spaces which they had grown to love were at first of little use for hopscotch or marbles or skipping. Some of the stray dogs and cats roaming the streets were objects to chase or to throw stones or tin cans at. All that had changed. Even the two boys had been close to tears when they had had to leave their pets with Dilys when their mother took them home.

On the same hot August day that Dilys was picnicking in the field with Tina, Kristoffer was lying on the grassy slope of Sticks Pass, six hundred metres above Lake Ullswater, on his way to conquer Helvellyn. Now a regular officer in the Norwegian army, he was making the most of a ten-day leave pass in the Lake District – the nearest he could come to the beautiful fjords of his homeland he missed so much. There was no denying the area was beautiful but it lacked the grandeur of the fjords with their towering mountain sides. He had hired a sailing boat the previous day when there had been a breeze and he had been able to believe he was on the water by Bergen where he and his father kept their boat. This day he had set aside to tackle the fifteen-kilometre trek to Helvellyn along Striding Edge.

He'd reached England not by Lysander but by the 'Shetland Bus', the sturdy fishing boats braving the danger of enemy attack. They ploughed regularly between the Norwegian coast and the Shetland Isles north of Scotland, carrying the many foreigners who wished to continue fighting the Germans. Kristoffer had been obliged to lie low after the Estridborgen explosion as one of Erik's men had been captured and it was feared that he might, under torture, reveal the identities of the other members of his cell and the part Kristoffer had played. It had been nearly six months before he had dared to go home to see his parents, and when he had finally done so he made up his mind to go to England like so many of his friends and continue the fight there.

Tired after the long day on the Helvellyn range, he made his way back to his hotel in Keswick, bathed, changed his clothes and went down to the tiny bar in the entrance hall. There was not much alcohol to be had in England these days but the landlord did his best to provide something, even if it was only cider.

There was a stranger at the bar, a tall, thin but good-looking man who turned out to be Polish. They exchanged names and Jerzy, who was on his way south from Edinburgh to Oxfordshire to meet up with his girlfriend, a WAAF officer, asked Kristoffer if he would like to see a photograph which he was obviously eager to display. He handed it to Kristoffer with a smile, saying in his own distinctive command of English, 'No, my friend, you are not seeing double. I have tricked many men who have too many to drink!' He laughed as he pointed to one of the two young women who stood smiling into the camera with their arms about each other's shoulders. 'This one I will marry if she will have me but she does not make up her mind. That one . . .' he pointed a finger at the identical girl beside her, '. . . is her sister. They are borned the same, you see, but they are not the same. My girl is officer in the air force but this one lives in the country with a little girl. I not meet her but I do tomorrow.' He smiled as he took a packet of cigarettes out of his pocket and offered one to Kristoffer. 'I tell you, one girl like Una is quite enough to manage, she is always laughing and ready for the happy time. Sometimes I am too tired to make love to her but she just laugh and shows me I am not so tired after all!'

He finally stopped talking, aware that Kristoffer was still holding the photograph, seemingly mesmerized by it. 'Something is wrong?' he asked anxiously, holding out his hand for the photo.

Kristoffer pulled himself together and shook his head. 'No, not at all. It's just that I used to know those two girls. We were in Germany together as students before the war. I . . . I was very much in love with the one who is sister to your girl, Una.'

Something in Kristoffer's voice caused his companion to look at him more closely. 'Was it not a happy time?' he asked.

For a moment, Kristoffer did not answer. Then, in a rush of words, he told the stranger how he had loved and lost Dilys; how he had tried to find her on a brief visit to England but had only found Una, who'd told him her twin was also in the air force and had almost certainly forgotten all about him.

Jerzy shook his head. 'That is sad for you, but life does not stand still. My Una tells me her sister has a daughter, but she has not spoke of a husband when she tell me we shall go this leave to the country where her twin lives.' He paused to light their cigarettes, then added: 'I do not mind where we go as long as we are together and I can make love to her so many times as I wish!'

'So Dilys cannot be in the air force after all,' Kristoffer muttered thoughtfully. His mind was racing. At long last, he knew where she was; that he could get on a train the next day and actually see her. But did he wish to do so? he asked himself. It would be like tearing the wound open which had never really healed. That unfortunate night in the *hytte* when he had submitted to Gerda's demands for sex had remained on his conscience, aware as he was that he had no love for her, that he had used her not so much for her but to satisfy his own need.

The following week had been a difficult one, Gerda smilingly attentive. This had made him sharper with her than he intended and that had served to make him feel even more guilty. It had been an enormous relief when one of Erik's men had come up to the *hytte* to inform them that Erik said the hiatus after the explosion had finally died down sufficiently for them to make their way back to Oslo.

During a brief visit to his parents in Bergen, Kristoffer had found that two more of the young men he had been at school with had left Norway to join the hundreds of others who were already serving in the Norwegian Brigade based near St Andrews in Scotland. He was now currently on embarkation leave prior to being posted to Italy where the Allies had gained a foothold in the south. He had made many friends among his fellow countrymen, who had wanted him to join them on a pleasure trip to Blackpool where they hoped to pick up some girls with whom to enjoy their brief leave. That he had opted for a solitary walking holiday in the Lake District now seemed like fate, for he would not otherwise have met Una's Polish boyfriend.

'Is it so hard to make the mind to come with me?' Jerzy was asking. 'I think you are still having feelings for this sister. If she is as beautiful as my Una, then I am not surprised.' He smiled encouragingly. 'Come with me, my friend! I have the car and petrol for the journey and we will have the jolly journey together.' He paused to refill their glasses once more, then said: 'I think we do not tell Una you come to visit with me. It will be surprise for her and this twin. If there is a husband, I do not think he is there as Una tells me I will have many tasks to fix as her sister has only the Land Girls at the farm who help when something breaks. You can help me to do the mends.'

Despite his uncertainty, Kristoffer smiled at his companion's strange grasp of the English language. He himself was bilingual, not only having studied the language at school and university but spoken it at all times with Dilys in preference to German, at which she was not very proficient.

Jerzy took his silence as an agreement and so, after they had eaten their evening meal together, each went to pack their belongings and pay their bills so they could make an early start next morning.

They awoke to brilliant sunshine, azure blue skies and a soft, gentle breeze. There were few other cars and only the occasional van or lorry on the A1, the main road leading south towards London. Kristoffer dozed from time to time, having had little sleep the night before as his excitement had escalated. During the wakeful hours he had steeled himself against the prospect of finding Dilys' husband with her. He knew there must be one because Jerzy had spoken of a daughter. He had not specified if it was a child or a baby but he presumed it must be quite young. If Dilys had married the year after leaving Munich, she would not have a child older than three or four.

The thought had been painful as he recalled how they had lain in the grass, his arm around her, and they had imagined their future and planned what they would call their children. This visit, he'd realized, was going to bring as much if not more pain than joy. He knew from Jerzy's photograph what she now looked like – older, thinner but still with her sweet, shy smile. His heart had started racing as he recalled how that smile could suddenly transform into laughter, her eyes sparkling and her mouth searching eagerly for his kisses.

By lunchtime Jerzy had turned off the A1 and they were now on the main A40 approaching Oxford. They had stopped briefly for a picnic lunch by the roadside and expected to be at Brook House by teatime.

'It will be the more the jolly surprise when they see you!' Jerzy exclaimed as he returned to the car.

Would it be a pleasant surprise or the reverse? Kristoffer wondered as they turned off the main road on to the country lane leading to Fenbury. Was he not totally out of his mind seeing Dilys again, knowing she must be married and that he would mean no more to her than a half-forgotten friend?

The nearer they got to the village the more apprehensive he became, but Jerzy was beaming as, turning into the drive, he drew up outside the front door of Brook House and jumped out of the car. Beckoning to Kristoffer to join him, he ran up the steps and rang the bell.

It was a minute or two before the door was opened by Una, with Tina beside her. The welcoming smile on her face turned to astonishment as she recognized Kristoffer.

'Oh, my God!' she exclaimed. 'Kristoffer . . .! Jerzy, wherever did you find him?'

In the hall behind her, Tina was shouting in her high treble to her mother who was in the kitchen. 'Mummy, Mummy! Come quick! Two mens are here and one is called Omygod but I don't know the other. Come and see!'

Una stood staring after her niece, her heart thudding furiously as she realized there was no possible way by which she could warn Dilys about the shock awaiting her. Jerzy was frowning as he tried to puzzle out why Una was looking so apprehensive, and Kristoffer's expression was one of utter astonishment as he, too, stared after the departing child whose features he had instantly recognized as identical to his own.

NINETEEN

The evening meal was over, Tina had been put to bed and the two men were enjoying the last of Scotty's gift of whisky in the drawing room while Una and Dilys had escaped to the kitchen, ostensibly to do the washing up. It was the first chance since Jerzy and Kristoffer had arrived for them to converse alone.

'I'm just so sorry, Dil!' Una was saying. 'What on earth were the chances of Jerzy running into Kristoffer in the Lake District of all places!'

Dilys put the last of the washed plates in the rack to drain and tipped the cutlery into the bowl of soapy water in the sink. Her face was very pale and her voice a little unsteady as she said, 'It's not your fault, or Jerzy's, who by the way I like very much. He's obviously crazy about you!'

Una nodded. 'I know, but I learned my lesson with Scotty: it just doesn't pay to give your heart to aircrew. Chances are it will be broken if you do. I believe their life expectancy these days is less than a month. I don't suppose it's a lot better for the troops, is it? Kristoffer told Jerzy he is on embarkation leave so I suppose he will be in the thick of it very soon.'

For a moment, neither girl spoke, then Una said, 'You still love him, don't you, Dil, and Kristoffer, poor devil, loves you. Try as he does, he can't hide it and, as for you, well, you haven't once managed to smile!'

Dilys handed Una some spoons to dry. Her voice was shaking slightly as she whispered, 'Una, I can't . . . I can't smile. I know it's wrong of me but I can't begin to count the number of nights I have lain awake thinking how it would be if I saw Kristoffer again, wondering whether he had forgotten me – forgotten the plans we made for the future when were married.' She put down the wet dishcloth and reached for the chain round her neck on which Kristoffer's ring still hung. 'And there's Tina,' she continued. 'I saw him staring at her and I know he must have guessed; she's so like him.'

Una drew a deep sigh. 'I'm afraid you're right! Those same azure blue eyes and that determined chin!' Momentarily, her lips curved in a smile as she said, 'Well, I suppose her insistence on calling him Mr Omygod kept the conversation from getting too serious. All the same, Dil, something has got to be done. I mean, do we put Kristoffer on a train to London – if there is one at this time of night – as he suggested? Or now he's here, do you want him to stay? Jerzy and I will sleep in the spare room – Tina isn't old enough yet to be shocked by the fact that we aren't married – and Kristoffer could have the other spare room.'

Dilys had finished her task of washing the cutlery and started helping Una dry everything and replace it in the drawer. After a moment's silence, she said, 'I received notification from the Red Cross yesterday before you arrived. They said James had recovered enough to be sent to a POW camp and I could write and send a parcel to him there. It means he won't be home now until after the war is over.' Her eyes suddenly filled with tears. 'Oh, Una!' she wept, 'how could I possibly be unfaithful to James after all he's been through and is still having to endure. I can't! I couldn't . . . But seeing Kris . . . Una, if it wasn't for James, I . . .' She took a handkerchief out of her pocket and wiped her eyes furiously, saying in a toneless voice, 'Of course I still love Kris. I've never stopped doing so. I thought he must have forgotten me but when he said he'd tried so hard to find me . . . well, I knew then that nothing has changed. Four years may have passed but when we looked at each other on the doorstep . . . I know it's wrong but I still love him. I always will!'

For several minutes, Una did not speak. Then she said in a quiet, steady voice, 'Dil, this is wartime! Nothing is the same as it used to be. Girls like us . . . good girls, are brought up to set huge store by our virginity, but what's the value of that when young men like Scotty are dying – some dying without knowing what it is to make love to a woman! Jerzy and Kristoffer may very well lose their lives like Scotty did.'

She put down her damp tea towel and walked over to the

window, drawing the blackout curtain a fraction to one side so she could see the darkening sky and the evening stars.

'I'm glad I made Scotty happy, and I shan't feel guilty making Jerzy happy during what might be his last leave, and Dil, I don't think you should worry about poor James as there's nothing you can do to make life happier for him. I think you and Kristoffer should have this one week together – something you can both always remember and which cannot hurt James.'

She turned back to look at her sister's tear-streaked face. 'Meeting Jerzy the way Kris did – it's as if fate meant you to be reunited. You are twenty-one years old, Dil, and apart from those months in Munich you have never had a chance for real happiness. Oh, I know what Tina means to you, the joy she gives you, but it isn't the same fulfilling of yourself as when you lie with someone who worships you.'

She drew a deep breath and then said in a quiet but firm voice: 'Jerzy and I will stay here and take care of Tina. She'll love that! You go off with Kristoffer. Live your dreams for a few days. Go back to the Lake District if that's what he wants – it's beautiful there at this time of the year. Go, Dil, darling! Live your dream while you can!'

Dilys stood perfectly still, her face now as white as the china cup she was holding. It was a full minute before she could find her voice. 'Una, I can't . . . I can't. James . . . it wouldn't be fair . . .' She broke off and then added in a whisper: 'Besides, Kristoffer might not want . . .'

'Of course he does!' Una interrupted. 'He hasn't once taken his eyes off you – except when he was looking at Tina. Obviously he has guessed she is his child. Jerzy did, too! Dil, listen to me! James won't know so it won't hurt him. Jerzy won't ever meet him and I won't ever tell him. Life's too short for the old conventions to apply. You, Jerzy, me . . . we might all be dead tomorrow if a stray bomb falls on us tonight. And how would you feel if you heard that Kristoffer had been killed and you had denied him this one week when he could have lived his dream? You'd never forgive yourself – and all for someone who would never know the sacrifice you'd made.'

Hesitantly, as if in slow motion, Dilys put the cup down on the table with unseeing eyes. The colour had returned to her cheeks and her heart was beating fiercely as her mind raced. She knew Una was right and that Kristoffer would be overjoyed at the thought of spending the rest of his leave alone with her. How many long months, years, had passed since she had last lain in his arms and he had claimed her for his own? His being here, now, under the same roof was all but unbelievable – as if fate had intended them to steal these few brief days together. Una was right. James would never know and, when he came home, she would be as good a wife as possible and let Kristoffer become no more than a treasured memory. Now, with Una and Jerzy miraculously on hand to care for Tina, there really was nothing whatsoever to prevent her going away with Kristoffer. Just the two of them . . . alone.

In the drawing room, Jerzy finished his whisky and, putting down his glass on the side table, looked over at Kristoffer. His cheerful face was serious for once as he looked at his new friend. 'I think I did the wrong thing!' he said. 'I was not knowing how much you love Una's sister when I told you to come here with me. Now no one is having the happy time!'

'I'm sorry!' Kristoffer said quietly. 'I should have told you when you suggested I come here with you how I felt about Dilys . . . how I've always felt from the day I met her. I knew when you told me she had a child that she must be married and that seeing her again would only cause me more heartache, but I had to see her . . . I had to . . . and now . . .' His voice was husky as he added softly: 'Now I wish— The child . . . she's mine, you see. I dare say you see the likeness! And Dilys . . . I suppose I will never stop loving her. And it's all too late – she is married to someone else!'

Jerzy cleared his throat. 'Yes, well, she is married but I have seen at once that it is you she loves. It is so easy to see in her face when she looks at you when she comes to the door and so big the shock she cannot speak. And then how she is always taking care not to come close to you. I think she is happy for escape where no one sees how she feels when she goes to prepare the supper, to put the child to bed, to prepare a room for you . . . Yes, indeed, my friend, she loves you like you are loving her!'

'Oh, God!' Kristoffer muttered. 'I should have guessed it

would be like this, but it was all so long ago I thought she had surely forgotten me, that I had only imagined how dedicated we were to each another . . .' He broke off, a faint smile replacing the look of despair on his face, and added: 'But she hadn't forgotten. She was wearing my ring. It was on a chain around her neck and when she leant forward to lift up the child it fell forward from the collar of her blouse! It's the ring I gave her four years ago.'

He stopped talking as Una came into the room, her arm round Dilys' shoulders as she smiled at the men.

'Jerzy, we have finished all the whisky and there is nothing else to drink. How about you drive me down to the Duck and Hen? I'm a special friend of the landlord ever since Scotty used to slip him a few bottles whenever he and his fellow pilots went there. Maybe he'll find something for us.' She smiled at Kristoffer. 'Give you and Dil a chance to catch up on your news!' Her eyes went to Jerzy, who rose quickly to his feet.

'That is the good idea!' he said. 'Your English pubs is one of many things I like most about your country – and always such funny names – Duck and Hen . . . why is it not Duck and Chicken, I ask myself!'

He quickly took Una's arm and, nodding to Dilys and Kristoffer, he led her out of house and walked her purposefully down the drive.

Neither Dilys nor Kristoffer moved and stood staring at one another until they heard the front door bang. Two seconds later, Kristoffer had stepped forward and taken Dilys in his arms. They stood silently, their lips and bodies pressed so close it was as if they had become one entity. Then Kristoffer drew his mouth from hers and his hands cupped her face as he kissed her cheeks, her eyes, her forehead. So overcome with emotion was he that he was whispering endearments in his own language: *'Min kjaere, min elskede, min kjaere, kjaere jente.'* And then in English, he said, 'Love you! I've never stopped loving you! I love you, my darling, dearest girl, so, so much!'

He pulled her down on to the sofa and with his arms tightly around her, he described how desperately hard he had tried to find her when she left Munich. He told her of the letter he had written to her father which he supposed could not have reached her, or which her father had considered unsuitable to forward to her. He spoke of his meeting with her mother and then Una in London; of the letter he had left for her at the RAF Club for Una to pass on. How Una had told him that Dilys had joined the air force like herself and was doing secret war work.

For a moment, Dilys looked horrified. 'How could she lie to you about me!' she whispered. 'She knew better than anyone how desperately I needed you; how much I loved you. Kristoffer, I never got your letter.'

Kristoffer was silent for a moment, then he said, 'If by then you were already married, it is possible she considered only that it could make us both so unhappy that we should meet again too late.'

Dilys nodded. 'Perhaps . . .'

'Why, why did you marry this man if you still loved me?' Kristoffer demanded. 'Was it because of the child?'

Slowly, Dilys related how she had discovered she was pregnant after she was back in England; how she longed to be able to keep his baby but was ordered by her parents to have it adopted.

'I was going to run away, hide somewhere . . . bring our baby up by myself but Una forced me to face the fact that I had no money, no training and, not least, I was underage and the police would find me and return me to my parents.' She drew a deep breath and then said, 'Una and I were working for James in his veterinary surgery here. She told him about me, about the baby. Kristoffer, he's such a kind man, so caring about animals and birds and helpless creatures. There was an old man who owned a very old dog which had heart problems, and the old fellow could not afford vet's fees or the dog's medication and James never charged him a penny; and once, when a stray, pregnant mongrel was dumped on his doorstep and it died having six puppies, he fostered them all himself, tending to them day and night, and found them all homes when he could so easily have just put them to sleep.'

She looked at Kristoffer, whose face was expressionless. 'When Una told James about me and the coming baby he offered to marry me . . . so I could keep it. His wife and baby son had died years ago and he said he'd be pleased to have

company in the house, that I would be his wife only in name
. . . We'd have separate bedrooms and so on, and he'd gladly
give my baby his name. He has been quite wonderful to me,
Kris, and I can't bear to hurt him.' She paused and then added
quietly, 'James has been badly wounded and he's now recovering in a German POW camp. Una says he need never know
you have reappeared in my life so long as we say goodbye to
each other at the end of your leave and promise not to keep
in touch . . .'

Her voice trailed into silence and for several minutes
Kristoffer, too, was silent. Then he said, 'It is difficult! I, too,
owe him so much. He has made it possible for you to keep our
baby, our little girl. She is so sweet, Dilys, so pretty and funny
and charming. If I am not to see you again, I shall not see my
little daughter growing up—' His arms tightened around her
and he drew a long, tremulous sigh. 'This I see is the price I
must pay if I am to have you for myself for the rest of my
leave. I have had two of the seven days so you and I . . . we
must manage somehow to have the whole of our married life's
happiness in five days. You will spend them with me, my darling,
won't you?'

Dilys was too close to tears to speak. Then she whispered,
'A lifetime in five days? It is so little I cannot believe James
would refuse me this chance of happiness. Afterwards, he will
still have me, and Tina who he loves as his own. He is such a
kind man, Kris, he may even allow me to send you a photo of
Tina once a year.'

Suddenly Kristoffer released her and, jumping to his feet,
pulled Dilys up beside him. His eyes were burning with excitement as he said, 'You will need shoes, enough clothes for five
days and must pack them now. We should go tonight, my darling.
Maybe Jerzy will drive us to the station so we can get a train
somewhere . . . anywhere. Maybe he will lend me the car if he
is staying here with Una. We will find a hotel . . . say we are
just married which is why you are not on my passport, which
they will demand.'

He grasped both her hands and looked into her eyes, his own
now alight with laughter. 'Una must tell Miss Omygod that I
have given you a lift to London to buy Christmas presents before

the Germans bomb them. How is that? I hope she will not be too sad without you.'

For the first time, Dilys laughed. 'I doubt it very much. Tina is quite accustomed to being left with my daily help, Mrs White. She loves Una and will, I suspect, flirt outrageously with Una's boyfriend.'

She drew a long, shuddering sigh and, reaching out her arm, traced Kristoffer's lips with a fingertip. 'I love you,' she whispered, 'and for five whole days and nights, I shall be yours.' As he pulled her back into his arms, she pulled away from him, smiling. 'Let me go,' she urged him, 'or I shall never get packed.'

By the time Jerzy and Una returned from the Duck and Hen, Dilys and Kristoffer were standing in the unlit hall ready to go.

TWENTY

Kristoffer had been driving for over an hour before he and Dilys reached the Gloucestershire village of Newgate, a small hamlet bordered by a slow-running stream which, now darkness had fallen, was reflecting the moonlight. The shaded headlights of Jerzy's hired car lit up the straggling few cottages and thatched roof of a single pub. No lights shone through the blackout curtains in the windows but Kristoffer drew to a halt when he saw a bicycle and a chained sheepdog curled up near the wall.

'Chances are that someone is still drinking in the bar!' he said. 'Although, it is an hour past your English closing time!'

Stopping only to kiss Dilys' cheek, he opened the car door and, crossing the narrow road, knocked on the sturdy oak door. It was several minutes before the door opened and a woman Dilys supposed was the landlord's wife opened it and stood listening to what Kristoffer was saying. Dilys could see her face break into a smile as she nodded and beckoned to him to follow her inside. Minutes later he reappeared and, opening the car door, took his kitbag and Dilys' small suitcase and helped her out of the car.

'The good lady has shown me the only room she has for guests!' he told her. 'It is not so large and has no carpet on the floor but it is very clean and . . .' he paused to kiss her once more, '. . . the bed is so big it fills up the room!' He laughed happily. 'I told her we are just married so quickly as I am to go overseas very soon, and she tells me this will be the first time they have had a honeymoon couple in the room. I think she is a romantic.'

Which, indeed, she was as she ushered them upstairs and opened the casement windows with a loud squeak to allow the soft summer night air to freshen the room.

She beamed at Dilys, saying she would bring her a cup of tea, and apologised to Kristoffer that her husband did not have any champagne in the bar and only a limited amount of beer or cider due to the wartime shortages.

Having produced Dilys' tea, she finally bade them goodnight and they were alone. It was the moment Dilys had been longing for but, now that it had come, she felt absurdly shy. As if Kristoffer had sensed her feelings, he pulled the only chair over to the window and sat down, saying, 'Why don't you unpack, *kjaere*, and as on this occasion I wish to spoil you, you may have the first visit to the bathroom, which the landlady tells me is at the end of the passage. When you are ready for bed, I shall take my turn!'

When Dilys had finished in the old-fashioned bathroom and returned to the room, Kristoffer immediately got up and disappeared down the corridor. She undressed and, realizing she had forgotten to pack a nightdress, she hurriedly scrambled beneath the bed clothes, pulling the eiderdown up to her chin. All she could think of was whether Kristoffer would notice how changed her body was since the last time he had made love to her. She was no longer the slim, small-waisted girl she had been then. Her breasts had filled out when she was feeding Tina and had never fully regained their shape. Would he be disappointed? It was easy to see that, if he had changed at all, he had become even fitter and more muscular, no doubt as the result of his training in the army. Other women would find him attractive. By comparison, would she seem gauche, a disappointment to him?

Stupidly she closed her eyes, pretending that she had dozed off and did not hear him return. She was holding her breath as she heard him cross the room and draw back the curtains, and then he was climbing into bed beside her, saying, 'Last time I made love to you it was in the sunlight, but now it will be in the moonlight . . .'

The night summer air had lost none of its warmth and Kristoffer quickly pulled the eiderdown and bedclothes away and began covering her with kisses, his hands caressing first her breasts and then moving down her trembling body to her waist. His body was burning hot against her naked flesh and hers filled with an answering passion. Her arms now clasping him to her, she kissed him feverishly, his lips, his chest and the taut muscles of his stomach, at which point he cupped her face in his hands and, parting her legs with his own, found his way into her.

They were now breathing in unison as Kristoffer moved slowly at first but quickened as she urged him wordlessly to move faster. For the first time in her life, she was swept away by the uncontrollable urge of desire. As the waves of pleasure swept over her, she held tightly to his body as he, too, climaxed. They now lay quietly, their arms tight about one another, their mouths exchanging gentle, loving kisses as their breathing slowed.

For one anxious moment, the thought shot though Dilys' mind: might she become pregnant again? But as if he had read her thoughts, Kristoffer said softly, 'I think God intended we should be man and wife! I think if we were married we would find ourselves with a house full of children like Tina. It is sad but just as well that I made sure this would not happen this time!'

He turned on his side and pulled her close to him. She could tell by his voice that he was smiling as he said, 'I think your sister has chosen wisely. Jerzy is a very kind, nice fellow, and but for him I would not have had with me the means to prevent a child.'

Just for an instant, Dilys was reminded of the two occasions when James had made love to her. He, too, was unprepared but explained that he would take great care not to climax inside her. Gently, he had described how babies could be prevented, adding that when he came back home again, he would make sure he was properly prepared. He had further implied that if she was agreeable, he would like her to have his child.

Quickly, she put thoughts of James out of her mind. She didn't want to think of anything but the fantastic stroke of luck which had made it possible for Kristoffer and herself to have these five precious days of his leave together. She wouldn't think about afterwards: how she could go back to living without him. She would treasure every moment, every kiss, every touch, every smile.

'I love you so much!' she whispered, but he did not hear her as he had fallen fast asleep.

The following morning they woke to another brilliantly hot August day. The sun was streaming through the uncurtained window when Kristoffer woke Dilys with a kiss which quickly led to more lovemaking. This time, Dilys was without any inhibitions and, to Kristoffer's delight, was as eager and passionate as himself.

Downstairs in the single room which served also as the bar, the owner, an elderly, grey-haired man called Jack Dawson who was deputizing for his son who had joined the navy, served them scrambled eggs on a slice of ham. Two of his neighbours had teamed up with him to buy a pig when food first started to become short, pooling their household waste with his to fatten it up. He added proudly that he had smoked it up his inglenook chimney and the three of them had shared the proceeds, which they hoarded for special occasions.

Kristoffer and Dilys were touched by the man's kindness in sharing his precious ham with them, and Kristoffer promised to send him a joint of *fenalår*, a Norwegian smoked mutton speciality, he explained, after the war was over.

It was yet another beautiful sunny day and when the landlord suggested they should take a picnic and explore some of the Cotswold countryside they quickly fell in with the idea. With the aid of a map roughly drawn by the landlady, they made their way across fields where herds of cows and sheep were happily grazing and down a lane void of houses. Kristoffer then turned into a spinney not on the map where the trees were sparse enough to allow the sunlight to penetrate the branches.

Smiling at Dilys, he found a soft mossy mound on the edge of a small, lazy stream and drew her down beside him. Without speaking, he removed his shirt and trousers and then pulled off her cotton frock and underclothes so that they were both naked.

'It is too long since I last made love to you, my darling!' he said softly between kisses.

Dilys traced his lips with her fingertip, her eyes smiling. 'But it's only a few hours since we woke up and . . .'

Kristoffer pretended to sigh. 'So already I am boring you . . .' he began but Dilys pressed her mouth against his and drew him to her. Such had been the loving intensity of Kristoffer's lovemaking the previous night and next morning that she had

lost all trace of shyness and, for the first time in her life, Dilys
was able to experience the full pleasure of a perfect sexual
union. Four years ago, when Kristoffer had made love to her
by the lake in Bavaria, she had been mentally happy that he
should do so but, physically, it had been painful and she had
been uncertain of how she was to respond. It had been enough
that she was making him happy and that they were behaving
like a married couple. It was so different when she had gone
to James' bedroom and lain with him those last nights of his
leave. Then she had just wished to thank him in the only physical
way she could think of for the huge gift of her beloved daughter
which he had made possible. She was happy to have made him
happy but had not herself felt or even wanted any pleasure from
the encounter. Now . . . now it was all different; she was as
hungry for Kristoffer as he was for her and had discovered the
intense joy of a union with a loved one.

For a while they lay with their arms about one another, the
midday sun hot on their naked bodies. Suddenly, Kristoffer rose
to his feet and went across to the stream. Dilys watched his
strong, muscular body as he bent down and started to collect
stones and pieces of wood to make a dam and, smiling, imagined him as a small boy and then, as the son she would never
have. Her mind went briefly to their daughter but without worry,
knowing that Tina adored her Aunt Una and would not be
missing her.

'Come here, *kjaere*!' Kristoffer called. 'I have made us a
little pool for bathing!' And he laughed.

Dilys took a quick glance round her to make sure they were
still completely isolated and then joined him in the small pool
he had created. Laughing happily, he kissed her quickly and
then splashed her with the clear cold water running into the
pool and seeping out through his roughly made dam.

'We are like Adam and Eve in the Garden of Eden!' he said,
smiling. 'You are so beautiful and I am so happy. I shall always
remember this day and how lucky we are to be here together.'

He seemed able to forget that, in four days' time, they would
be parted and never see each other again. Dilys tried to hide
her own unbearable thoughts of a life without him. She at least
had Tina, a part of him. Last night Kristoffer had spoken of his

daughter and told her he did not wish to see her again before he left, that the hurt would only be greater knowing he could never be her father. It would have been easier if he had never seen her, he'd said sadly, but then added that he could find some happiness in knowing that part of him would always remain with her, Dilys.

True to his resolve, when their idyllic few days together came to the end and he drove her home, he remained in the car unseen when Tina came rushing out of the front door to greet her mother. She was in her nightdress ready for bed, her small face alight with excitement as Dilys hugged her.

'Aunt Una let me stay up till you came!' she said excitedly. 'Have you brought me a present? Uncle Jerzy gave me my very own watch. Look! It tells the time and you wind it like this . . .'

She did not look at the car but, clinging to Dilys' hand, followed her mother indoors.

He and Dilys had already said goodbye to one another when he had stopped the car half a mile away. White-faced, Dilys had been too unbearably sad to cry as they had clung to one another. She knew Kristoffer was right when he said it would be easier for them both if they made a clean break, never to see each other or communicate again. He did not suggest that they should try to forget one another as he knew it would not be possible.

His throat tightened and hot tears stung the back of his eyes as he watched them disappear into the house. It was all he could do not to wrench open the car door and go running after them. That last night together, it had taken a huge effort of will not to renege on their agreement when, after their lovemaking, he had tasted the tears on Dilys' cheeks and known that she was as conscious as himself of how little time they had left.

Now the parting was done and, mercifully, the front door opened again and Una came out with Jerzy carrying their suitcases. All three were travelling back to London together. Their leaves over, they would be returning to their wartime duties – Jerzy to his airfield, Una to her Filter Room and Kristoffer to his regiment. Tactfully, no mention was made of the days he and Dilys had spent together and conversation was for the most part about the massive carpet bombing by the Allies over

Germany and whether this would lead to the invasion for which everyone had waited for so long.

It crossed Kristoffer's mind that when the invasion happened there would inevitably be a huge loss of life and both he and Jerzy might not live to see victory, but as far as he was concerned, he could see no joy in a future without Dilys. Such was his despair that it even crossed his mind they might both have been happier had he never found her and, as the years went by, they had become distant memories.

When finally they reached London, Jerzy drove Una to Victoria where she was staying the last night of her leave with her parents. He then drove Kristoffer to King's Cross station where he intended to catch the night train to Scotland to rejoin the Norwegian Brigade, the 52nd Division, of which he was part. It was a mountain training division who were preparing men for the ultimate reclaiming of his country.

While Jerzy was driving the car to a nearby garage where he would leave it, Kristoffer sat in the station waiting room waiting for him to return. Ordering himself a beer, he took from his pocket a folded sheet of notepaper Una had placed there as she was saying goodbye. His drink lay untouched as he read it not once but several times, his heart beating furiously as he did so.

> *Dil just told me you agreed not to keep in touch but I said it wasn't fair on you and she agreed that I could write to you every Christmas to let you know she was OK, and to send you a photo of Tina so you could see her growing up. Dil thinks you might not want them, in which case, just chuck them away. She doesn't want you to write to her. Take care of yourself.*
>   *Love, Una*

Kristoffer's depression lessened as he realized he was not going to lose all contact with Dilys and his daughter after all. It might be painful to see how they were continuing their lives without him but at least they would not be entirely lost to him. Kristoffer's whole body, which had been tensed so tightly he had had difficulty breathing, now relaxed and an expression of pure happiness spread over his face. He felt like a condemned man who had been told that he had been reprieved: not released from a life sentence but at least with something now to live for.

When Jerzy returned he found with great relief a different companion for the journey north. The sad, unhappy man was now happy to listen to him singing Una's praises and telling him what unexpected fun they'd had playing mother and father; a happily married couple. They had laughed and made love and been so happy, he told Kristoffer, that on their last day together he had proposed to Una and she had agreed to get engaged.

'So many WAAF girls have been so sad when their boyfriends not come back safe, she telled me. So she never love anyone too much again after Scotty died, so a big surprise for me when I ask her to marry me and she say yes. I am the very, very happy man, and it make me sad that you and the nice Dilys have not the same happiness.'

The train rattled its way northwards, filled as always with uniformed men with their kit bags, clunking every now and again to a standstill when a heavily laden string of wagons carrying vital supplies shunted past in the darkness of a blacked-out station. Some of the men slept in the corridors when the carriages were full; some on the overhead luggage racks. Nearly all were smoking and, until the early hours, there was a continuing noise of chatter, laughter and, occasionally, singing.

After several hours, Kristoffer finally managed to doze off, his head against the rough upholstery, his right hand in his pocket clutching the lifeline Dilys' twin had thrown him.

TWENTY-ONE

Two long years later the war had finally ended and the liberated countries were celebrating their first peacetime Christmas for seven years. If anything, living conditions were even worse as the countries started picking up the pieces after the invasion; as they tried to re-establish their depleted economies.

Kristoffer's father, Herr Holberg, had regained control of Holberg Tømmer AS, the family timber company, and with the surrounding forests, wood for heating at least was plentiful. Kristoffer was sitting in a chair by the warm stove when his mother came into the room with an airmail letter in her hand. The stamp was English and her expression was far from happy as she handed it to him.

On her son's return from Scotland, he had told her of his love for Dilys, a married woman, and the existence of his child. Both shocked and dismayed, she had been only partially relieved to hear that they had agreed never to see each other or communicate again. Now she feared that the woman was trying to get in touch with him once more as he took the envelope from her eagerly, his expression full of joy.

As he had hoped, it was from Una. When they had parted company in London, she had promised to send, unknown to Dilys, news of her twin and Tina once a year at Christmastime so he could be reassured that they were alive and well. No letter had come that first Christmas of 1943, but one had come in 1944 saying briefly that all was well with Dilys and the child. The rest of the letter referred to the progress of the Allied invasion and her hope that Norway would soon be liberated. The letter had been delivered by a member of the Norwegian Resistance returning from England and was six weeks' out of date. Now, with his beloved country free at last, when the Germans had finally surrendered, Una's letter arrived before the end of the year.

Disregarding his mother's presence, he tore open the envelope and drew out a snapshot of his little girl. Now five-and-a-half years old, she had lost the chubbiness of babyhood and bore a slight resemblance to her mother. She was laughing into the camera and was holding out her two little arms as if she was about to be embraced.

Watching her son's expression and all too painfully aware of the reason for the sadness and longing he was feeling, Fru Holberg waited until he had read the letter before saying, 'This is not right, Kristoffer. You know you should forget this English woman and the child! You know nothing can ever come of it and you are wasting the years when you could be happily married with children of your own and . . .'

Kristoffer silently handed the letter to his mother to read. 'No, *Mor!*' he said sharply. 'I have told you this many times: I shall never marry. My heart is not mine to give and I am quite happy living here with you and *Far*.'

Finishing reading, his mother handed the letter back to him with a sigh. 'It is not right, Kristoffer! Your father and I always thought when you and Gerda . . . You were so close as children . . . That you would marry one day, and I know she loves you. When you were wounded, Gerda was beside herself with worry and told me she would not want to go on living if you died. Mercifully, you recovered, but often your temperature was so high those weeks before the liberators gave me medicine for you, you were delirious. Gerda was so good, helping me look after you. I could see how it tormented her when all the time you called the name of the Englishwoman.'

Kristoffer hesitated, then he said quietly, 'I am sorry, *Mor*, but I cannot forget Dilys, and I'm sorry that Gerda and I will never give you the grandchildren you wish for, but perhaps Gerda will find a husband in America. From what she wrote to you in her last letter, the family in California for whom she is now the au pair sound very pleasant. Gerda is both pretty and intelligent and it may not be long before we hear she has met someone she fancies who might wish to marry her.'

Fru Holberg sighed. 'I hope you are right and that she will be happy married to an American. If that happened, I should miss her very much. She has always been like a daughter to me. Before she left, I promised her I would write regularly to tell her how you were recovering and, more importantly, to let her know if I thought you were at last putting away the memory of your affair with this Englishwoman. I should be so happy that she would then return home. I miss her very much. She is a good girl, Kristoffer, and she would make you a good wife.'

Kristoffer shook his head. 'It will never happen, *Mor*. It is as a sister that I love Gerda. My heart will remain always with Dilys.'

Fru Holberg sighed again before asking, 'How is your leg feeling today? I was happy when I dressed your wound this morning to see there is no further sign of infection. Now that we have the telephone service again I will speak to the doctor and see if he will recommend you to walk without the crutches.'

Kristoffer watched with relief as his mother finally left the room and then he eagerly reread Una's letter.

Dilys has been helping out at the village infants' school where Tina now goes but the boys' prep school, which had been commandeered by the army when they were evacuated at the outbreak of the war, has now been de-requisitioned and Dilys applied for the job of first-year teacher. Because of the shortage of teachers after so many were killed in the war, the school were pleased to employ her and agreed that Tina could join in the six- to seven-year-old boys' classes as she is very forward for her age.

As he read on, Kristoffer caught his breath. Dilys' husband, James, had been repatriated when his prisoner-of-war camp, Oflag IV-D, situated north of Dresden, was liberated by the Russians in May. Sadly the shrapnel wound in his head had led to confusion and loss of memory and he was currently in a London hospital, where Dilys could visit him every Sunday. No one yet knew if or when he would be allowed home as he had yet to hear when the surgeons considered it safe to operate on his head to extract the fragment of shrapnel that had not been removed by the German doctors the previous year. The letter continued:

Sometimes Tina goes with Dilys but every other weekend our parents go down from London to oversee the renovations to Hannington Hall, now that it has been de-requisitioned. Then Tina spends the afternoon in her grandmother's care and a surprisingly close bond has developed between them. As for my father, he pretends not to find Tina enchanting but it's obvious he does!

The letter finally ended with the news of her recent demobbing from the WAAF, that Jerzy was applying for a British passport and that they would settle in England when they were married, and the usual good wishes for Kristoffer's well-being.

For a few minutes, Kristoffer sat with the letter between his hands, his emotions in turmoil. In some ways, the news was almost unbearable knowing that Dilys' and his little daughter's lives were being lived without him. There was also a sharp stab of jealousy when he'd read of Dilys' weekly visits to her husband. He forced himself to curb such emotion, knowing as he did that James Sherwin's war injuries were far, far worse than his own leg wound. His doctor had said that in six months' time he should have the full use of his leg again. Mental confusion was a cruel permanent handicap.

His thoughts returned momentarily to his mother's understandable antipathy to Dilys and perhaps, even more so, to the child he could never claim as his. He knew only too well how much Gerda had hoped, when she was helping to nurse him, that he would turn to her on the rebound. Far from it, the night he had spent with her in the mountain *hytte* was something he tried to erase from his memory, aware as he was that it should never have happened. Dilys had never asked him if he had made love to other women before her but there had been no need for an answer as she was never in doubt during those halcyon days together that their love for one another was for a lifetime.

Occasionally, one or another of his old fellow resistance fighters called in to see him during his convalescence. Inevitably they asked him if he was thinking of going back to England now the war was over. He pretended uncertainty but he knew he never would go, that were he to do so he would not be able to prevent himself from seeing Dilys and his child.

He picked up the snapshot Una had enclosed from the table where he had placed it and wondered at the little girl's resemblance now to her mother. The only time he had seen her, he had seen at once that she looked like him. He smiled, happy about the transformation and proud of her prettiness.

After reading it once more, he carefully put the letter and photograph in the breast pocket of his jacket and tried to regain the interest he'd had in the papers his father had given him to pass the time and, more importantly, to bring him up to date with their family business. As soon as he was back on his two feet he would be initiated into the tasks of export manager, a job that had lapsed during the war when ninety-five per cent of the firm's output had gone to Germany.

However, he could not concentrate and finally he put the folders back on the table and took up the book he was reading. It was an English novel by Graham Greene called *The Ministry of Fear*, a thriller taking place in London during the Blitz, which had so far kept him enthralled.

Meanwhile, his mother was busy in the kitchen, not cooking which she enjoyed doing every morning, but writing the promised letter to Gerda while the news was fresh in her mind.

> *Dearest Gerda,*
>
> *You were quite right: the letter Kristoffer expected did arrive from England this morning, three days after the celebrations. I am so sorry to have to tell you that things have changed. As I promised before you left, I tried to persuade Kristoffer to forget the Englishwoman and make a new start to his life with you, but he continues to live in the past and tells me he will never marry anyone if he can't marry her.*
>
> *We have to accept, Gerda, dear, that there is no hope. The sister writes that the husband is waiting to*

*hear if the English doctors can remove the shrapnel which
is lodged too close to his brain for safety. If the husband
should not survive such an operation, his widow would
be free to marry again.*

*I am so sorry, Gerda, to have to write and tell you this
news. You must try now to forget about a future with
Kristoffer and please try to have a happy time with your
new Swedish friend, Birgit. Do you converse in Norwegian
or Swedish? I hope your skiing holiday was fun and I
wait to hear if the terrain was very different from our
mountain slopes here.*

*All my love and very best wishes for 1946, dearest
child, and you have my word, I will continue to do what
I can to knock some sense into my senseless son.*

Helena Holberg

Fru Holberg drew a deep sigh as she took her mixing bowl
off the shelf, then flour, eggs and sour cream from the larder
cupboard and began to prepare *fløtelapper*, which would be
eaten with her homemade, delicious fruit sauce, at their evening
meal. Kristoffer was her only child and throughout the war,
knowing how dangerous were his activities, she had lived in
fear of his death. Since his and Gerda's childhood, she had
nursed the idea that they would eventually marry and give her
the grandchildren she wanted. For a while, when they were
teenagers, it had looked as if that might come about. Then had
come the fateful year in Germany before the war and he had
fallen in love with the English girl with the funny name, Dilys.
It had not bothered her too much at first, certain as she was
that when the war separated them he would quickly forget her,
but she had not known then, any more than he did, about the
child. His daughter. It was only when he returned from England
in 1943 that she had learned of the child's existence and it was
then that she – and, of course, poor Gerda – had begun to lose
hope.

Fru Holberg recalled the tears Gerda had shed at the time
and how sensibly she had dealt with the news, vowing not to
waste her life hoping for the impossible and deciding to spend
a year in the United States. As she continued to beat the flour

and eggs it never once crossed her mind that her letter and the news it contained, now awaiting on the hall table to be posted to America, would have such a devastating effect upon the girl she had hoped would be her daughter-in-law.

Ten days later, when Gerda read the contents, every muscle in her body froze and her eyes narrowed. *No hope*, *Tante* Helena had written. There was no such thing as no hope. In this instance, as far as she was concerned, there had to be hope. Somehow she must find a way of removing the English girl from Kristoffer's life. There had to be a way and she would think of it.

TWENTY-TWO

n two months' time it would be Tina's sixth birthday, Dilys reminded herself as she dried the last of the lunch dishes. She must start thinking of something really nice to do by way of a party for her. She sighed, wishing that dear old Mrs White was still with her, not just to help with tiresome domestic chores but because she always made splendid birthday cakes for Tina. James' faithful servant had been forced to retire at the end of the war due to severe rheumatism.

Stacking the clean plates on the dresser, she wondered what it would be like owning a dishwasher. She had seen one in an American film but as far as she knew no one as yet had one in England. Although the war had ended when Japan had surrendered last September, shortages of nearly everything still continued.

Through the kitchen window, Dilys could see James wandering round the garden, a garden devoid of all but a few flowers as she was still growing vegetables, a necessity during the war. She also still had her chickens. She could see James staring down into the enclosure where a broody hen was sitting on a clutch of eggs, listening to hear if the chicks had hatched. Ginger, the cat, was winding itself between his legs.

Dilys paused, her eyes momentarily stinging with tears of pity as she watched him. He looked so completely normal: so like the James she had kissed goodbye when he had departed after his embarkation leave four-and-a-half years ago. He was thinner, of course, which was only to be expected after two years as a prisoner of war, but unless he was drawn into a conversation, people were unaware of his damaged brain. The English doctor in the prisoner-of-war camp at Elsterhorst had concealed the fact from their captors, fearing what might happen to James if his mental state was known.

Physically, he had no visible scars, his only wound being on his head where a piece of shrapnel was lodged in his brain. The result of that injury was an almost total loss of memory. He only recalled his former work as a vet. His personal habits were unchanged, and he seemed most at ease when he was smoking his pipe. He greeted people who came to the house for one reason or another as if they were clients and seemed confused if they did not have an animal with them requiring his treatment. His good manners were the same as they had always been – automatic.

When James had first been repatriated after the Russians liberated his prison camp, he had been sent to one of the big London hospitals where his condition had been assessed. During those weeks when Dilys had visited him every Sunday, he had behaved towards her not as a husband but as her employer, wanting to know if Mrs Anstruther's Labrador's broken leg had healed; if the young Peter's rabbit had recovered its appetite. She had not always taken Tina with her on those visits, and her daughter had spent Sundays with her grandparents at Hannington Hall. Tina loved going there and both her grandparents now doted on her, her origins conveniently forgotten.

As she told Una on one of her twin's frequent visits, she had little time to dwell on the past, halcyon days with Kristoffer. Her visits to James, looking after Tina and her teaching job at the prep school sufficed to make life a tolerable routine which kept her busy but reasonably content, she said. The only nagging worry was when James was sent home after the brain specialist said an operation was far too dangerous for him. He'd explained it would be safer to leave the shrapnel where it was as it might never move. At the same time, he warned her that should it do so, it would almost certainly cause James' death.

At first, Dilys had feared she would have to give up her job at the school. She loved working with the small boys, thinking up ways to make their lessons interesting so they were fun as well as instructive. Tina was accepted by the boys as one of them but still maintained her femininity, loving pretty dresses and fairy stories and even dolls, although these were never taken to school to be ridiculed by her masculine classmates.

Dilys' worry that she would have to give up her job to take care of James was quickly solved by Una. She suggested that

Dilys employ someone such as an au pair to live in and help with the extra work and cooking needed by James' return home and, more importantly, to keep an eye on him when she was at the school. It was not as if he required nursing. If the weather was fine, he would wander outdoors to look at the animals, the cat, Tina's rabbit, the chickens and the tortoise. When he examined or stroked them his face would lose its strained look, and Dilys realized he was reliving his former life as a vet. His manner towards her was polite, grateful and friendly but never intimate. Once, when she had gone to his bedroom to make sure he had everything he needed for the night, she had bent and kissed his forehead and his reaction was one of surprise, as if he was not quite sure who she was and what his response should be. He'd finally said, 'Thank you!' and she had decided not to confuse him again.

Tina's reaction to James' homecoming was, Una declared, entirely understandable. The child had no memory of him and referred to him frequently as the 'Wounded-Man-who-lives-with-us'. She knew he was someone she was supposed to call 'Daddy', but she seldom did so. At times, if she had nothing else she wanted to do, she would join him in the garden and then he would begin giving her instructions about the animals' welfare. He never remembered her name. She learned quickly that he seemed not to object when she chatted to him but that she must not expect a reply unless it was how many pills she must give a sick animal or what to feed her rabbits.

The first months James had been home from hospital had been difficult. He would wander off without saying where he was going and, for all Dilys knew, might go out of the garden on to the road. It was like having Tina as a toddler again. During those busy days she had no time to think of the past, of Kristoffer and what he might be doing with his life. When she was drifting into sleep she would allow herself to remember those five days when the two of them had been briefly reunited, but to her disappointment she never dreamed of him.

Dilys was finding her new au pair, a Swedish girl called Birgit, a huge asset. She was always smiling, always willing to help with cooking as well as housework and got on splendidly with Tina. She was happy to read her stories or play games

with her. Her manner with James was unobtrusive and she had
even been able to persuade him, on one or two occasions, to
join her and Tina on walks to the village. She sat with them
after Tina had been put to bed, and although she found it difficult to hold a coherent conversation with James, Birgit would
chatter happily to Dilys about her life in Sweden in her broken
English. How much of her conversation James understood
remained a mystery as he invariably sat in silence smoking his
pipe, his face impassive as he listened to her.

It was not exactly an exciting life, Dilys admitted to Una
when she came to stay on one of her weekends – certainly not
compared to the life Una now led in London. Jerzy had applied
for British citizenship and Sir Godfrey had found him a job
helping to sort out the post-war lives of the many Polish men
who had come to England to fight but were now unable to
return to their own families and homes. Stalin had cleverly
manipulated the formation of a provisional government in
Warsaw and Jerzy was far too anglicized to wish to live under
Communist rule. He was grateful to Sir Godfrey for supporting
his application for citizenship.

It was a bright spring day in April when Una arrived unexpectedly with the news that she and Jerzy had fixed a day for
their wedding. As his family were unable to leave Poland, the
ceremony was not going to be at the fashionable church of St
Margaret's in Westminster, which their mother favoured, but at
the Wren church St James' in Piccadilly. It was a smaller church
at which some of his and Una's former RAF and Polish air
force colleagues could be present and it was conveniently near
the RAF Club for the reception. Tina, she announced to the
child's delight, would be her only bridesmaid and Dilys her
matron of honour.

Tina was wildly excited when her aunt told her she could
wear her princess dress, a full-skirted, frilled pink satin
garment Dilys had made for her out of an old taffeta petticoat
which had once been the underskirt of one of her mother's
old ball gowns.

'I've chosen a pale cream brocade wedding dress from
Norma Cave!' Una announced to Dilys with a secret smile
at her twin. The shop, well known to Una and other society

friends who were desperate for something 'new' to wear, had resorted to buying expensive second-hand couture clothes being sold by the rich women whose wardrobes were still full of fashionable dresses which had been made for them before the war. All but the most basic of materials were still unavailable and the stigma of wearing second-hand clothes had conveniently disappeared.

'I don't imagine James would want to come to the wedding,' Una said, glancing at the silent man seated by fireside.

Dilys shook her head. 'I think he's getting worse!' she said softly. 'Two nights ago he suddenly got out of bed, dressed himself and went downstairs. Fortunately Birgit heard him and found him in the drive heading for the road. He had no idea where he was going and let her lead him back to bed. He also keeps trying to open the door to the surgery which we locked after he was called up all those years ago. As a matter of fact, that particular incident gave Birgit and me the idea of opening it up, putting everything that might be useful to another vet in storage somewhere and using it as a playroom for Tina when she brings friends home. As you know, I'm planning a birthday party for her here the first week in May. What with work and James and everything, she doesn't have many treats so I want to arrange something special.'

Listening to Dilys' simple plans for her daughter, it crossed Una's mind how totally different her twin's life was from her own. With her flat in London and her engagement to Jerzy, there was seldom a night when she was not out enjoying herself. Despite the continued austerity as the country tried to recover from five years of bitter war, London was doing its utmost to regain its former reputation as an exciting capital city and theatres, cinemas and restaurants were busy once more.

Whenever she came to see Dilys, it left her feeling guilty that her twin should be leading such a dull, barren life without fun, without love or sex. She knew Kristoffer was still as devoted to Dilys as she was to him and it seemed tragic they could not be together. Dilys, of course, had refused to listen when she, Una, had speculated as to what might happen were James to get worse and be put in a secure hospital. Even if James' deterioration were to happen, she knew her twin would never desert him, the man who had once come to her rescue when she'd been about to lose her baby.

Last month, she had written again to Kristoffer. Although it was understood at the end of the couple's stolen week's 'honeymoon', that she would only write to him once a year at Christmas with news of Dilys and the child, his letter of thanks for last December's letter had sounded so desperate, so despairing of the future, that she had written again, although she had been unable to offer him even a glimmer of hope.

It was a constant worry to Una that there was so little she could do to better her beloved twin's life. At least, she consoled herself, Dilys' life had been greatly improved by the advent of the Swedish au pair. Birgit was not just a 'mother's help' as were most au pairs, but had become a friend and companion to Dilys as well as being James' and Tina's carer when she was needed.

Before she departed back to London, Una helped Dilys plan Tina's birthday party. It was the first time the child had celebrated the occasion with a party, but now, with Birgit's help, Dilys was organizing it for eight small boys from Tina's class at school. It was Birgit's idea that the party should be held in the old surgery. The reception room was large enough for the energetic youngsters to enjoy party games and, devoid of furniture, it needed only Birgit's dusting and polishing to be ideal for the party.

Together with Birgit, Dilys made a list of games to play and Birgit volunteered to make the birthday cake. They would decorate the room to look like a smuggler's cave with a treasure chest of fake silver coins. Meanwhile, Una telephoned to say that she and Jerzy would visit that day and Jerzy would dress up as a pirate, this because Tina insisted her party should be a boy's affair, not a girly one.

As usual, Birgit was as enthusiastic a planner as Dilys, all the preparations being undertaken after Tina had gone to bed. Both she and Dilys had saved their sugar ration so Birgit could make a heap of circular peppermint creams which she meticulously covered with silver paper to make them look like pirates' stolen silver coins. She said she would wire up an eerie, green light, saying that the smuggler's cave would look more realistic if the curtains were drawn and there was only a dim, green glow when the children first went into the room. Birgit's enthusiasm was infectious and Dilys was only too happy to leave her to prepare the room.

She was almost as excited as Tina when the day of the party finally arrived. Tina opted to travel with the eight small boys she had invited to her party who were to follow Dilys home from school in the headmaster's old, pre-war Bentley shooting-brake normally used to take the older boys to cricket and football matches. As soon as afternoon games were over, the sports mistress who had volunteered to act as chauffeur bundled all the children into the vehicle and followed Dilys down the drive.

Keeping her eye on the shooting-brake behind her, Dilys let her mind wander over all the preparations she and Birgit had made and reassured herself that nothing had been forgotten. Her thoughts then turned to Kristoffer as they so often did on special occasions involving Tina, and she thought how sad it was that he could not be with them. Her happiness at such times was always tinged with a sense of loss for what might have been had Kristoffer's letter to her all those years before the war not been lost.

A quick glance in her mirror reassured her that the Bentley was not far behind as she drove through the village. Then, as she neared her home, her thoughts went to James and how he would react to the sudden appearance of eight noisy little boys. It was a really good idea of Birgit to reopen the surgery for the party venue where they would all be happily confined and not getting under his feet.

Dilys would have been surprised had she known that James had noticed something unusual was happening because of the activity in his old surgery. During the past few days, when he had seen Birgit going in and out of that wing of the house, he had grown increasingly anxious that clients were bringing in their animals for him to examine and he was not there to attend to them. Such thoughts, though, seldom lasted more than a minute or two.

James was now sitting in the kitchen by the window, watching the ducks as they waddled in a line across the newly cut lawn. He felt a little uneasy without knowing why. Birgit seemed to be so busy, and Dilys, too. There was an air of excitement in the house. Somewhere in his brain he remembered being told that it was Tina's birthday. It worried him that he had not bought the child a present. He was fond of the girl – a pretty little thing, and she was always happy chatting to him.

Turning his head, he saw Birgit go once more into his old surgery. Again he felt confused. One part of his brain told him that he no longer used his surgery, that it was a long time since he had been a vet, that he had been in hospital, ill, and his memory was not as good as it used to be. Nevertheless, people should not be in that room. He'd closed it up and locked it. It didn't really make much sense. The house was certainly big enough for the three of them that lived in it. He must ask that girl why she was going in there so often when she next came into the kitchen.

The confusion in James' mind was such that he decided it was high time he got back to work. Putting down his unread newspaper, he made his way to the surgery. There was no sign of Birgit.

Birgit was standing at the front door watching for the cars to arrive. She wanted to make sure that Dilys was the first to go into the surgery and not young Tina or the other children she had brought with her from school. Her heart was beating furiously as she heard the noise of the cars turning into the drive. She was unaware that James was about to open the surgery door.

As Dilys drove into the drive, at the same moment James opened the surgery door. He had no time to register the brightly coloured party decorations, or hear the shocking noise of the explosion which instantly killed him.

On the doorstep, Birgit heard the noise of the violent explosion. Clapping her hand over her mouth, the colour drained from her cheeks; she realized there had been a ghastly mistake. Never once had she contemplated that someone else would open the door and set off the skilful explosion she had learned to engineer during the war when she had been in the Norwegian Resistance.

The young Swedish girl, Birgit, was still safe and sound in America, where Gerda had also gone to work as an au pair when she'd realized there was no hope that Kristoffer would return to Norway and marry her. After months of deliberation,

Gerda had stolen Birgit's passport with the intention of going to England, determined to rid herself of the one barrier to her neurotic need to possess the man she loved and, in order to do so, to kill Dilys.

Once she had arrived from America, using Birgit's passport, Gerda had registered with a domestic agency in Oxford, asking if there was any chance of employment in a local school. Fate had played into her hands. Una had only three weeks previously asked the agency to find an au pair for Dilys. There being no domestic vacancies at the school, would she consider this instead, they asked Gerda.

It was, she told herself, a sign that God had always intended Kristoffer to be hers. Once installed in Dilys' home, she was quite happy to wait for the right moment to carry out her plan. The knowledge of explosives she had acquired in the Norwegian Resistance was at the forefront of her mind. She had no wish to harm James or the child, and it was when Tina's birthday party was planned that she saw her opportunity to finally dispose of Dilys once and for all.

It was six months before the truth came to light. Gerda had managed to escape in Dilys' car but had forgotten that in the British Isles drivers used the left-hand side of the road. After the inevitable car accident that ensued, she was taken to hospital and the terrible truth emerged.

Sadly, it was Gerda's parents who suffered most as a consequence of their daughter's horrifying actions and the fact that she would no longer be a part of their lives. Fru Holberg blamed herself for writing those regular letters to Gerda in California reiterating that Kristoffer's love for the English girl was irreversible.

Dilys was so distressed that her parents insisted she close up the house and live at Hannington Hall with them, and that she resign from her job at the school. Tina, young as she was, understood very little of what had happened and remained her usual cheerful self, her only worry being the transfer of her rabbits to her grandparents' home.

In Norway, Kristoffer was so deeply shocked it did not immediately occur to him that Dilys was now free to marry him.

TWENTY-THREE

Dilys stood at the rail of the ferry as it ploughed its way past numerous small islands, her eyes fastened on the distant port of Bergen. It was a beautiful, clear September morning, the sunshine sending dazzling shafts of light off the surface of the sea. The crossing from Scotland the previous night had been calm and both she and Tina had managed to get a good night's sleep despite their excitement.

It was seven years almost to the day since she and Kristoffer had said goodbye to one another in pre-war Germany, and three years since their stolen week together during the war. Both of them had believed on that occasion that they would never see each other again.

Momentarily, tears stung Dilys' eyes as the memory returned of James' lifeless body lying on the floor of the old surgery and the doctor's voice saying, 'I'm so sorry, my dear, but there is nothing I can do for him.' He had gone on in an attempt to soften the shock by saying that James had been a very sick man with no real quality to his life: that, for him, death would have been a relief as he could only have deteriorated had he lived longer.

Dilys had known the doctor was right but it had taken her nearly six months to get over the shock – not just of James' death but of learning that the explosion had not after all been accidental but a deliberate attempt by Gerda Magnusson to kill her. People had become accustomed during the war to the so often unexpected loss of life, of whole cities destroyed in horrific bombing raids and the unbelievable revelation of the mass destruction of Jews and gypsies in German concentration camps. Men had died in their thousands in the air, at sea and on land, but James' death at the hands of the Norwegian girl and her subsequent trial and imprisonment had affected Dilys very deeply.

Recalling those six months, Dilys reflected how much support

Una and her parents had given her, her father dealing with all the police and legal problems that had ensued.

The situation had become clear when both passports were discovered. They had been in Gerda's possession when she had been apprehended.

Were she to have succeeded in escaping in Dilys' car after the explosion, her real name and guilt might never have come to light for, with Dilys dead, she had planned to return to Norway using her own passport.

What Gerda had not taken into account when she realized she had killed James instead by mistake was that in England drivers used the left-hand side of the road. In her hurry to avoid questioning, she had driven too fast and hit a lorry approaching her on a bend.

Gerda had spent several months recovering in hospital before she had stood trial for dangerous driving, stealing a car and driving without a licence. By then, her use of the Swedish girl's name and passport had come to light and the police had gathered from her incoherent ramblings that her intention had been to kill Dilys, not James. This fact was confirmed at the trial. Una and Jerzy had been able to verify Dilys' testimony that Gerda had been attentive, kind and caring towards James, and would have had no reason what-soever to wish him dead, whereas she'd every reason to want Dilys despatched to another world. After an abortive attempt to kill a prison warder and then herself, Gerda had been sent to Broadmoor for an indefinite period.

'Honestly, Dil, it isn't any of your fault!' Una had repeatedly told her. 'You didn't know who Birgit really was and you befriended her, trusted her. Suppose she had done something ghastly to Tina! She wanted you dead so she could get Kristoffer, and as for poor James . . . well, you know that he was never going to get better. I know the accident was terrible but, in some ways, it was a kinder end to his life than just getting slowly worse and worse.'

Recalling those words now, Dilys was no longer in doubt that Una was right. Fortunately Tina had been very little affected. For a start, the Bentley shooting-brake she was in had not yet arrived at the house and, after the incident, she had been allowed to join the boarders at school for the next two weeks, to her intense delight.

Now, half a year later, Dilys had replied to Kristoffer's many letters, telling him that she would bring Tina to Norway for a holiday. How long that holiday would last was a decision she would make when they met one another again. She knew she had changed . . . the war, her marriage, Tina . . . that she had finally grown up. What she did not know was if Kristoffer, too, had changed. In his letters he had had no doubt whatever about his feelings, but so much had happened to both of them that she could not be certain they could go back in time. Some of the wives she knew in Hannington and Fenbury, whose husbands had been abroad throughout the war, were finding it hard to adjust to their return, in most cases to resume their place as head of the household which the wives had been running single-handedly for five or more years without them.

Her reminiscences ceased as she caught sight of Kristoffer waiting on the quayside. As the boat edged nearer she could see his face and arms were tanned a deep brown by the summer sun, contrasting with the open-necked white shirt he was wearing. His trousers were blue, cut in the current American style. Hatless, his tanned face was creased in smiles as he caught sight of her and waved.

It was another twenty minutes before Dilys and Tina disembarked and he came hurrying to their side. Taking her suitcase from her he kissed her cheek, smiled at Tina and said, 'Welcome! *Wikommen* to Norway!' Then, meeting Tina's curious stare, he held out his hand, his eyes twinkling. 'And how do you do?' he asked formally. Then added: 'I bet you do not even know my name!'

'Yes, I do!' Tina replied. 'Mummy says I met you when I was three. You are Mr Omygod!'

Across the top of Tina's blonde head, Kristoffer's glance met Dilys'. They were both smiling.

'Yes, well, I do have another name,' Kristoffer said. 'Here in Norway you could call me *For*!'

Tina's large blue eyes widened. 'Well, that's just silly!' she announced. 'You can't be four. I'm six and you're much, much, much older than me. I was six last May but I didn't have a birthday party because of the 'splosion but Mummy let me be a boarder at the boys' school and then let me go and stay with Aunt Una in London for a treat instead of my party, and Aunt Una took me to see all the animals at a zoo called Reason's Park and we met a vet man who used to know the Wounded Man, I mean Daddy, when he was a vet and—'

'Darling, we can't stand here talking. You can tell us all about the zoo later!' Dilys broke in.

'Yes, we should go!' Kristoffer said. 'I thought as it is such a beautiful day that we might stop by the fjord and have a picnic lunch before we go home to meet my parents. What do you think, young ladies?'

Tina giggled and Dilys smiled her agreement. She was beginning to feel as if a huge load was being lifted from her shoulders. This was Kristoffer, the same man she had known and loved since she was in her teens. The long years and events between then and now were quickly vanishing.

Having got through customs, Kristoffer helped them into his car and drove away from the harbour. It crossed Dilys' mind as he did so that although he had done no more than kiss her cheek, his tone of voice and his expression had been full of love and her heart now leapt in response.

Neither spoke as they drove through the outskirts of Bergen. Leaving the urban suburbs behind them, the road wound up through the hills and then descended towards the sea at Hardangerfjord. From the back seat they could hear Tina's excited chatter remarking on the strange wooden houses, the forests, the fjord, the little islands, the boats. An hour later Kristoffer stopped the car by a field still full of summer flowers where they ate the picnic lunch Fru Holberg had provided. After packing the utensils away, Kristoffer and Dilys lay down side by side in the warm sunshine, Tina squatting beside them and now chattering excitedly about their voyage to Norway on the ferry. Aware suddenly that Kristoffer's gaze was on her mother rather than her, she demanded to be told a story.

'Do you know any good ones, Mr Four?' she asked. 'My fav'rits are about princesses. It used to be fairies but the boys at my school said there aren't any so now my fav'rit is princesses. I'm going to be a princess when I grow up.'

Kristoffer nodded, his face serious as he said, 'I do have a very special story about a very special princess. I'll tell it to you, shall I? It goes like this. One day a prince came upon a beautiful seventeen-year-old princess from a foreign country picking flowers in a meadow . . .'

'A handsome prince?' Tina interrupted excitedly.

'Well, I don't know if he was all that handsome but he fell instantly in love with the princess and wanted to marry her, but . . .'

'But what? Why couldn't he marry her? Why not?' Tina demanded impatiently.

'Well, because all of a sudden a war started in her country and the king, the princess's father, hurried her back home where she would be safe. The prince wanted to follow her but he didn't know where she lived. Instead he went off to fight the enemy and tried to forget her.'

'Yes!' declared Tina, now hopping from one foot to another. 'So when the war ended, did he go and find her?'

Kristoffer shook his head. 'Not for a long time, but he never gave up hope. Then, suddenly, after a long, long, long time . . .'

'How long? A hundred years?' Tina broke in.

'Perhaps not quite as long as that, but he did find her and . . .'

'And he asked her to marry him,' said Tina, her eyes shining.

'Yes!' said Kristoffer and, taking Dilys' hand in his, he said, 'Please will you marry me, Princess?'

'No, not like that!' Tina shouted excitedly. 'You have to go down on one knee and take her hand and put a ring on her finger and—' She broke off, her eyes even wider as she turned to her mother. 'Lend Mr Four your ring, Mummy; the one you wear round your neck.'

She watched with a delighted smile as Kristoffer took the ring Dilys removed and handed to him and, bending down on one knee, said softly, 'Most beautiful of all princesses, will you give me your hand in marriage?'

Slowly, their eyes locked and Dilys nodded.

'Say yes, Mummy. You have to say yes,' Tina urged. Smiling, Dilys did so.

Tina drew a long, satisfied sigh. 'That was a good story,'

she pronounced. 'I always like it when it ends "and they lived happily ever after".' She paused briefly and then sighed. 'I wish you lived in our country, Mr Four. Then you could come and tell me lots of good stories . . .'

'I've got a better idea!' Kristoffer said. 'Why don't you and Mummy stay in my country? We could build a big house which would be our palace and I'd be king and Mummy would be queen and you'd be the princess!'

Tina's eyes widened as she turned to Dilys. 'What do you think, Mummy? I know it's only pretend but I'd like being a princess and I could wear my pink party dress what I wore at Aunt Una's wedding and—'

'And I think it's a wonderful idea!' Dilys broke in, her gaze meeting Kristoffer's.

'It's the way a good story should end,' Kristoffer said, looking into his small daughter's blue eyes. 'You know, the king and queen get married and they all live happily ever after.'

'But aren't you and Mummy too old to be king and queen?' she asked anxiously.

Kristoffer shook his head. 'No,' he said. 'I think Mummy and I are just young enough,' and was rewarded by his small daughter's radiant smile.